ROBERT B. PARKER'S
IRONHORSE

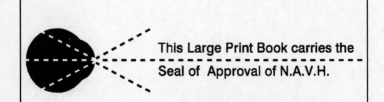

This Large Print Book carries the
Seal of Approval of N.A.V.H.

ROBERT B. PARKER'S
IRONHORSE

ROBERT KNOTT

WHEELER PUBLISHING
A part of Gale, Cengage Learning

GALE
CENGAGE Learning·

Detroit • New York • San Francisco • New Haven, Conn • Waterville, Maine • London

GALE
CENGAGE Learning·

**LIBRARY OF CONGRESS CIP DATA ON FILE.
CATALOGUING IN PUBLICATION DATA FOR THIS BOOK
IS AVAILABLE FROM THE LIBRARY OF CONGRESS.**

ISBN-13: 978-1-4104-5491-1 (hardcover)
ISBN-10: 1-4104-5491-6 (hardcover)

Published in 2013 by arrangement with G. P. Putnam's Sons, a member of Penguin Group (USA) Inc.

Printed in the United States of America
1 2 3 4 5 6 7 17 16 15 14 13

FOR JULIE

1

Virgil was sullen. Other than "yep" and "nope," he hadn't said much in the last few days. We crossed the Red River and entered the Indian Territories aboard the St. Louis & San Francisco Express out of Paris, Texas. At just past five o'clock in the afternoon, Virgil broke the silence.

"A good pointer don't run through a covey," Virgil said.

I tipped my hat back and looked at him. He was gazing out the window, watching a line of thunderclouds spreading across the western skies.

The St. Louis & San Fran Express was a new breed of train. It was the nicest we'd been on since we traveled up from Mexico, with automatic couplers, Westinghouse air brakes, and a powerful Baldwin ten-wheel engine capable of pulling twice as many cars as other locomotives. The fourth and fifth cars back were first-class Pullman sleepers with goose-down beds and leaded-glass transom windows. The coaches were fancy, too, with luminous pressure lamps, mahogany luggage racks, tufted seats, velvet curtains, and silver-plated ashtrays. Virgil and I sat at the back of the last passenger car. Behind us was a walk-through freight car followed by a stock car that carried livestock, including Virgil's stud and my lazy roan.

After near twenty years doing law work with Virgil Cole, I knew well enough he wasn't talking about hunting, but I obliged.

"No, a good pointer takes it slow. Moves steady," I said.

Virgil continued looking out the window and nodded slowly.

"They do, don't they," he said.

"They do if they're trained right."

Virgil watched the clouds for a moment longer, then looked back to me.

"What was the name of the philosopher we were reading about in the Dallas newspaper the other day?" Virgil thought some, then answered his question: "Peirce?"

"Charles Peirce."

"Charles. That's right," Virgil said. "What was it they called him the father of?"

"Pragmatism . . . He's a pragmatist."

"That's right. Pragmatist . . . Hell, Everett,

that's you, too. You're a pragmatist."

"Charles Peirce is a pragmatist," I said.

"You went to West Point, Everett. You're educated."

"About some things."

Virgil glanced back out the window again.

"You never said nothing."

"Said nothing about what?"

A dark thundercloud in the far distance flashed a hint of white and silver lightning, and for a brief moment, the western horizon lit up some.

"We're talking about Allie; this is about Allie?"

"Of course it is."

"What are you getting at?"

"What I'm getting at is, you might have apprised me not to run through it over a woman who's got the disposition to do the things she does."

"Could happen to any man."

"Not Charlie Peirce."

Virgil hadn't talked about Allie since Appaloosa, and his comment took me by surprise. Not so much by the elapsed time since he'd last talked about her, but by the comment itself. Virgil never asked, needed, or took advice from anybody, including me.

"Better to pull up short than to run

through it like a pup, you know that, Everett."

"I do."

"You never said anything."

"I did not."

"Why not?"

"Not my place."

Virgil narrowed his eyes at me as if he'd eaten something that didn't taste so good. He focused his attention back out the window.

Virgil Cole was always steady — never rattled, never bothered, and incapable of confusion — but at the moment, something was sitting sideways with him.

He shook his head a little.

"I love that woman," Virgil said.

2

After our shoot-out with Sheriff Amos Callico and his clan in Appaloosa, Virgil was appointed territory marshal, and I was appointed his deputy marshal. The position was better suited for Virgil and me. It was better than being town sheriffs or city police. The job didn't restrict us to one town. Our duties were to oversee everything within our territorial jurisdiction.

On the third day after our new commission, we got orders to carry out the assignment we were on.

Before we departed on this mission, Virgil selected Chauncey Teagarden and Pony Flores as interim deputies of Appaloosa. Chauncey and Pony were good gunmen. They had helped us in the altercation with Sheriff Callico and proved to be trusted allies.

Our job was to collect two Mexican Wall Street con artists and deliver them to

Mexican authorities in Nuevo Laredo. The job was a simple matter of transporting top-priority criminals. This was not something Virgil and I were accustomed to doing, but it was part of our new marshaling duties, and we did just that, transported criminals.

Though there was a considerable amount of train travel involved, the journey was less than formidable, and Virgil and I got along with our prisoners.

Virgil figured any man who could make money from people who stole the money in the first place couldn't be all bad.

The Mexicans spoke good English, were polite, and knew nothing about firearms. We played cards and even shared a bit of whiskey.

Virgil intended to ride horseback on the return to Appaloosa, seeing the country, as he preferred to see it, from the view of the saddle, but a telegram he received the day we dropped off our prisoners to the federales in Nuevo Laredo changed our plans.

I was not privy to the details regarding the telegram or who it was even from, but I figured the content of the telegram wasn't good, and it had everything to do with Allison French. The devil is always in the details, or, better put, the devil is in Allison French.

We had barely made it to the train station in Nuevo Laredo before we received word our prisoners had been placed in front of a firing squad and shot. Mexicans have a swift way of dealing with other Mexicans.

It had been four full days on the rail before we were close to getting out of Texas. We had traveled up through San Antonio and Austin City, crossed the Brazos, changed to the Texas Pacific, and stopped for a spell in Dallas. There, we got a big T-bone dinner near the Trinity River, walked the horses a good bit, and hoteled for the evening. In the morning, we got a plateful of food at a Hungarian café near the depot and boarded the Missouri, Kansas, and Texas line heading north into Indian territory.

We had been within roping distance of the Chickasaw Nation and were leaving Texas behind before we got detoured just south of the Red River. The MK&T track running north from Sherman was under repair, so we had to catch the Pacific Transcontinental line, a sixty-mile jaunt east to Paris, Texas. We made a final stop in Paris. It took a while to make the changeover there, so I walked the horses again before we transferred to the St. Louis & San Fran Express and headed back north.

■ ■ ■ ■

Currently, the Express was struggling a bit up a steep grade.

Virgil slid a cigar from his breast pocket, bit off the tip and spat it out the window. He fished out a match, dragged the tip of it on the iron frame of the seat in front of him, and lit the cigar. After he got it going good, he repeated what he'd previously said.

"I do," he said. "I love her."

"Except for the unfortunate stint of whoring, you or me have killed all the men she has been with," I said encouragingly.

"Got no guarantee," Virgil said.

I thought about that for a moment.

"No," I said. "I suppose you're right about that."

Virgil shook his head slightly and turned, looking out the window.

"Been enough, though," Virgil said.

"There has."

"Can't say there might not be more."

"No, we can't."

Virgil got quiet. After a moment or two of silence I leaned forward a bit, looking at him.

"That what this is about?"

Virgil looked at me.

"You thinking she's fucking Chauncey Teagarden?" I said.

3

Virgil didn't answer my question. He focused on the cigar in his hand and rolled it back and forth between his fingers and thumb. Then he looked out the window at the rocky terrain passing by.

Besides the rail we were riding — the St. Louis & San Fran — the Atchison/Topeka, Santa Fe/Burlington, Rock Island & Pacific, and the MK&T railways connected all the Five Civilized Tribes that made up the majority of the territories: Cherokee, Chickasaw, Choctaw, Creek, and Seminole. The sixty-mile detour east had us crossing the river and entering the Indian Territories into the Choctaw Nation, as opposed to the Chickasaw Nation. Other than the additional sixty miles of travel, the only real notable difference for us taking the St. Louis instead of the MK&T and entering the Choctaw Nation was the wooded and rough terrain ahead. The rail leaving Texas and heading north was a treacherous winding rise up, up, and up, following the swift waters of the Kiamichi River.

"We've been gone a good while," Virgil said.

"We have."

"Just how long have we been gone?"

"Well, 'bout two months," I said. "Give or take some days."

Virgil turned his attention out the window again.

A swell of blackbirds appeared, traveling parallel with the train for a while. They dipped down out of sight behind a section of quartz cliffs. After some distance the birds drifted back up again, lifting above us and out of sight.

"Just because we have been away for a long while doesn't mean Allie's with Teagarden," I said.

"Proof is in the pudding," Virgil said.

"That'd be a matter of your sampling."

"Normal circumstance, I'd be interested in that proposition," Virgil said. "But at this very moment, I ain't."

"I can understand that."

Virgil gave a sharp nod.

I didn't say anything else. I understood Virgil well enough to know when a conversation had paused, lingered, or ended, and this one had ended.

Virgil looked back out the window. The lowering sun flickered behind a ridge of evergreens.

"I'm gonna tend to the horses," Virgil said.

He took a long draw from his cigar and placed it in the silver-plated ashtray on the seat back in front of us.

"I'll be right here."

Virgil stepped out the back door as the train chugged slowly up a narrow pass of juniper, quartz, and sandstone. I looked out the window, thinking about how much weight the engine was pulling, thinking of my days of service in the area we were currently passing through. This was the edge of the Fourth Military District. I worked under General Adelbert Ames and had been stationed throughout the Indian Territories during the Reconstruction, following the war. Not real good memories to be conjuring up on such a beautiful sunny summer afternoon, but the territories were different now. Even though there were Kiowa, Comanche, and Apache living in the assigned Indian Territories, there was no longer any real threat of hostiles. Trains, or "little houses on wheels," as the Indians called them, were as common in the Indian Territories as they were in most states.

18

The locomotive was chugging unusually slow now. I tipped my hat, shading my eyes from the flashing patches of sun, and started to feel slightly dozy. For some reason, the hot sun on my cheeks made my thoughts drift to Katie from Appaloosa — her sheets, her liquor, her long legs, her dark hair, her womanliness. I yawned, and when I did, I heard the front coach door open, followed by the back door, followed by, "Hands in the air! This is a robbery!"

4

The robber's accent was thick, Scottish, maybe Irish, Welsh maybe. I lifted my hat to see a large man wearing a billowing white shirt and a flat-pressed felt hat with a flip-front brim. Behind him stood a very large man with a long red beard. They both carried late-model Hopkins & Allen revolvers and had bandanas covering their faces. Standing next to me was a tall man who'd come through the rear door. He was wearing a duster and carrying a Schofield revolver in each hand.

By now the passengers were screaming, which prompted the Scot, possibly Irish or Welsh, robber with the flip-front brim to bark, "Everybody, hands in the air! Reach! Hands in the air and shut your mouths! Anybody who doesn't do as we say will be killed! Hands where I can see 'em!"

Everybody did as he demanded. For the moment, I figured there was no reason not to comply with his demands and have a bullet sent in my direction. I raised my hands up where they could be seen.

I was trying to place the foreigner. There was something very familiar about him. Maybe we had been stationed together. Maybe . . .

"Everyone keep your hands where I can see them," he shouted. "Everyone!"

I'd been stationed near here, in Fort Smith. I was familiar with this rugged country and most of the outlaws that were part of it. I was certain this foreigner was from my diary of disregards.

"The only time I see your hands drop is when you put your money, watches, and rings in these hats!"

When the robber and the big bearded man took off their hats to be used for collection plates, I recognized him and the bearded man both. I knew if Virgil did not somehow do as he was accustomed to, show up and change these thieves' course of direction, or if I didn't make a move soon, I'd be shot when they recognized me.

The man with the Schofield revolvers standing next to me did not say a word or remove his hat. He was the watchman, and I did not oblige him by looking up and exposing my face.

I wondered how he got past Virgil. Nothing gets past Virgil, ever. He must have come from the top of the train, or maybe he was hiding in the freight car, and Virgil walked past him. Maybe he got the jump on Virgil, and Virgil was thrown from the train, or was dead.

"Put all your valuables in these hats!" Vince yelled.

That was his name, Vince. Vince was Randall Bragg's right-hand man in Appaloosa. He was as bad as they came. Given that I was the one who killed Bragg on the porch of the Boston House Hotel in Appaloosa, I was certain when he got to me, he'd be none too happy to see my face. Vince and Redbeard moved down the aisle, collecting passengers' belongings.

"Don't anybody do anythin' stupid!" Vince shouted. "When we get to the top of this rise, we'll be gone and you'll be safe!"

I assessed my options as Vince and Redbeard walked the aisle, prodding each passenger to give up their valuables. My eight-gauge leaned against the window frame but was certainly too cumbersome for swift movement. I could not reach for my Colt or dingus because the man with the Schofields was standing just to my right, towering above me. He was no more than a step

22

behind me, and he'd be sure to see my actions.

Vince and Redbeard were halfway down the aisle, getting closer and closer to me as they gathered money and jewelry from the passengers. Redbeard was collecting faster and was ahead of Vince by a step when he looked directly at me. He stood tall, and I knew he recognized me. He turned his head slightly, looking back to Vince.

"It's Everett Hitch," Redbeard said.

When Redbeard turned back to me, I could tell by the wrinkling around his eyes that he had an evil smile under his bandana. But the wrinkles smoothed out quickly when he heard Virgil speak up: "And Virgil Cole!"

5

Virgil was behind the man with the Schofield revolvers. His bone-handled Colt nudged into the man's back.

Redbeard jerked quick and inadvertently fired off a shot. It hit the man with the Schofield revolvers square in the chest.

The name Virgil Cole sort of did that to people. It made people flinch and do things they otherwise might not do. Redbeard might have been trying to pick off Virgil where he was standing behind the man with the Schofields, but the man with the Schofields went down.

The next shot came from Virgil and located itself in the forehead of Redbeard, sending him backward into Vince. Redbeard's big body made for good cover, and Vince was quickly out the front coach door. Virgil moved fast up the aisle, chasing after him.

I grabbed my eight-gauge and followed

Virgil in pursuit of Vince. By the time I made it to the door, the door had swung back closed and Virgil was on the platform of the forward coach. He turned quick.

"Down, Everett!"

A fast succession of shots rang out from the forward coach. Virgil moved quick to the side, out of the line of fire, as bullets came flying down the aisle, busting through the glass of the front car door and through the glass of the rear coach door. I shifted to the right and promptly dropped in a seat next to a heavyset woman. The passengers were screaming and crying as the bullets whizzed down the aisle, catching pieces of glass and wood. After a moment the shooting stopped. We waited. I was on the opposite side of the coach from Virgil. I could see him clearly through the busted glass. The passengers were distressed. Some of them were crying, and others started chattering nervously.

"Everybody quiet! We're marshals," I said. "Just remain quiet!"

Most of the folks stopped clamoring, but some kept talking.

"Quiet!"

Virgil looked at me as he reloaded his Colt.

"Who we dealing with, Everett?" Virgil

said. "That hoss called you by name."

"Not sure about the lot of 'em or how many they are, but that fellow shooting back at us is Vince."

Virgil snapped the loading gate of his Colt closed with the palm of his hand.

"Vince! The Irishman from Bragg's gang?"

"None other."

"You sure?"

"It's him."

"He's no good," Virgil said.

"No, he's not."

Virgil shook his head some.

"What the hell is he doing down here?"

"Until you showed up," I said, "trying to rob this train."

"Vince!" Virgil called out loudly.

Vince did not reply.

"Vince!" Virgil shouted. "You hear me?"

Again, there was no reply.

"You already got two of your hands killed, Vince! You'd do best to give yourself up so we don't have to kill any more of you! Including you!"

Nothing. Either Vince was waiting for us to make a tactical error and expose ourselves or he was going forward through the train.

"Might be on the move," I said.

"Could be."

"Don't think it'd be a good idea to go

26

through that door and find out, though," I said.

Virgil shook his head.

"No, it wouldn't," Virgil said.

"No telling how many they are."

"Big train," Virgil said. "Three in this coach might be a hint the whole slew of that bunch are on board."

"If they've not already got control of the engine," I said, "they're gonna try."

Virgil looked to the ladder by his shoulder, then back at me. He pointed up the ladder.

I nodded and pointed to myself, then pointed to the rear door of our coach.

Virgil nodded. Then he climbed the ladder to the roof of the train.

6

I dropped to the aisle floor, then stayed low and moved toward the rear door. I passed over the top of Redbeard and the dead man with the Schofields and made my way out the door.

By the time I climbed the ladder to the roof of the car, Virgil was ahead of me by two cars. He was heading to the front of the train, to the engine. The locomotive was belching heavy smoke as I walked forward on the roof of the coach, following Virgil.

The train was still on an uphill grade, chugging through a deep gorge of red sandstone and quartz. Through a cloud of thick smoke ahead, Virgil stopped and crouched down. He was all the way to the front end of the first coach, just behind the tall tender car that carried the rock coal. I kept on the move and made my way over the top of the next car, and the next, and the next.

As I jumped to the forward car, the train cleared the gorge and started slowing down. To my left, there were three riders with a number of saddled horses keeping pace with the train.

No sooner did I see them than they saw me. The rider in the front pulled a Winchester from his scabbard, swing-cocked it, and rounded it in my direction, but before he could pull the trigger, Virgil shot him.

The rider tipped over in the saddle and fell under the herd, which prompted the other two riders to pull up.

I kept walking steadily forward and moved up next to Virgil, who crouched behind the tall tender. I looked back behind us; the riders faded away in the distance as the train continued moving north.

Besides being a steady and confident gunman, Virgil was one hell of a shot, best I'd ever seen, and that was one hell of a shot.

Virgil looked at me, rose up a bit, and pointed over the top of the tender toward the engine cabin. We could barely see the engineer and his fireman, but we could see enough to know they were being held at gunpoint by two of the bandits. The engine was loud, but the bandits had heard Virgil's shot. They were looking out from one side of the cabin to the other. Virgil pointed, motioning for us to move up over the top of the tender to the engine cabin, and in an instant, we did just that. We moved fast and rushed the cabin.

Virgil shouted, "Drop 'em!"

The bandits did not drop their guns. They raised them instead, but they were too late. Virgil shot the one on the left. I shot the one on the right. They never fired a shot. By the time the thieves hit the cabin floor, Virgil and I were to the front end of the tender, looking down into the engine cabin at the shocked faces of the engineer and his fireman.

We kept our pistols on the bandits as we climbed down into the engine cabin. One bandit lay sideways on the floor — he'd been shot in the head — and the other was on his back, shot in the chest. They were both dead.

Virgil showed his badge.

"I'm Marshal Virgil Cole. This is my deputy, Everett Hitch."

The engineer and the fireman were both huge men, with strong arms and overalls covered in soot.

The engineer slid up his goggles, revealing white circles around his eyes.

"Thank God you showed," the engineer said.

7

The train was chugging slowly as it moved up through the heavily wooded river valley. The wall of mountains to our left blocked what remained of the setting sun, and we were closing in on dark. Virgil opened the loading gate on his Colt. He replaced the spent rounds with lead-filled casings and undented primers as he looked out of the cabin, watching the woods passing by.

I reloaded my Colt as I looked closer at the dead gunmen on the cabin floor. Neither of them wore bandanas hiding their faces. I put the heel of my boot to the shoulder of the man lying on his side and turned him over.

Virgil looked back to me.

"Bragg's hands?" he said.

"Don't recognize either one of 'em," I said.

"The others back there?" Virgil said.

"Not sure 'bout the hand you came up

behind with the Schofields," I said. "But the big red-bearded fellow you shot rode with Bragg. The other shooting at us was damn sure Vince."

"Vince is a bad hombre," Virgil said.

"Not afraid to pull the trigger," I said.

"No, he's not."

Virgil shook his head and leaned out of the cabin a bit and looked back behind us.

Before I killed Randall Bragg on the porch of the Boston House Hotel, Bragg had his way with Virgil's woman, Allison French. Virgil had a profound dislike for Bragg and his gang. The name Bragg or anyone associated with Bragg was not a welcome recollection to Virgil's memory, especially the big Irishman. Vince challenged Virgil outside the jailhouse in Appaloosa, and Virgil backed him down in front of the whole gang. Vince threatened he'd kill Virgil one day, and Virgil didn't much care for that notion. Virgil Cole did not take threats lightly.

"Looks like Vince finally got the opportunity he's been waiting for," Virgil said.

"Opportunity to kill you?"

"Yep," Virgil said.

"Been a bunch that have had such opportunities before."

"There have."

"They didn't fare so well," I said.

"No, they didn't."

"Wasted opportunities."

"Don't see a reason to disappoint Vince of not having his opportunity," Virgil said.

Virgil looked out of the cabin again to the solid stand of trees passing by, and then turned to the engineer.

"How long this land stay like this?" Virgil said.

"Rugged like this, you mean?" the engineer said.

Virgil nodded.

"Well, right back there, where those horses were, was the last of the open terrain. Nothing but woods going north now. Rail snakes through thick woods all the way up to Tall Water Falls, and it's uphill to boot. After that, the woods open some. By the time we get to Division City you're in fairly open country."

"Can you make it to open country without stopping?"

The engineer looked at the fireman.

The fireman shook his head.

"No," the fireman said. "Got the biggest tender of any train running, four thousand gallons. But uphill like it is, I doubt we'd even make Tall Water Falls."

"When's your next water drop?" Virgil said.

"Standley Station," the engineer said. "Two hours."

"There a town there?" Virgil said.

"Small one," the engineer said.

"Right now," Virgil said, "keep moving; don't slow down any more than you have to. Don't want these robbers getting off this train, busting free into the woods, understand?"

"I do," the engineer said. "There's something you should know, though."

"What's that?" Virgil said.

"We got the governor of Texas and his family on board," the engineer said. "Wife, two daughters."

"That's why you took so long boarding in Paris," I said.

"I reckon so," the engineer said.

"What car they in?" Virgil asked.

"First-class Pullman sleeper," said the engineer. "Fourth coach back."

"Daughters?" Virgil said. "How old?"

"Grown women, that's for sure, in their twenties."

"Texas Rangers with them?" I said.

"No," the engineer said. "Pinkertons."

"Pinkertons?" Virgil asked. "How many?"

"That I don't know."

34

"Well, all right, then," Virgil said. "You boys take care of what's in front of us, and Everett and me will take care of what's behind us."

8

The fireman and engineer didn't waste any more time with talk as they took to task doing what Virgil instructed. Virgil grabbed one of the bandits we'd shot and slid him off the side of the train. Virgil's move was not to remove the dead from the living as much as it was a warning sign to the other bandits. It would give them something to think about, seeing their fallen friend crumpled next to the rail. It was doubtful, though, they could see much of anything. By now, daylight had slipped away, and except for the eerie reddish light that filled the cabin when the fireman opened the firebox, it was near dark. Virgil dragged the second bandit and slid him off the opposite side of the engine cabin like he was throwing out saloon trash.

"Whether Vince and the gang see their dead lying on the side of the rail or not," I said, "they know we got control of the engine."

"Not stopping for their horses," Virgil said. "They most assuredly do."

"What do you figure we do?"

"Gonna have to go at 'em."

"Judging by the number of horses those riders had," I said, "we got us a handful back there to deal with."

"We do."

"Not just Vince we have to be concerned about," I said. "The whole of that Bragg bunch are no good."

"They're mean," Virgil said. "Bad as they come, and we can't just wait to get bush-whacked by 'em, either. We're gonna have to go right at them. Have to be the spider on the fly."

When the fireman opened the firebox, I looked back behind us, down the side of the tender. The light from the boiler made it possible for me to see a narrow ledge just wide enough to get a foothold running down the length of the tender. The fireman closed the firebox, and again it was dark.

"Open that door again," I said to the fireman.

The fireman opened the door. I pointed out the narrow ledge to Virgil.

"I'll make my way back," I said. "Take a look."

Virgil leaned out and looked at the ledge.

"Reconnaissance," I said.

Virgil looked back to me.

"See what I can see," I said.

Virgil stepped back and tipped his head toward the ledge, giving me the go-ahead.

"Take her easy," he said.

I leaned my eight-gauge against the cabin wall next to the engineer, stepped off the platform and onto the narrow ledge. I crawled sideways down the side of the tender toward the front coach. When I got to the back of the tender, I could see light coming from inside the first coach. I edged my eye around the corner to see what I could see and almost fell as I jerked back, seeing what I saw. I quickly took a step back toward the engine, but my foot slipped, and this time, I fell.

After all the Indians I'd been up against and the years of taking on gun hands, a damn night train was gonna get me?

I was headed for the fast-moving earth below, but I caught a grab iron, a goddamn short piece of bar that attached to the side of the tender, and pulled hard, pulling myself back up to the ledge. I caught my breath, settled, and worked my way back to the front of the tender. By the time I made it to the back landing of the engine cabin, I was breathing hard. I pulled my Colt and motioned toward the coach.

"Four men in the breach of the door," I said. "Got two women, both wearing white dresses."

"The daughters," Virgil said.

"They dragged them from the Pullman," I said. "Brought 'em to the forward for a reason."

"By God they did."

"Using them as barter."

"Or shields," Virgil said.

"Force them to come over the tender in front of them," I said. "We drop iron or they toss the women. We shoot, we risk the women getting shot or falling."

"Not if we go at 'em first, quick like," Virgil said. "Like you did, down the side. They won't figure us coming at them from the flank."

"Don't expect they will."

"That's it, then," Virgil said. "Let's get after 'em."

Virgil looked to the engineer and pointed north.

The engineer offered a sharp nod, and answered by giving the engine a bit more throttle.

9

We started off. Virgil stepped from the cabin, walking the narrow ledge on the right side of the tender, and I moved back down the ledge on the left. It was hard to know exactly how this would go down. Virgil and I had been in many distressing situations, but crawling down the side of a fast-moving train in the middle of a dark night posed tall complexities. I thought about Virgil's bum knee, and how long he would take before he'd get to the back of the tender. One thing I always knew about Virgil was that when his sights were set, time slowed down. I thought of Virgil's words, *spider on the fly,* as I worked my way along the narrow ledge of the tender. When I got to the end, the first element I slid around the corner of the tender was my Colt with its hammer back; the next was my eye looking down its barrel.

I let lead fly as I locked target and jumped

to the platform. My shot made its way to the chest of a large man wearing an open shirt and holding one of the women. He fell back and she dropped to the floor. I saw someone duck out the back coach door.

Virgil was on the platform from the other side, and his first shot caught the side of a robber's head, splattering blood onto the daughters' white dresses.

A fat man got off a shot. The bullet hit the doorjamb, splintering pieces of wood onto the platform.

My second shot caught the fat man in the throat. I did not see Virgil's second shot, but a tall robber fell backward and dropped in the aisle.

Swiftly, in a matter of fleeting moments, there were four dead gunmen and we were in the open doorway of the coach. Both of the young women were safe and on the floor in front of the first passenger seat.

"One hand made it out the back, Virgil," I said.

Virgil and I stood side by side with our Colts trained to the back of the coach, looking for other robbers. The car was thick with smoke and there was not another bandit left standing. Many of the passengers were covering their ears, eyes, or mouths and, for the most part, were silenced by the instant carnage.

We reloaded. Then I gathered the weapons off the men we'd shot. Virgil looked to the passengers.

"I'm Marshal Virgil Cole; this is my deputy, Everett Hitch. Everybody stay seated and remain quiet. We'll do our best to rid this train of these thieves."

Virgil looked down at one of the young women and offered his hand. She looked up and grasped his hand. Virgil helped her to her feet. He took his handkerchief from his pocket and gently wiped blood from her face. She was pretty. Her face was similar to that of an angel you might see in an old biblical painting. She had rosy cheeks and large eyes. I helped up the other woman, who was also pretty, but more womanly, more slender and tall.

"You two the governor's daughters?" Virgil said.

The girl with the rosy cheeks and big eyes clutched Virgil's arm. She was shaking hard and could not say anything. The taller woman spoke.

"We are. I'm Emma; this is my little sister, Abigail."

Abigail burst into tears. Emma was also shaking but breathing easier than her sister.

"Our . . . our mother and father are back

there somewhere," Emma said and pointed.

"How many guards are with your family?" Virgil asked.

"I don't know for sure," Emma said. "Two that I know of. Pinkerton men, maybe there were others elsewhere on the train, I don't know."

"The two Pinkertons are in your car?" Virgil said.

"They were," Emma said. "One was stationed at the front of the coach and the other at the rear."

She looked at me and back to Virgil. Water filled her eyes.

"I'm not for certain," Emma said, "but I'm pretty sure they are both dead."

10

Virgil was without a doubt listening to Emma, but his attention had turned toward the rear of the coach. He moved from Abigail's clutch and positioned himself square-shouldered, looking at something I had not seen. He took a few steps and stopped. Then he raised his Colt with his arm extended out straight in front of him.

"Dean," Virgil said. "Get up. Real easy. Keep your hands where I can see them."

I leaned to the side for a clear look around Virgil, and sitting in the second-to-last row was a lanky gun hand named Dean. Virgil knocked out his tooth years ago on top of the rocky rim above Appaloosa when Dean was riding lookout for Bragg.

"I got my pistola in the side of this here lady's corsetta," Dean said. "You take one step closer and I'll ruin it."

"Why?" Virgil asked.

"What do you mean, why?" Dean said.

"I'll kill you if you do," Virgil said. "So why?"

Dean's eyes moved from side to side.

"Let me tell you how this will go down, Dean," Virgil said. "You drop your pistola in the aisle there, stand up with your hands where I can see them. Do like I say."

Dean didn't move.

Virgil pulled back the hammer on his Colt. A few of the passengers gasped.

"Okay!" Dean said. "Okay!"

Dean held his pistola out into the aisle and dropped it. He stood up with his hands in the air, stepped into the aisle, and faced Virgil.

"Take a few steps back," Virgil said.

"What?"

"Right now," Virgil said.

Virgil was using Dean to block the door. Dean took a few steps and his back was to the door.

"Good," Virgil said. "What are you and the others doing down here?"

"What do you mean?"

"Just that."

"Um . . . just travelin' the train."

"Don't test me, Dean."

Dean swallowed hard.

"Vince the boss?" Virgil pressed.

Dean looked at Virgil and frowned a bit.

"Is he?"

"He . . . he is," Dean said.

"This his idea?"

"It is."

"What's the plan?"

"Um, we was to ride down to Paris, Texas, and get on this train and . . ."

"And what?"

Dean was sweating. He swayed his head from side to side.

"Rob it."

"Why this train?"

"Vince said because of the land run happening in the Indian Territory that there would be a lot of people on the train going that direction with money."

Virgil moved a little closer to Dean and stopped.

"What else?" Virgil said.

"Um . . . well, we did that. We got on back in Paris. We was gonna gather folks' belongings, then get off and meet our horses right back there, but you and Hitch done changed all that."

"Lot of horses," Virgil said. "Your fellow thieves from Bragg's gang?"

"For the most part."

"How many are you?"

"Twenty-one."

"Twenty-one?" Virgil said. "Why so many?"

"Don't know," Dean said. "Big train."

"Including the rider," I said. "We killed nine."

"That'd leave eleven," Virgil said.

"It would," I said.

Dean looked at Virgil and closed one eye.

"Counting me," Dean said. "That'd be twelve."

"We ain't counting you," Virgil said.

11

Dean was thinking hard about why he wasn't being counted when Virgil interrupted his thought process.

"Turn around, face that door," Virgil said. "Pull the shade, put your hands above the door."

Dean did as he was instructed.

Virgil walked down the aisle and picked up the Orbea Hermanos pistola Dean had dropped.

"Don't think about nothing but keeping your nose to that door, Dean," Virgil said.

"I won't."

Virgil looked to the passengers.

"Anybody here good with a gun and not afraid to use it?"

A sodbuster sitting with a frail woman lifted off his seat slightly and removed a floppy-brimmed hat from his head.

"I don't got no gun, but I ain't afraid to use one, 'specially on them," the sodbuster said, pointing at Dean.

"What's your name?" Virgil said.

"Ness," the sodbuster said.

Virgil looked at the young woman by his side.

"This your wife?"

"She is."

The frail woman offered a nervous, thin-lipped smile.

Virgil checked the chamber of Dean's pistola. He spun the cylinder to see if it was full, then handed the pistola to Ness.

"That skinny fellow at the door," Virgil said. "Shoot him if he moves."

"Yes sir," Ness said.

An older, dandy-looking gentleman wearing a finely tailored suit stood up from his seat toward the rear of the coach.

"Marshal," the dandy said. "I'm heeled."

The dandy pulled a .38 plated short-barrel from his vest pocket and showed it to Virgil.

"I'm a retired veteran of the Army," the dandy said. "I've killed before, and I'm not afraid to do it again."

"What's your name?" Virgil asked.

"Cavanaugh," the dandy said. "Captain Lowell Cavanaugh."

Virgil pointed to Dean.

"Do the same, Captain," Virgil said. "Point that short-barrel at him. He makes a move, pull the trigger."

"That I will do," Cavanaugh said.

"Hear that, Dean?" Virgil said.

"I do," Dean said with his nose to the door. "I ain't moving."

The locomotive was working hard, chugging up a long, gradual grade. Virgil reached down with one hand, grabbed the collar of one of the dead robbers. He dragged him out of the doorway and slid him off the side of the platform. I followed suit, and a big elderly man gave me a hand. We dragged the dead men out of the doorway and discarded them off the side of the platform and onto the hardscrabble earth passing by.

Virgil stood tall, looking at the passengers.

"Everybody just remain calm. My deputy and I will be best suited if you stay seated and don't fret."

Abigail and Emma were standing together in front of the first row of seats, holding hands. Abigail was still shaking. She took a deep breath.

"Marshal," Abigail said. "What about our mother and father?"

Her voice was much different from her sister's. It was husky, yet she sounded like a little girl.

Virgil tipped his head to the seat.

"Why don't you and your sister have a

seat," Virgil said.

Abigail did as Virgil asked and lowered herself onto the seat with her shoulders held back and her chin up, as if she were royalty. Emma stayed standing for a moment, then sat next to her sister.

"We're gonna do everything we can to get everyone off this train safely," Virgil said. "Including your mother and father."

"Thank . . . thank you," Abigail said with a trembling voice. "I'm sorry, I'm sorry, I . . . I'm just frightened."

"I know," Virgil said. "But me and Everett are here now, and we're not."

Abigail lowered her chin. The small move made her eyes appear bigger than they already were as she looked up at Virgil.

"We have been doing this kind of work a long time," Virgil said. "We are good at it. It's what we do."

Emma looked at me.

"These men have broken the law," Virgil said. "Going against the law is the same as going against me and Everett. We don't take kindly to notions like that. Understand?"

Abigail dipped her head slightly.

"Also," Virgil said, "I don't like them. None of them. Neither does Everett."

12

Virgil tipped his head for me to move toward the door. I followed him out to the platform. We stood just outside the doorway, where we could talk out of earshot of the others.

"What do you allow, Everett?"

"They're rough company."

"They are."

"We've shot 'em up pretty good, though," I said.

"We have."

"Got more to go."

"We do," Virgil said.

"The hand that made it out the back will be spreading the gospel of what went down."

Virgil shook his head a bit as he looked back into the coach.

"Most assuredly he will," Virgil said.

"They'll be buzzing 'round like wasps," I said.

"Yep," Virgil said. "Chewing on their

next move."

"What do you figure that'll be?"

"Shot up like they are," Virgil said, "I'd imagine they're more than interested how they're gonna get off this train."

"They might jump."

"Don't think so," Virgil said, shaking his head. "Not in the dark with no horses."

"They're well aware the train didn't stop for their horses."

"That they are."

"They're none too happy about that," I said.

"Nope," Virgil said. "Don't expect they are."

"What do you think the riders will do?"

Virgil shook his head a bit.

"Hard to say."

"Don't think they'd stay where they were going to meet up."

"No, don't think they would."

"You shooting that getaway rider might have got the other two riders running the opposite direction."

"Might," Virgil said. "Or keep on riding north to the next water drop?"

I pulled out my watch.

"That'd be about an hour twenty from now," I said. "Standley Station."

We thought about that for a moment.

53

"One thing for certain Vince and them know and don't like," I said.

"That you and me are on board?"

"That, and the fact they lost control of the engine," I said.

"That's right."

"What do you think their move would be if this train don't stop at the next water drop?"

"They got two choices," Virgil said. "Come at us, or wait till the engine runs dry and the train stops."

"This train passes the next drop," I said, "they'll come at us."

"More than likely," Virgil said. "Vince has got bargaining chips, too."

"The governor."

"Yep," Virgil said. "And his wife."

"We could stop at Standley Station and play it out there," I said.

Virgil thought about that, then shook his head.

"Better off with them sequestered on this train," Virgil said.

" 'Spect that's right."

"Is," Virgil said.

"Don't want them spread out," I said, "holding the governor and his wife as hostage."

"No, we don't."

I stepped on the grab-iron ladder toward the edge of the coach. I took a few steps up and edged up just a little, looking back over the top of the train. It was dark, but there was enough light to see there was nobody coming at us. I dropped back to the platform.

"Keep lookout for me," I said. "I'll make sure the engineer keeps us on the move, get my eight-gauge while I'm at it."

Virgil nodded and climbed the ladder, looking back over the coach with his Colt at ready. I climbed the ladder on the tender and made a fast trip to the engine cabin.

13

Virgil came down from the coach ladder when I returned with my eight-gauge. The train was now in a full crescent bend, moving slowly upgrade. The cars were stretched out behind us, trailing off to the left in a semicircle, and the lighted windows of the cars shined brightly in the dark night. We could see all the way back to the caboose.

"There's more to this," Virgil said.

"What are you thinking?"

"Don't know exactly," Virgil said, shaking his head slowly, "but this ain't Vince, Dean, and the others' territory."

"No, it's not."

Virgil looked at the cars circled behind us.

"Think Dean's lying?" I said.

"Yep."

" 'Bout what?"

"Don't know," Virgil said. "It's all he knows how to do."

"Reckon it's hard for him not to."

"Been doing it so long," Virgil said, "he's grown particular to it."

"He's not very good at it."

"No," Virgil said. "He ain't."

I looked to Dean, and thought about what Virgil was saying.

"I suppose it's just a matter about how much he's lying about," I said. "And about what."

"That's right."

"What do you speculate?" I said. "You think they are down here for something else?"

"They knew the governor was on board," Virgil said.

"Think they targeted the governor?"

"They're after something else."

"Vince and the bunch are a back-shooting bunch," I said, "capable of doing bad things, but I wouldn't figure they'd have the smarts for doing an ambitious job that requires too much thinking."

"Me neither."

Virgil looked at Dean standing facing the door at the other end of the coach.

"Me neither," Virgil said again and reentered the coach.

He walked halfway down the aisle and stopped.

"Dean?" Virgil said.

"What?" Dean said.

"What are you boys doing down this far?" Virgil said.

"What do you mean?" Dean asked.

"Next time you answer with a question," Virgil said, "me or Everett will throw you off this train. Turn around."

Dean turned and faced Virgil.

"I will ask you a few questions," Virgil said, "and you're gonna answer me straight."

"Wha—" Dean stopped, afraid he was about to ask a question.

"You boys are outside of your where-abouts," Virgil said. "How come this train, this far?"

"I told you."

"What else ain't you telling me?"

"Nothing."

"Don't get sidetracked with your lies, Dean."

Dean shook his head. "I ain't lying."

"This was not Vince's idea," Virgil said. "Coming down this far and robbing this train, was it?"

14

Dean looked at Virgil with a blank look on his face. His knees worked toward each other like he needed to pee. Dean's face was wet with sweat.

"Was it?" Virgil said.

Dean slowly shook his head.

"Whose idea was it?"

"I don't rightly know."

"What do you mean you don't rightly know?"

"Vince tol' us, but I ain't sure who tol' Vince."

"No."

"No? I mean, I swear! I don't know! We was in Wichita Falls, we just moved a bunch of cattle for a cow-calf outfit there. Vince's horse came up lame, and he peeled off 'fore the rest of us. He said he met a fellow playing Seven-Up at the Bluebell Pool Palace. A Yankee. It was the Yankee's plan."

"You're lying to me, Dean."

"No!"

Virgil took a few steps toward Dean and stopped.

"I ain't lying! It's the truth!"

"A Yankee?" Virgil said.

"Yes!"

"What's his name?"

"That I don't know! Vince was the one who met him. Vince said this Yankee knew about trains. About this train, I swear . . . the rest of us was just doing what Vince tol' us to do."

"What did Vince tell you to do?"

"To ride down to Paris. Board a long train with a bunch of cars. This train! He said 'cause of the land run happening in the Indian Territory that there would be a lot of people on the train going that direction with money and we'd make a lot of money."

"What else?"

"That was it," Dean said. "I swear."

"What does this Yankee look like?"

"Don't know. Never saw him."

"You don't know his name? You never saw him?"

The Adam's apple in Dean's skinny neck moved up, then dropped down.

"That's right."

Virgil walked a few more steps closer to Dean and stopped.

"You did not come down here to rob wallets and watches," Virgil said.

Dean backed up a bit, hitting the door. He was dripping with sweat. Drops were falling from the tip of his nose.

"Did you, Dean?"

Dean blinked hard a few times and shook his head.

"No."

"Go on," Virgil said.

Dean took a deep breath.

"Well, we was getting the money, everybody's money, like I tol' you," Dean said. "But . . . um, there's supposed to be some loot on board."

"Loot?" Virgil said.

Dean nodded.

"A bunch of loot," Dean said.

"How do you know this?" Virgil asked.

"That's what the Yankee tol' Vince," Dean said. "Vince tol' us there was a lot of money being carried on this train."

"What else do you know, Dean?" Virgil said.

"Honest to God, nothing!" Dean said.

"Don't go using words like *honest* and *God*. They don't sit well by you," Virgil said. "Makes me think you are lying to me, Dean."

"I ain't lying," Dean said. "All I know is

61

Vince said we was gonna rob a train carrying a bunch of loot, that's all I know. That's what the Yankee told him, and Vince said when we all got off back there where we was supposed to get off that we was going to divvy up! That's all I know!"

"Turn around, put your nose to that door."

Dean just looked at Virgil.

"Now," Virgil said.

15

Dean was facing the door again. Virgil walked back up the aisle to where I stood by Emma and Abigail. They were seated in the front row. Lightning lit up the interior of the car as Virgil turned to face them.

"Do you know if your father was carrying a large amount of money?" Virgil asked.

Emma looked to Abigail. Abigail shook her head.

"Not that we are aware of," Emma said. "No."

"Where were you and your parents traveling?" I said.

"We are headed to our grandmother's home," Emma said. "In Kansas, near Wichita. Father, Mr. Lassiter, and Mr. Hobbs were going elsewhere on business."

"Who are Mr. Lassiter and Mr. Hobbs," Virgil asked.

"Friends of our father," Emma said.

"You know where they were headed?" I said.

"No, I'm not sure, business meetings with businesspeople," Emma said.

"I know this is not easy for you," Virgil said, "but try and tell Everett and me what led up to you being in this predicament."

Emma looked to her sister and then to Virgil.

"Well . . . I was sitting in a chair at the front of the carriage across from our berth, reading. Abby was sleeping. You were asleep, weren't you, dear?"

"Yes," Abigail said.

"And the others?" Virgil said.

"Father, Mr. Lassiter, and Mr. Hobbs were playing cards on the center table," Emma said, "and Mother was in her berth."

"Go on," Virgil said.

"The conductor walked in from the rear of the carriage. He was talking to the Pinkerton man. The conductor's back was to me. I think the conductor was telling a joke or something, because they were laughing. Then a hard-looking man stepped through the door, behind the Pinkerton man. He had a big knife. The Pinkerton man was stabbed."

"What about the other Pinkerton guard?" I said.

"He rushed to his partner's aid and then the conductor shot him," Emma said. "He just shot him. . . . It was loud."

"What about your father?" Virgil said, "and the other two?"

"The conductor told them to keep their hands up," Emma said.

"The conductor?" I said.

Emma shook her head.

"I have to say, I don't think he was the conductor," Emma said. "He was wearing a conductor's cap, but . . . I don't know, he and the man with the knife threw the Pinkerton men from the train. It all happened so fast."

Emma stopped talking. Tears welled up in her eyes, and she started to cry. Abigail grabbed her hand. They both were crying.

"Okay," Virgil said. "Okay . . ."

Emma stiffened up, determined to continue. "The man with the knife pulled Mother out of her berth. He was mean and rough with her. He put the knife to her throat."

Abigail spoke up: "The conductor, or whoever he is, told Father to get his luggage down."

"Then there were gunshots," Emma said.

"That's right," Abigail said.

"There was gunfire coming from the car

behind us," Emma said, "and then a big Irishman came running through the rear door."

"He was followed by two other men," Abigail said.

"The Irishman told the conductor there were lawmen on board," Emma said, "and they'd shot two of their men."

"Then what," Virgil said.

"The conductor told him to go back and kill them," Emma said. "Kill the lawmen."

Lightning cracked loudly. Abigail jumped. Emma grabbed my hand. Bright light briefly flooded the coach.

Virgil looked to the ceiling. He called to Ness and the dandy as he pointed up.

"You hear something?"

Ness looked to the dandy; the dandy shook his head. Ness looked back to Virgil and shook his head.

16

I stepped out onto the platform to have a look back on top of the coach to make sure there was nobody trying to crawl their way forward. I climbed the ladder and peeked over the top, looking back behind us. It was dark, and the only thing I could see was the light coming from the interior of the cars shining on the trees passing by. I felt a drop of water on my face, followed shortly by another drop and another. A distant flash of lightning briefly illuminated the whole of everything for me, the train, the trees. There was nobody, at least for the moment, on his way to ambush us. The sprinkling continued as I came down the ladder and reentered the coach.

Emma was talking but stopped when Virgil looked at me.

"Nothing," I said. "Rain coming though."

Virgil turned his head slightly, listening for a second, then looked back to Emma.

Emma continued. "The conductor man told Mr. Hobbs and Mr. Lassiter to get off the train or he'd tell the man with the knife to cut Mother's throat."

"And they did that," I said. "They got off?"

Abigail and Emma looked at each other and nodded.

"It . . . it was so awful," Abigail said as tears rolled down her cheeks.

"Does your father always travel with Pinkertons?" Virgil said.

Emma looked to her sister, and they shook their heads.

"As far as I know, this is the first time," Emma said.

"Daddy generally has security," Abigail said. "Just not the Pinkertons . . . I think they were maybe Mr. Hobbs' men."

"How was it you and your sister were brought forward?" I said.

"Another man came from the front, a big heavyset man. He said that the train had passed where it was supposed to stop," Abigail said. "He said he had seen two men jumping into the engine cabin."

"The conductor man became incensed and yelled at the big man. He told him to take us, me and Abby, and to use us to get control of the engine," Emma said, "with

68

whatever means necessary."

"And he brought you here," I said, "to the first car?"

"Yes," Abigail said.

"He did. There were other men, too," Emma said.

Virgil pointed to Dean. "That skinny fellow there," he said. "Was he one of them that brought you to this car?"

"No," Emma said. "He was already here when the others brought us forward."

Virgil looked at me. Then he walked back toward Dean.

"Dean," Virgil said.

"What?"

"Turn around."

Dean turned to face Virgil.

"Who came on this train posin' like he was the conductor?"

Dean didn't reply.

"Answer me."

"I don't know 'bout no conductor."

Virgil walked closer to Dean.

"How were you boys split up?"

"What do you mean?"

"How many in each car?"

"Oh, um, three of us in each car."

"Who was in the Pullman?"

"I don't know," Dean said. "I was just tol' by Vince to get in this first car and holler

69

robbery at five-thirty."

"Go back there and tell Vince to come up here," Virgil said.

"Huh?"

"Tell him I need to talk with him," Virgil said. "Tell him he's got one chance to back out. He gives himself up right now and I'll be nice. He don't, I won't."

"I'll do that," Dean said and turned toward the door.

"Dean?" Virgil said.

Dean looked back at Virgil.

"Tell him if he don't, me and Everett will kill the lot of you. All of you together, a few at a time, or one by one. Makes no difference."

Dean turned toward the door.

"One more thing. Do like I tell you, you might have a chance to be counted. You don't, you'll be dead like the others."

Dean swallowed hard.

"I'll go get Vince."

Dean moved to one side out of the center of the aisle and called out loudly, "It's Dean! I'm coming out! If y'all is there! Don't shoot! I'm coming out! It's Dean!"

Dean opened the door a little. Then he opened it a little more, just enough for him to get through. There was no gunfire, just the partially open door, and without

incident Dean left, closing the door behind
him.

17

Virgil spoke to the dandy and Ness as he walked back up the aisle toward the front of the coach.

"You two keep your guns pointed at that door and be ready to shoot," Virgil said.

"Thought you told that man to have another man come and talk with you?" Ness said.

Virgil shook his head.

"There is not gonna be anybody come through that door interested in talking," Virgil said. "Just be ready."

Ness and the dandy trained their pistols to the door.

Besides the fact Virgil was tired of Dean's stupidity and his inability to offer much in the way of worthy information, his ploy of releasing Dean was only to buy us time. He knew it would give Vince and the others some fat to chew on as they figured out what they should do.

"What did he, this conductor, look like?" I asked.

"He was rather tall and slender," Emma said. "He wore spectacles and had a thick drooping mustache."

"I'm not certain, but he might have been crippled," Abigail said. "Or injured. His left arm seemed limp."

"And he was educated," Emma said. "He spoke very proper."

"What about the other man with the knife?" I said. "What did he look like?"

"Well . . . he looked as if he were a trapper," Emma said.

"Yes," Abigail said. "He was wearing full buckskin with fringe."

"His hair was long," Emma said. "Shoulder length. He had a long beard, and he wasn't wearing a hat."

"He had one of those beaded parfleche pouches on his waist, like Indians carry," Abigail said. "But he was not an Indian."

"No, he spoke English," Emma said. "His voice was very rough and raspy."

Virgil looked at me. He narrowed his eyes slightly.

Emma looked at Virgil and back to me.

"I know you will do everything in your power to help us," Emma said, "and for that we will be forever grateful."

73

"It's what we do," Virgil said.

Virgil walked out the door. I turned to follow Virgil to the platform, and Emma reached out, taking my hand.

"Thank you," she said.

I looked at Emma's hand holding mine, then looked into her eyes. She squeezed my hand and remained looking at me for a time. I touched the top of her hand in my hand, then walked out the door.

18

The sprinkling had now turned to light rain as I stepped out of the coach and joined Virgil on the platform. He wasn't pacing, but he wasn't still.

"That's Bloody Bob Brandice they're talking about," I said. "With the pouch and knife."

"None other."

"That's not good news."

"No," Virgil said. "It's not."

"Can't think of worse news, really," I said.

" 'Specially for those within an arm's length of him intent on living," Virgil said.

Virgil was a man of solid resolve, a man who did not hold a grudge. There was no reason for such nonsense. He took one moment at a time, one situation at a time, and had no reason to haze his focus by allowing feelings to be part of a task at hand. *Feelings get you killed,* Virgil always said, but the thought of Bloody Bob Brandice primed the hell out of Virgil's intentions and sharpened the bead of his aim. If there was any one association more disturbing, more unfortunate, more nagging, to conjure up than Randall Bragg's gang it would be Bloody Bob Brandice, and now it appeared we had them both to deal with.

"Thought the son of a bitch was in prison," I said.

"Evidently, he ain't."

"He got life."

"He got out," Virgil said.

"He's not part of Bragg's outfit," I said.

Virgil shook his head.

"Don't seem likely."

"Don't think he'd be part of anybody's outfit," I said.

Virgil shook his head.

"Don't either," he said.

"He's not capable of taking orders, riding with an outfit."

"Even if it was his *own* outfit," Virgil said.

"He's nothing but a hard case. A murderous loner."

"He is," Virgil said. "Even murderous loners got a price."

"Hired assassin, you think?"

"Might be," Virgil said.

"He's no Yankee."

"Far from it."

"Don't make much sense," I said.

"No, it don't."

"Got Bragg's outfit to sort out," I said. "And now Bloody Bob."

We thought about that for a moment.

"Don't get much worse," I said.

"It don't," Virgil said.

Virgil shook his head some. Then he looked back through the door to Abigail and Emma.

"It by God don't."

"What do you figure we do?"

Virgil leaned out over the platform rail and looked back behind us.

"Go after him," I said.

Virgil looked back to me.

"We do," Virgil said. "Sooner we get to him. More lives will be spared."

I looked back through the coach to the rear door.

"We open that back door we'll have a gun or two pointed at us, hammers back," I said.

Virgil looked to the ladder. He got close to it and looked to the door window, gauging if he could be seen through the window.

"We go back over the top," Virgil said, "come down on the platform between the first and second cars, staying tight to the ladder, they won't see us. Least not through the door window they won't."

I looked at Virgil, looked at the ladder, and thought about what he was saying.

"We won't be expected from the top," Virgil said.

"I suspect you are right, and if they're on the platform we'll see them before they see us."

Virgil nodded.

"All right, then," Virgil said. "We go."

19

I followed Virgil back into the coach. He called out to the dandy as he walked halfway down the aisle.

"Captain Cavanaugh, keep your eye to that door," Virgil said. "Shoot anybody who opens it."

The dandy saluted.

Virgil looked at the sodbuster, Ness, and pointed him toward the front of the coach.

"You, Ness," Virgil said. "Like you to come up here with me."

Ness turned, saying something to his wife.

Emma stood up in front of me as I turned to walk back to the front platform.

"What will you do?" Emma said. "What are you planning?"

She was close to me. So close I could feel the warmth of her breath on my face.

"Virgil and I have been doing this kind of work for a long time," I said. "At this very moment all I can readily allow is we don't have any plans on quitting."

Emma didn't move. If anything, she moved slightly closer to me, just looking in my eyes.

"Here," I said.

I handed her one of the pistols I had picked up.

"Take this," I said. "Keep it at ready."

Emma looked at the pistol. She took it in both hands, then looked in my eyes again.

Virgil and Ness started back toward me.

"If you feel the need to use it," I said. "Use it."

Emma kept looking in my eyes as she took a step back. I offered her my most reassuring look and stepped out onto the platform. The rain was falling steadily now. Virgil followed me out, followed by Ness. Virgil turned to Ness. He spoke fatherly-like to him.

"Everett and me are going back over the top of this car. Mix things up a bit. What I want from you is, climb this ladder after us, position yourself with Everett's eight-gauge there. Everett, hand him that brush hog."

I handed Ness the shotgun, unbuckled my shell belt, and draped it over his shoulder.

"Keep watch," Virgil said. "Any one of the robbers get around us somehow, tries to come over the top of this car, send them

lead from this side-by-side."

"Yes, sir," Ness said.

"I can count on you to do that?" Virgil said.

"Yes, sir," Ness said. "You can."

Virgil looked at me and tipped his head sharply to the ladder.

"Let's go," Virgil said.

I climbed the ladder and peeked back over the roof. It was difficult to see much, but I could see well enough to know there was no one in sight. I hoisted my body to the roof, and Virgil followed. I started moving toward the rear of the coach and quickly realized it was a hell of a lot easier walking in the direction the train was traveling than walking in the direction from which the train came. I figured Virgil felt the same as he grabbed a handful of the back of my coat, stabilizing himself as we walked slowly with the strong wind and rain pushing at our backs. The rain started coming down harder and harder as we moved slowly, one solid step at a time. When we got toward the end of the coach we crouched low. As we got closer we dropped to our bellies and inched up so we could see between the cars. The rain started coming even harder, and water was rushing by us, channeling off the coach and onto the platform.

No bandits were on the platform. I quickly slid myself toward the platform ladder and, shrouded in water, dropped down the ladder and onto the platform. I stood off to the side of the platform and could see the door window of the rear coach was completely fogged over.

I looked up and motioned for Virgil to come down the ladder.

For having a busted knee, Virgil's ability to maneuver always surprised me.

Virgil positioned himself sideways and slid one leg down to the ladder, followed by the other, and, in an instant, he was now on the platform beside me and we each had a Colt in each hand with their hammers back.

I ducked under the window and positioned myself on the opposite side of the door from Virgil.

From inside the coach, a hand wiped the fog from the window and a pair of bandit eyes peered out. With Virgil and me off to each side of the door and the bandit keeping watch on the front coach door, we were unseen.

The water was falling off the front coach and pouring over the top of us like a waterfall, making it difficult to see, but I could see Virgil well enough to see him nod *Go!*

20

In an instant, I swiveled back a step and kicked the door right under the brass lever, knocking the bandit on the other side backward. He raised his pistol, but I shot him first. Virgil shot a skinny bandit behind him who managed to clear leather with his pistol. Vince had just entered the rear door but was backing out. Dean was with another robber, five rows from the rear of the coach. He had another revolver and got off a shot as he backed up. The bullet pinged off the ceiling. Virgil's shot hit Dean in the chest. The fourth bandit also got off a shot, but it hit the back of the seat just to my left, and I sent two shots to him and he fell back. Vince got his Hopkins & Allen pointing at me. He fired a shot that registered just above my head. Then he ducked back out the rear door before I could get a clear shot. Virgil shot just as Vince closed the door, and we could hear Vince yell, "Goddamn it! Goddamn it!"

The coach was full of blue smoke, and except for the cowering and stunned passengers, the car was now empty of gun hands.

A fearful freckle-faced woman clutched a preacher holding up a tattered Bible like it was a shield as Virgil and I moved down the aisle.

"I'm Marshal Virgil Cole; this is my deputy, Everett Hitch!"

"God bless you," the preacher said as I followed Virgil. "God bless you!"

We moved swiftly down the aisle. An old fellow with a beard stood, offered his hand. "Much obliged, Marshal."

"Sit down!" Virgil said. "Stay seated! Everybody stay seated!"

The old man promptly sat down.

"We got them on their heels," I said. "They're backing up."

"They are," Virgil said.

We stepped over Dean and the other robber's body. I thought about what Virgil had said to Dean. Virgil was a man of his word. He kept his promise to everyone, including Dean. He gave Dean a chance to be counted, but Dean did not take it, and now he was dead.

When we got to the rear door, Virgil

shifted to one side and I shifted to the other. Virgil edged his body over so he was not in front of the door and lowered himself to where he was sitting back on his heels. He opened the loading gate on his Colt and reloaded.

"If it weren't for that telegram you received in Laredo," I said, "we'd be riding through hill country, watching dancing girls in San Antonio, taking our leisurely time getting back to Appaloosa. Fact, though, we've wound up on a train, chasing some of the meanest no-goods we've ever come across."

"It's what we do, Everett," Virgil said. "We're lawmen."

I opened the loading gate on my revolver and dumped the empty casings.

"Beside that fact," Virgil said, "we got unsettled business with the lot of them."

"That we do," I said as I reloaded bullets back into the Colt's chamber. "Some point, though, I 'spect you'll be telling me about that damn telegram?"

Virgil didn't say anything. He slowly cracked open the door.

21

I did not see what Virgil saw until he stood up and opened the door wider. Vince was nowhere in sight, and the door of the next coach was wide open. Even though the hard falling rain blurred our vision, there wasn't anyone moving about. Virgil moved out, and I followed onto the platform. We took post on each side of the door of the next coach, and again we were under a deluge from the pouring rain. I peeked around the door and saw no gunmen. Toward the rear of the coach a woman was kneeling over a man lying in the aisle. I stepped in the car, followed by Virgil. We trained our pistols on everybody and nothing.

An older man sitting at the second-row aisle started shouting, "We've given you all our money, just leave us!"

Another passenger, a chubby man sitting across the aisle, held his hands in the air.

"Don't hurt us," he said. "Please!"

"We are not here to harm you," Virgil said. "We're here to protect you!"

Again, Virgil told the passengers who we were. A young fellow wearing spectacles pointed toward the rear door.

"One of them came running back through here! Bleedin' like a stuck pig!"

"Where was he shot?" I asked.

"Side of his head! He had his hand over his ear! He yelled at the others to go back, and they ran out the back door!"

"How many others," I asked.

"Two other men."

The young fellow pointed back down the aisle to the woman kneeling over the man and spoke quietly: "They shot that lady's husband 'bout a half-hour ago. He tried to put up a fight when they wanted his wife's ring, and they shot him. She's been sittin' over him, talkin' to him, but he ain't alive."

We moved down the aisle with our pistols pointed toward the rear door.

"Everybody just try and remain calm," Virgil said.

When I got to the woman kneeling over her husband, she turned and looked at me. Her face was streaked with tears. I showed her the badge on my vest but kept my gun pointed toward the rear door.

"We are here to help," I said.

The man she was leaning over was sure enough dead. His eyes were open. He had a bullet hole in his cheek, and behind his head, a puddle of blood pooled in the aisle floor. She looked to her husband.

"It's going to be okay now, darling," she said. "Law officers are here now to help us."

I moved on toward the door. Lightning flashed again, and the coach's interior brightened for a brief moment. I glanced back to Virgil. He reached out his hand to the woman kneeling over her husband.

"Be better if you took a seat, ma'am," Virgil said.

The woman looked at Virgil as if he were something curious, unrecognizable. Then, in almost a moment of haste, she took his hand.

"There you go," Virgil said. "Just stay seated, that'd be best."

Virgil moved on.

"Everybody!" Virgil said. "Just stay in your seats!"

A tall gent wearing expensive but tattered clothes leaned out into the aisle. He pointed to the dead man and spoke to Virgil.

"This is my trade. Name's G. W. Tisdale, mortician. I tried to console her, tried to let her know her husband was with God, but she has her own agenda," he said. "Women often do."

"Might need your services in a bit," Virgil said. "Right now, stay seated, don't do nothing."

Virgil's focus remained in the same direction his Colt was pointing, the rear door, as he moved next to me.

"Next car is the Pullman," I said. "The governor's car."

"Yep," Virgil said. "Providing him and his wife are still among us. No guarantee. No telling what to expect with Bloody Bob on board."

"What do you want to do going in there," I said. "How do we go about it?"

"Just gonna have to be quick," Virgil said. "And shoot straight."

"Won't be our first time."

"No," Virgil said. "It won't."

Virgil positioned himself on the right of the door. I was on the left. I nudged behind the doorjamb, lowered myself to one knee, cracked opened the door, and what was in front of me was on one hand predictable but on the other unfortunate.

22

I stood up and swung the door open wider for Virgil to see what I saw. The back half of the train, from the first-class Pullman car to the caboose, had been disconnected and, along with the governor and his wife, was rapidly drifting away from us.

"Good goddamn," Virgil said.

Lightning cracked across the dark sky, and we could see the Pullman. It was at least one hundred feet behind us now. I could see someone. It looked like Vince, but I was not sure. He was getting up off the platform from closing the angle cock air valve on the coach brakes.

"They closed the air valve on the brakes," I said. "We're not slowing. They obviously closed us off first."

I got on my knees to open the valve.

"What are you saying, Everett?" Virgil asked.

I reached for the valve and it wasn't there.

"Got no lever," I said. "The son of a bitch!"

I stood up and looked back. The cars were no longer visible. They had vanished as we continued forward.

"He closes that valve, Virgil, he overrides the automatic safety brakes. Without a lever, our valve stays closed and it does the same damn thing, overrides the brakes and we keep going. They keep going south, we keep going north."

Virgil shook his head slowly, and the rain swirled up around us as we powered ahead.

"We've been traveling on an uphill grade ever since we crossed the river leaving Texas," I said. "By them bypassing the safety brakes, they will roll freely downhill. Using the handbrakes to control their speed as they go."

"So the air brakes," Virgil said, "work disconnected from the engine?"

"According to George Westinghouse, they do."

"George Westinghouse?"

"The fellow who invented the air brake."

Virgil just shook his head, looking south into the dark night.

"The air line runs from the engine all the way back," I said. "If that line loses pressure, the brakes close automatically on any

91

coach that is disconnected, and that coach
—"

"— stops by itself," Virgil said.

"Yep, that's right," I said.

"Next thing you know they'll be putting wings on these damn things and we'll be flying around like birds."

"Well, there's one thing for certain those robbers will be thinking, Virgil."

"The farther away from us, the better for them," Virgil said.

"Yep, they are going to roll back as far as they can go," I said.

"You think they planned this somehow?" Virgil said.

"Hard to figure," I said. "Must have. Might have been a backup plan. Seems likely, more than likely, one or some of them are train hands, know what they're doing."

Virgil shook his head.

"What do you figure we do?" I said.

"We get up to the engineer. Get this train that's rolling forward to get going backward," Virgil said. *En este momento.*

23

Virgil wasted no more time with words or thought. He started moving forward up the aisle at a quick pace, and I followed. He spoke to the undertaker as we stepped over the dead man: "Take care of this fallen fellow. And be diligent about it."

We continued walking forward. When we crossed through the rain from one platform to the next, there was a hard jolt in the movement of the train.

When we reentered through the rear door of the uphill coach the passengers turned in their seats and looked back at us. They were wide-eyed watching us as we hurried up the aisle.

Virgil opened the front coach door, and when he did we quickly understood why the train had previously jolted.

We had been disconnected and were drifting away from the first passenger car and engine. Rain was swirling and it was dark, but we could vaguely see the silhouette of someone on the back platform. He was watching us as we faded away from the front section of the train.

"Hellfire," I said.

Whoever it was, whoever had disconnected us, whoever had outmaneuvered us, was now traveling on into the distant darkness.

Virgil said nothing.

The train was now in three separate sections: the engine and first coach with Emma and Abigail on board, the second and third coach with us, and the fourth coach back to the caboose with Vince, the remainder of the bandits, Bloody Bob, and, if they were still alive, the governor and his wife.

I got down on my knees to check the airline valve and quickly determined it had already been closed.

We were still moving forward from the momentum, but in no time we would soon be rolling backward.

"Looks like we're now gonna be bumping into Vince and Bloody Bob sooner than we expected," I said. "That's a fact."

I got back to my feet.

"And a hell of a lot sooner than they expected," I said.

Virgil just shook his head slightly.

"They will roll slower than us," I said. "With us in just these two coaches, we'll be rolling downhill faster."

Virgil didn't say anything. He just remained looking forward.

"And when we do," I said, "we'll need to ride these handbrakes, controlling our speed."

Virgil continued looking up the track as if he didn't believe what was happening.

"They got a head start, but we'll catch up to them," I said. "Hopefully before they bottom out. They got more friction, more cars."

I felt as though I was just talking so Virgil wouldn't think what he was thinking.

"Vince and the others on those cars back there have to control their speed; otherwise, there will be a train wreck if they don't," I said. "Us too, we have to control our downhill speed or we will get to rolling too fast and lose control. We should turn off the lamps so we are dark. Don't want them to see us coming up on 'em."

"The fox got in the henhouse," Virgil said as he continued looking up the track.

"The Yankee?"

"Might well be the Yankee," Virgil said.

"You're not thinking that sodbuster we left with my eight-gauge," I said, "or the dandy had a hand in this, do you?"

Virgil stayed looking up the track.

"You didn't see that preacher fellow back there, did you?" Virgil said.

"Preacher fellow?" I said.

"In this car. The preacher fellow that had been sitting row five, west side, aisle," Virgil said.

24

I turned and looked back into the coach, row five, west side aisle. The seat was empty.

"No," I said.

Virgil moved his head up and down very slowly.

"He's not there," I said. "There is no preacher sitting there."

"That's what I figured," Virgil said.

Virgil did not turn around; he just remained looking forward up the dark track in front of us. We were still rolling north from the train's forward momentum.

"I remember him, too," I said, "but he's not there now. There's a freckle-faced redhead by the window."

"Yep, she was holding on to him and was crying when we came by."

Virgil had already identified the culprit. The fact that Virgil knew the man who had held up the Bible was not sitting where he was previously did not surprise me. Virgil saw way more than most. Even when things were on tenterhooks, Virgil had the ability to remain perceptive and steady.

Virgil turned and looked back through the open door into the coach. Except for the preacher who was previously sitting in row five, the west side aisle, everyone was looking at Virgil as if they needed some sort of answer. Virgil gave it as he crossed the threshold and walked a few steps down the aisle.

"Everybody get your this and thats in order," Virgil said. "We will need you to turn off these lamps in a bit, and it will get dark."

We dragged the dead gunmen out to the platform and slid them off the side. Virgil moved back down the aisle to row five. The redheaded freckle-faced woman who had previously been crying and holding on to the preacher was sitting by the window, looking up at Virgil. Sitting in the west side aisle seat was the preacher's discarded Bible. Virgil picked it up. He opened the Bible and leafed through it as if he were looking for a passage or verse, then closed it. He looked at the back side of the Bible. Then he dropped it into the seat.

The freckle-faced woman offered Virgil a crooked smile.

"The preacher fellow who was sitting here

holding this Bible," Virgil said. "Was he somebody you knew?"

She shook her head.

"No, sir."

"How long had he been sitting here?" Virgil asked.

"Not long," she said.

She looked around at a few passengers sitting near her.

"He just plopped down here, short time before y'all two come through the front door shooting them robbers."

"He came through the rear door here?" Virgil said.

"Yes, sir," she said. "The robbers pointed their guns at him. I thought they was gonna shoot him, but he held up his Bible, talking about Jesus, and they didn't."

The other passengers sitting nearby nodded in agreement.

"Just preaching he was," she said, "talking about going to hell. Spewing like it was just shy of noon on Sunday. The robbers told him to sit down and shut up."

"And the preacher fellow just sat here?"

"He did . . . but I'm not real sure he was a preacher," she said. "Well, if he was a preacher he was rather unpreacherly."

"What was unpreacherly about him?" Virgil asked.

"When the shooting started, I grabbed on to him and I could feel he was carryin' guns."

"Guns?" Virgil said. "More than one?"

"Yes," she said as she looked back and forth between Virgil and me. "Two I know of. One on his hip, one in his coat pocket."

"When he left this seat," Virgil said, "was he carrying anything?"

The woman looked up to the luggage rack overhead, then to a few of the passengers that were watching her.

"He had a fancy black suitcase," she said. "He took it with him when he left through the front there."

"Thank you, ma'am."

Virgil tipped his hat and started to move, but the freckle-faced woman spoke up.

"It was hard for him with the luggage," she said. "He had but one arm. His left arm was wood, and he had a hand that was carved and painted to look normal, but it was not."

"Thank you," Virgil said. Virgil looked a me. Then he looked to the rest of the passengers.

"We need to get these lamps off, folks," Virgil said.

25

I followed Virgil to the rear of the coach, and the passengers did as they were instructed and started turning off the lamps. With the exception of Virgil being downright hornswoggled by Allie French, he was a man who did not get the wool pulled over his eyes, ever. The mere fact that we were now coasting and eventually would be rolling backward in disconnected coaches down the track in a rainstorm because of an oversight wasn't setting well with Virgil.

"If there is a Yankee," I said, "that must be him masquerading as a conductor, masquerading as a God-fearing preacher?"

"Hard to say," Virgil said.

"He must have double-crossed the others," I said.

"Might have."

"Looks like he made off with the loot," I said.

Virgil stopped at the rear door and looked

back to the passengers turning out the last few lamps.

"That's not all he's made off with," Virgil said without looking at me.

"I know," I said.

The notion we left the governor's daughters in harm's way prompted Virgil's eyes to narrow and grow cold. I'd seen that look on Virgil's face many times before, but it was always right before he killed somebody.

"Emma's got fight," I said. "She's got six rounds in a short-barrel Colt; she's got a steely resolve and she's got fight."

"One thing for certain," Virgil said. "They're heading north, we're heading south, and there ain't nothing we can do about the inevitability of that fact. Least not at this very moment there ain't."

Virgil opened the door. We stepped into the falling rain and crossed to the next coach. I followed Virgil down the aisle. The undertaker had done what Virgil had asked him to do. The dead man had been laid to rest on a seat and was covered by a blanket. An old Apache woman wearing a stove-collared black dress was now sitting with the grieving widow.

"Everyone," I said. "We need you to turn out the lamps. So take care of what you need to take care of, then do just that, turn 'em out."

By the time we stepped out the rear door the rain had subsided some, but it was still coming down solid as if it had settled in for the night. The two coaches we were riding were now rolling very slowly backward down the slightest grade. Virgil was looking down the track, but there was really nothing to see other than darkness and rain.

"This is it," I said.

"It is," Virgil said.

"Now we just ride the brake," I said. "Ease up on Bloody Bob, Vince, and the others."

Virgil nodded.

"First sign of that rear section," I said, "we stay back, watching 'em. Stop when they stop."

"Sounds right."

"Mix things up a bit," I said.

"We will," Virgil said.

For the moment we didn't need to brake; we were traveling very slowly, but I released the foot latch on the handbrake wheel and gave the wheel a slight test turn to the right. The wheel turned, but there was no friction, no braking.

"No good," I said.

"No good?" Virgil said.

I turned the wheel again, this time a few revolutions, thinking maybe the chain to the brakes might have just slacked off, but there was nothing, the wheel just turned.

"Don't work?" Virgil asked.

"No," I said. "It don't."

"You think with the George Westinghouse brakes," Virgil said, "they're no longer hooked up?"

"Don't know. We'll need to stop, though, figure out what is what," I said. "I'll open the air-line valve on the other end, get us stopped, have a look."

26

Virgil stayed on point on the downhill platform, and I worked my way back through both coaches. Nobody was talking. The passengers were settled and the lamps had all been turned off. It was quiet except for the sound of the slow rolling wheels on the track.

I thought about the many brakemen who lost their jobs because of George Westinghouse; brakemen with the dangerous job of helping the engineer regulate a train's speed by moving from coach to coach, tweaking the wheels of the handbrakes.

With the exception of the faint glow from a passenger's cigar or cigarette, we were now traveling in complete darkness. When I opened the door and stepped out onto the uphill coach's platform it was obvious we were rolling faster. Not a lot faster, but some. I got down on the floor plate of the platform and opened the angle cock valve and heard nothing — nothing happened, no braking, no slowing, nothing.

I got to my feet and released the foot latch on the handbrake and gave the wheel a turn.

"Son of a bitch," I said out loud.

The wheel just turned, like the other end, it just turned.

"Son of a bitch."

I got down to look under the coach. It was dark, and nothing was visible on the underside. I reached under to feel underneath the shaft of the handbrake. There was no chain connected to the brake. I got to my feet quick, stepped back through the door and down the aisle toward the other coach. My mind started to race. Had this been by design? Were we dealing with a train hand? A saboteur? Was there a getaway plan? A backup plan?

Whatever, whoever, however, we were rolling without any way of stopping or controlling our speed. I stepped into the next coach and grabbed a conductor's lantern hanging by the door.

"A match!" I said. "Who's got a match?"

The undertaker pulled out a box of matches. He struck one and cupped his hand around the flame. I lifted the reflector glass. He lit the wick, then slid the matchbox into my breast pocket. I turned up the lamp flame and stepped out the door and back onto the platform.

"We got a situation, Virgil!" I said.

"What sort of a situation?"

"The back wheel brake is not working," I said. "It's disconnected."

"What about the George Westinghouse brakes?" Virgil asked.

"Not working, either."

"Not?" Virgil said.

I shook my head.

"That's not good," Virgil said.

"No, it's not."

"And this one here," Virgil said. "It's busted, too."

"Is," I said. "I'm going to get down and have a look at this handbrake. See if I can make out what's broke about it. Hold this."

I handed the lamp to Virgil.

"Hold it down here," I said. "Below the platform."

We were picking up speed as I leaned out over the platform and looked back under the coach. Virgil held the lamp down under the platform so I could see. I was upside down, the ground passing by swiftly below my head as I tried to figure out what the problem was with the brake. It was hard to see, but there was enough light to determine what the problem was right off. The chain

107

had separated from the wheel shaft and was dragging back under the coach between the tracks. I lifted myself up quick.

"The chain is free of the wheel, dragging behind us," I said.

"No way of reaching it?" Virgil said.

"No."

"What do you figure?"

"We get to the end of the other car," I said. "If we got the same situation, at least the chain will be dragging behind. Maybe we can get ahold of it and somehow stop us. Otherwise —"

"Otherwise, we'll have to ask everyone to jump," Virgil said.

"We will," I said.

27

Virgil and I moved quick through the door. Virgil carried the lamp as we hustled with pace up the aisle. The lamp's shadows twisted and turned as we moved through the two coaches. The faces of the passengers looked back at us, and we moved toward the uphill end of the coaches: the undertaker, the Apache woman, the widow, the young fellow with the spectacles, the old man, the chubby man, and in the uphill coach the freckle-faced woman watched as we moved briskly past her. The moving light made the passengers' faces look eerie, almost dead-like. When we exited out the front-end door we had picked up speed. I quickly lowered myself onto the platform floor and Virgil was by my side with the lamp. Right away it was obvious we had the same situation we'd had on the downhill coach. The chain was trailing us, dragging between the rails.

"Same thing. The chain is off the wheel," I said. "Get ahold of the back of my belt, Virgil, let me see if I can reach it."

I leaned over the rear of the platform. Virgil grabbed the back of my belt, and I reached, stretching out, trying to grab the snaking chain as it moved back and forth over the railway ties. After my third, fourth attempt, I snagged it.

"Got it," I called out.

Virgil gave a pull on my belt and I was back up, secure on the floor. The chain, however, was short.

"There's no way this will reconnect to the wheel, Virgil!"

"Let's get the folks off before we get going any faster," Virgil said.

I nodded.

The young fellow wearing spectacles poked his head out the door.

"Sir? Marshal?" the young fellow said. "Maybe I can be of some help. I'm a train hand for Frisco, well, in the Fort Smith yard. I figure we got a situati—"

I interrupted, "You got any idea why when I open the valve on the air pipe the brakes don't apply?" I said.

He shook his head.

"Must be for some reason the K-triple valve is bypassed," said the young fellow.

"How do we fix that?" I said.

"You don't," he said. "Unless you're stopped."

I held up the chain.

"The chain is not connected to the wheel," I said.

"Both ends," Virgil said.

"That ain't good," said the young fellow. "This track is downhill for a long ways."

The young fellow leaned over for a closer look at the chain.

"I got an idea," he said. "Be right back."

The young fellow moved off quickly just as a bolt of lightning cracked across the sky. We could see we were in heavily wooded country, with trees close on both sides of the train, and it was obvious we were rolling faster.

The young Frisco yard hand came back through the door with a long iron bar that was flat on one end and pointed on the other.

"Slip the chain end over this end," he said. "Keep a strain on it, pull like hell, leveraged against the platform. It ain't easy, but it might work, unless we get a goin' too darn fast!"

I understood the method and followed his instructions. I slipped a link of chain over the pointed end of the bar, and the kid

111

pulled back steady on the bar, leveraging it against the platform. We could hear metal-to-metal grinding and could see sparks flying. I stood and added my strength on the bar, helping the yard hand.

"Thing is," said the yard hand, "gotta keep the pressure steady yet firm. If the chain snaps or the bar bends, well . . ."

"We jump," Virgil said.

"Yes, sir," the yard hand said. "Believe that'd be best."

The bar was being used as a lever pulling on the chain that connected to the coach brakes and the upper edge of the platform, but we were rolling faster. The yard hand and I pulled harder on the bar, causing more flying sparks and louder grinding.

"Don't want to break it!" the yard hand said as he was straining, red-faced. "Don't want to break it!"

"Come on! Come on!" I cried out as I put my weight firm but steady on the bar.

It was a matter of odds now: the downhill grade, the strength of the chain, the make-shift brake handle, the coaches' weight, and Newton's law, but thankfully, miraculously, we started to slow, and eventually, very slowly, the coaches came to a creeping stop.

The young fellow and I kept holding the pressure on the bar.

"Marshal," the young fellow said. "There's a set of chalk blocks there under the first seats."

Virgil grabbed the two wooden wedges made of oak that were bound together with thick rope. He jumped from the platform to the ground, knocked one block under one wheel and, after a moment, wedged the other under another wheel.

"Okay," Virgil called out.

The yard hand looked to me, and we let off on the leverage of the bar. The coach moved a bit, but no more. We were stopped.

"There you go," Virgil called out.

The yard hand and me leaned back against the coach platform wall and breathed a deep sigh of relief.

Lightning flashed again, and it was shockingly bright as Virgil climbed the steps. He growled like a coyote as he set foot back on the platform.

"George — by God — Westinghouse."

28

"What's your name, son?" Virgil asked the young yard hand.

He took off his spectacles and wiped the sweat from the lenses with a pocket handkerchief.

"Lee, as in Robert E.," he said. "Folks, though, call me Whip, on account I'm good with one."

"You work on trains?" Virgil said.

"I do."

"I got a question, Whip," Virgil said.

"Sir?"

"As you know, we got a hell of a situation with this train. Part of it is headed north, part of it headed south, and of course this part, these two cars, are sitting stopped right here in the middle."

"Yes, sir."

"Do you think there's a way for you to repair the handbrake on the downhill coach?" Virgil said.

"I can have a look underneath," Whip said, "see if I can figure out what the situation is."

"Good," Virgil said. "What we need to do is leave this uphill car right where it is with the women and the law-abiding others and get the downhill coach disconnected, rolling freely and headed south on this downgrade."

Whip gave Virgil a sharp nod.

"I'll have a look," Whip said.

Whip gathered up the lantern and the pinch bar and stepped off the platform.

"Need a hand?" I said.

"I'll holler at ya if I do," Whip said, and he was off.

I stepped into the coach, took out the matches the undertaker had stuffed in my coat pocket, and got one of the lamps burning. The passengers were, for the most part, wide-eyed and uneasy. Some of them were asking questions about what was going to happen, some were just talking to be talking, and some remained silent, but they were all unsettled and afraid.

Virgil moved past me, and I followed him as he walked slowly down the aisle.

"Everybody," Virgil said. "Let me vow to you, right here where you are is the safest place you could be. So do me the good deed of remaining pleasant and unparticular."

The chubby man offered us a cigar as we walked by.

"No, thanks," I said.

"Don't mind if I do," Virgil said.

Virgil lit the cigar and, after he got it going good, thanked the fellow, and we walked out the back door. Virgil shared the same safety information with the passengers in the rear coach, and then we stepped out the door and onto the downhill platform.

Light was shining from underneath the downhill coach, where young Whip was already fussing with something. It sounded like he was trying to break some piece of metal away from another piece of metal.

Virgil and I stood on the platform under the coach overhang, watching the rain continue to fall.

"Hell of a ruckus we got ourselves in," I said.

"Is," Virgil said.

"Bad bunch we are dealing with."

"Don't get much worse," Virgil said.

"Somebody," I said. "The governor or his cronies had something somebody wanted."

"That being money. Money somebody knew about, too," Virgil said.

"We've killed a number of those somebodies," I said.

"We have," Virgil said.

116

"We've been up against a good number through the years, but nothing like this," I said. "Lot of hombres all in one place."

Virgil smoked his cigar for a bit. He held up three fingers.

"The two in the car we started out in and the getaway rider," Virgil said.

"The two in the engine compartment," I said.

Virgil added his thumb and little finger.

"Then the four that were holding the girls when we jumped to the platform of the first coach from the tender," I said.

Virgil included four fingers from his other hand.

"The four in the next coach, including Dean," I said.

Virgil added his tenth finger to his nine. I brought up three fingers.

"Thirteen."

"We're not done," Virgil said.

"No, I know it," I said. "We're not."

"Worst are yet to come, too," Virgil said.

"They are," I said. "We know for sure we got Vince and most likely Bloody Bob to contend with, or someone capable of his deeds."

"I believe it is most assuredly him," Virgil said.

"Counting those two," I said, "I'd say

there are at least five, could be six, maybe seven, more, depending on whether Dean was counting the other two getaway riders."

Virgil nodded slowly as he puffed on his cigar.

29

Whip crawled up from under the front of the downhill coach. He looked up at Virgil and me standing on the platform. His face and hands were smudged with grease. He was holding the lamp in one hand and the brake chain in the other.

"I think I might be able to get this fixed," Whip said.

"Might?" Virgil said.

"More than might," Whip said. "I got the chain from the other car. And with this one here, I think I can piece the two together with this bolt."

"What can we do to help?" I said.

"Hold this lamp for me, I reckon."

I stepped off the platform and got the light from Whip. I held it up for him so he could see what he was doing as he ducked back under the platform.

Virgil was looking down from the platform over the rail. He blew out some cigar smoke.

The smoke drifted into the light, showing the direction of the slanting rain.

I moved the lantern closer for Whip as he scooted back under the coach. Whip pulled and tugged on the chain connecting to the brakes and then called out, "Turn that wheel, take up the slack!"

I looked up at Virgil on the platform. He turned the wheel about a half-revolution.

"That's good," Whip said.

I watched as Whip pieced the two chains together with the bolt. After he nutted the bolt he looked over to me.

"Have him turn the wheel some more," Whip said.

"Turn her some more there, Virgil," I said.

Virgil turned the handbrake wheel, and the chain went taut.

"That's it," Whip called out. "There ya go!"

Whip crawled out from under the coach.

"So that's it?" Virgil said. "This wheel brake will work?"

"It will," Whip said. "The thing is, this track is good and downhill. You just don't want to get going too fast."

"You know this line pretty well, Whip?" Virgil said.

"I do," Whip said. "Before I went to work in the terminal yard I worked section gangs on this rail, spikin', keepin' tracks straight, trees cut back, rocks cleared off, that sort of thing."

"There towns nearby?" Virgil said.

"Got two way station depots near," Whip said.

Whip lifted the cap off his head and scratched his scalp under his shaggy hair.

"That way there, up the Kiamichi a piece," Whip said, pointing north with his cap, "is a place called Standley Station, ain't much of a town. Post office, dry goods, switch-yard, a bar hotel."

Whip raised his hat up higher, pointing north.

"Yonder, farther that way, is a bigger town called Crystal Creek," Whip said. "Another switchyard, bigger hotel, more people, more outfits. Next town after is Tall Water Falls; it's bigger yet. Then there's Division City, and that's the division line on the track. Turntable and telegraph loop is there, and it's like five, six blocks big."

"You said this track is good and downhill," Virgil said, "but it's got to flatten out someplace between here and Texas."

"Does," Whip said. "Where we are right now, though, is the most downhill stretch of this whole track. You could roll like, oh, twenty, twenty-five miles or so, probably stop just before Half Moon Junction."

"Junction?" Virgil said.

"Yes, sir. This line meets with the Denison and Washita Valley Railroad in Half Moon Junction. That'd be for sure the biggest stop on this run."

"I remember seeing the half-moon painted on the water tower," I said.

"Yes, sir," Whip said, "that's it."

"Looked like a busy town," I said.

"It's busy, and it's a pretty big place. It gets bigger all the time, with all of the mining goin' on. Don't know I'd necessarily call it a town, though. Oh, there are a number of hotels and plenty of businesses there, but overall it's more of like a place written about in the Bible where God got mad. Mostly whorehouses and saloons with all the mining traffic from the D and WV and all . . . gets worse all the time."

"And that'd be twenty miles?" I said.

"Yep," Whip said. "There's a dynamited cut in a tall rock butte just past a big westward sweep. Right after that, the grade flattens out before you get to Half Moon."

"All right, then," Virgil said. "Let's get these folks that are in this rear car moved to the front car. And get on with this."

30

By the time we got the passengers from the rear coach settled into the forward coach, it was not a comfortable sight. The aisles were full, and the passengers were practically sitting atop one another. Virgil stood at the back door, looking at everyone.

"Ladies, gents," Virgil said. "Me and my deputy have business to take care of south of here. It's better than a good idea you all remain here, stay dry."

Virgil looked back to Whip.

"This young fellow here, Whip, knows these parts well and can get you to safety, but for now it's best to wait out this rain and wait for daylight."

There were a few passengers with questions and a few others who hemmed and hawed, but Virgil provided no more comfort than he'd already allowed.

The rain continued to fall as we readied ourselves to disembark from the uphill coach. I stood on the back platform of the downhill coach next to the wheel of the newly reconnected handbrake. Whip was on the back platform of the uphill coach, and Virgil was on the platform of the downhill coach across from Whip. Whip uncoupled the uphill coach from the downhill coach, and Virgil called out, "Release the brake, Everett."

I released the wheel brake. Whip used the pinch bar and wedged it between the coupler. He pulled back on the bar and we broke free of the uphill coach and started moving away from it.

"Good luck, Marshal," I heard Whip say as we drifted away from the coach full of passengers.

I heard Virgil say what I heard him say many times before.

"Luck most often is accompanied with knowing what you are doing, son," Virgil said.

And just like that, we were off and moving down the track and into the night. Virgil walked down the aisle of the now-empty coach toward me on the back platform. I looked back down the side of the coach.

Whip picked up the lantern and moved it in a circular motion, the conductors' signal for reverse, and that was exactly what we were doing. We were reversing into the dark.

"Don't this beat hell?"

"Does," Virgil said.

"Train's cut up like a worm."

We thought about that for a moment.

"Yep," Virgil said. "Four living sections."

The front section with Emma and Abigail had been commandeered by someone, maybe the mysterious Yankee. I thought about Emma, about looking into her eyes, and I wondered if I'd ever look into them again.

The next section was full of passengers not knowing what would happen to them. The grieving widow, the old toothless man, the chubby man, the Apache woman, the undertaker, the freckle-faced woman, and Whip, all hunkered down in a coach, sitting stock-still on the tracks in the pouring rain. The next section, the single coach carrying Virgil and me, was now rolling freely downgrade. The last section held the governor, his wife, Bloody Bob, Vince, the remainder of the bandits, and the stock trailer with my bony dark-headed roan and Virgil's chestnut stud. Even though it was raining and it was dark, Virgil and I could see each other. There was a full moon above the rain clouds providing us with an eerie hint of silver light. The whites of Virgil's eyes had a subtle glow. We stood side by side, looking down the track into the darkness. I turned the wheel, adjusting the brake, keeping our speed steady as the blowing rain swirled around us.

"Like sailors," I said.

"It's wet enough," Virgil said. "I'll give you that."

"Fact remains, though, we're on a hard damn rail that ain't leading to the open seas."

"That's a fact."

"We go at it alone," I said.

"We do."

"Like we've done many times before."

"We have."

"Can't think of anybody I'd rather be going at it with."

"Me neither," Virgil said.

I thought of Virgil's words. *Luck most often is accompanied with knowing what you are doing.*

We rode in silence for a while before I asked, "You want to tell me about what was in that telegram?"

31

"No," Virgil said.

"But you will."

Virgil nodded.

"Yes, I will."

"It was about Allie," I said.

"It was."

"Not from Allie, though."

"Pony Flores," Virgil said. "It was from Pony Flores."

"About Allie," I said.

"I already said it was about Allie."

"What about Allie?"

"I ain't said yet, Everett. You let me tell ya, I'll tell ya."

"Okay, go right ahead, but you already told me you think she's fucking Chauncey Teagarden."

Virgil just looked at me.

"My apologies, go right ahead."

"The telegram was, as I previously said, from Pony. Pony wrote, Allie started working at the Boston House Saloon again."

"Doing what?"

"Pony's telegram said Widow Callico took up working at the Boston House first," Virgil said, "and encouraged Allie to join her."

"Sheriff Callico's grave is still warm," I said.

"Allie obliged Widow Callico, and they started up a duo."

"A duo? What kind of duo?"

"Allie sings and plays the piano, and Widow Callico dances some and plays the fiddle," Virgil said.

"I'll be damn. A duo."

"That's what the telegram said."

"That's not that bad," I said. "Not necessarily good for those listening, but there's no reason for jumping to conclusions."

"Pony's telegram said they draw a lively crowd."

"Maybe Widow Callico is a bit more musically inclined than Allie."

"It's a nightly mus-A-cal," Virgil said.

"Well, how about that," I said. "Maybe she's found her calling; maybe this attention will do her some good."

"Let's have a nudge of your spirits, Everett."

I pulled my flask from the inside breast pocket of my jacket and handed it to Virgil.

128

"Maybe she's making some money," I said. "That's not a bad thing."

Virgil uncapped the flask and took a nip.

"Seems after this nightly mus-A-cal, Widow Callico and Allie have both been spending time upstairs in Teagarden's room," Virgil said. "Allie told Pony's wife they play cards, pinochle."

32

Virgil passed the flask back to me. I took a drink and thought about what he was telling me. I kind of figured by Virgil's demeanor since we left Texas and him not really wanting to talk about the telegram that this story might not turn out to have a very good ending, but I provided the best understanding and encouragement I could muster.

"Pinochle?" I said. "Pony's wife said that, they play pinochle?"

"That's right," Virgil said.

"Well, there ya go, Virgil. No reason that's not the fact of the matter."

"According to Pony, rumors 'round town are they ain't playing pinochle up there."

I handed Virgil the flask.

"Rumors are called rumors because they are rumors," I said.

Virgil took another pull of the whiskey.

"One thing to remember," I said. "Allie's

a pretty good hand at pinochle. Bidding, melds, and tricks of the game, she's a good hand."

"Pony's telegram said this has been going on night after night."

"Just cards and a little music, Virgil."

"Pony said he wanted to make sure the rumors were rumors, like you say. He went up there and peeked in the keyhole."

I really did not want to ask, and I had a pretty good idea what was on the other side of that keyhole, but I asked anyway.

"And?"

"They weren't playing pinochle," Virgil said. "Pony said it was noisy and he really didn't need to look in the keyhole, but he looked in anyway, just to make sure they weren't playing pin the tail on the donkey or something."

"Damn," I said.

Virgil took another nip and passed the flask back to me, and I took a pull.

"I'm sure this is just a situation she's going through, Virgil. You know how she gets lonely. Widow Callico, I'm sure, is also a bit lonely herself, with her husband being dead and gone 'n all."

Virgil nodded a bit.

"And who knows, hell, maybe Pony wasn't seeing so good," I said. "Maybe Allie was not involved. Maybe she was just, I don't know, watching."

"Watching?"

"Could be. Maybe it was just Teagarden and Widow Callico getting into their grits, and maybe Allie was . . . just in the room. You know, like watching a rodeo, or an opera."

Virgil looked at me as if I were an idiot, and I kind of felt like an idiot for saying something that was stupid and frankly far-fetched.

"Allie and Widow Callico started up a side business, too," Virgil said.

"Side business? You mean another business besides the music duo?"

"Yep."

"What kind of side business?"

"You know the Callico place, the big two-story on Second Street?"

"Sure. What about it?"

"With the mines reopened, and Appaloosa being full with miners, Widow Callico and Allie turned the place into a rental," Virgil said.

"Well, there you go," I said. "That's a big house; doesn't sound like a bad business renting to miners."

"They're not renting to miners," Virgil said.

"Who they renting to?"

"The miners just stop by 'n visit."

"Visit who?"

"Working ladies," Virgil said. "Widow Callico and Allie turned the place into a whoring establishment."

"A whoring establishment?"

"Yep," Virgil said.

I took another drink and thought about what Virgil was telling me some more. I wished I hadn't asked about the telegram now, but it was too late to turn back.

"What's the name of it?"

"The name of it?" Virgil asked.

"The establishment?"

"Hell, I don't know, Everett," Virgil said. "What difference does that make?"

33

"Queen of Storyville was where Widow Callico worked when she was the Countess."

"Queen of Storyville?" Virgil said.

"Yep, that's where Widow Callico worked before she was Mrs. Callico," I said. "I was drinking a beer with Chauncey Teagarden in the Rabbit Saloon. He told me Widow Callico was the Countess at the Queen of Storyville, a big whore palace in New Orleans."

"Countess?"

"That's what Chauncey said. Said she wore fancy dresses with nothing underneath. No pants on her queen."

"She called herself the Countess?" Virgil said.

"Chauncey used to visit her, he said, before he was old enough to shave. Said she was a busy Countess. Said that was where she met Amos Callico. Amos took away the title of Countess and gave her the title of

Mrs. Callico before you took away the title of Mrs. Callico and gave her the title of Widow Callico."

The coach slowed up some; I turned the wheel and released some of the friction I had on the brakes so we would not slow up too much.

"So, are Allie and Widow Callico selling pieces, too, or are they just running the business side of things?"

"I'm not real sure of the particulars about that," Virgil said. "But with Widow Callico's background as the Countess and Allie's history of whoring, I wouldn't put it past them."

"Pony didn't say?"

"No," Virgil said. "He did say she was living there."

"Living there?"

"Yep."

"You mean she moved into Callico's place?"

"According to Pony's telegram, she did," Virgil said. "She moved in after our house burnt down."

"What? Damn, Virgil, your house burnt down?"

"Allie was cooking some fat belly, pan caught on fire, the curtains took to burning, and the whole place went up."

I looked at Virgil. Virgil was looking down the track, and he did not look at me.

"Damn, Virgil. Appaloosa burnt up something good after our fight with those renegade Chiricahuas, and it took a long while and a lot of money to put the town back together. Your house was one of the few places that did not get burnt and now this?"

"Yep," Virgil said.

"And all because Allie was cooking fat belly?"

Virgil nodded.

"Allie's never been much of a cook, you know that, Everett."

"Fat belly?" I said. "Pony said she was cooking fat belly?"

"According to the telegram," Virgil said. "Fat belly."

I turned the wheel ever so slightly, keeping us from slowing some more.

"Allie doesn't eat fat belly," I said.

"I know," Virgil said. "She don't like it."

"So who was she cooking the fat belly for?" I said.

"I don't know," Virgil said.

A gust of wind swirled the rain around a bit more. We were on a wide, fairly flattened curve, and the coach slowed. I thought we might stop, but there was no sign of the back end of the train cars with the bandits that had drifted away from us. I knew there would not be a possibility of stopping as we slowly rolled on.

"Is that it?" I asked.

"It what?" Virgil said.

"Is that the all of the telegram?"

"Yes," Virgil said. "That's all the telegram said."

"Damn," I said. "That's one helluva telegram."

"Yep, Pony wrote the code himself. He wrote it after the telegrapher left the office, on account he didn't want to spread the news around town any more than the news was already spreading," Virgil said. "I imagine it took him all night. Pony's coding wasn't really up to snuff. Western Union fellow in Nuevo Laredo deciphered it the best he could. I picked up a copy of the *World-Wide Travellers' Cipher Code* book at the Western Union office there when we crossed the border and went through the whole thing myself just to make sure the telegram was deciphered correctly."

Virgil stopped talking.

34

I pocketed my flask, and we rode the rail in silence for a long while as I worked the brake regulating our speed downhill.

"I suppose it could be worse," I said.

Virgil looked at me.

"The telegram," I said. "Not sure how exactly, but it could."

"No matter," Virgil said. "Don't change the fact Chauncey Teagarden can go about town doing as he pleases while we're out marshaling."

"No, it don't," I said, "especially since you left him in charge of peacekeeping duties."

"Especially," Virgil said. "Not much peaceful about the whole of it, though."

"Not," I said.

"But it's just the way it is, it's the way things go. Some things are certain and some uncertain," Virgil said. "Most being uncertain. You know that, Everett, and it's an uncertain thing we do."

"Is," I said.

"So," Virgil said. "We keep one eye open on the certain things and the other open on the uncertain."

I thought to myself about the certainness of what to expect from Allie French as we coasted in the dark. There wasn't much uncertain about Allie. Fact being, Allie French was as predictable as sundown.

"But," Virgil said, " 'what lies before us and what lies behind us are small matters compared to what lies within us.' "

"Emerson?"

"Yep," Virgil said. "Ralph Waldo."

After that, Virgil stopped talking. We rode in silence for the next few miles.

I understood the nature of Virgil's dismay. When Virgil's mind was set, it was granite. He believed in Allie. His mind was set on that simple fact, and he cared for her deeply, whether she was whoring or not. It was never actions that shackled Virgil's interest, but more to it, the nature behind the actions.

Virgil was more capable than anyone I ever saw in a struggle, but Virgil always valued strategy over struggle. I always thought if Virgil had fought with the Army he would have made a hell of a general. There would be no other place for him besides the top. In a way, Virgil maneuvered as a general in everything he did. Not all generals, but the ones who were fearless and thoughtful. Virgil was selfless, matter-of-fact, always knowing there was nothing more to the future than the present, and that fact made him stand taller than most.

"Dead hand," Virgil said, almost quiet-like.

Virgil was signifying the fact we were rolling past a dead gunman tossed off the train.

"Not much of a burial," I said.

"No, it's not," Virgil said.

"Not much of a life, either."

"Not," Virgil said. "There's another."

"Seen a lot of dead men, especially in the Army," I said. "Never comfortable with the fact, really."

"Killing a man is one thing," Virgil said. "Getting comfortable with it is another thing. Living among the dead is altogether something else."

"Never was much for religion. Or really considered such a thing as living forever, but seeing crumpled dead men always makes me think there's got to be something more to it. Especially if the poor bastard was just that, a poor bastard, which most of the time are the dead people we come in contact with."

"You live," Virgil said. "You die."

"Indians seem a bit different, for some reason."

"Indians got a foot in and one foot out of life from the get-go," Virgil said.

I thought about that. That seemed right. We rode for a bit and Virgil was quiet.

"What do you figure happened with the men that were traveling with the governor," I said.

"Lassiter," Virgil said, "and Hobbs?"

"What do you think?" I said. "Slow as the train was going, unless they landed in a deep gully, I don't think the jump would have hurt them."

"Hard to know," Virgil said.

"Maybe they took a road, made it to a farm or ranch or one of the other places the yard hand Whip was talking about."

"Might have," Virgil said.

35

The rain started to let up some. There was an opening in the thunderclouds, and we could see moonlight on the tracks. Far away to the east there was lightning. We rode in silence as the coach made a wide switchback loop following the bend in the river. We were rolling very slowly, with no applied pressure to the brakes.

I was about to offer a few words of encouragement about Allie and the pinochle situation when I heard the window in the back of the coach shatter, followed by a loud report in front of us, an obvious sound delay, rifle shot.

"Down!" Virgil said.

The bullet had traveled between where Virgil and I were standing, through the open door behind us, down the aisle, blowing out the glass in the front door. The fact it was a bullet was confirmed when a second bullet exploded the window just behind where I had been standing. I was already down and low to the platform floor.

"Inside!" Virgil said.

I hurried behind Virgil through the door to the interior of the coach. Virgil was off to one side of the aisle, and I was on the other.

"Who the hell is shooting," I asked.

Another shot pinged loudly on a piece of iron.

"Somebody," Virgil said. "That's a fact."

"Why?" I said. "A single coach rolling quiet could not be expected by Vince and his gang or anybody, for that matter."

"Those shots sounded the same," Virgil said. "Sounded like the same rifle."

"Hell, and it's dark," I said.

"It is."

"Doesn't make good sense," I said. "To just shoot in the dark when they got no idea what or who they're shooting at. It's not like we are expected."

"That's a fact," Virgil said.

"No good sense at all."

Another shot rang out. The bullet ricocheted through the car and busted out another window.

"Good sense or not," Virgil said, "got a feeling sense don't have nothing to do with this situation."

"Maybe it's just some Indians don't like

train coaches," I said. "Shooting at the little houses on wheels."

"Might be."

"Some superstitious Comanche, thinking this coach is some kind of bad sign," I said.

"Don't know," Virgil said. "Seems like maybe we're dealing with a lone shooter, though, Comanche or otherwise."

"Yeah, there'd be more bullets coming, that's for sure."

"There would."

Another shot rang out, followed by another.

"Same rifle, all right," Virgil said.

Another shot hit the platform rail.

"Whoever it is," I said, "they're peppering the hell out of us."

We coasted for a bit longer, and there were no more shots being fired.

"Maybe they're done," I said.

We were traveling slow, so slow I thought the coach was going to stop.

"Maybe we passed them by, maybe —"

Virgil gave me a sharp nudge to my shoulder; he heard something.

"Uphill platform," Virgil said quietly.

I turned around and trained my attention to the door between the platform and us. I did not say another word. I listened. Except for the sound of the wheels on the track, it

144

was quiet. I heard nothing, but Virgil had
heard something, and it appeared there
were some others, or somebody, now on
board with us.

36

The door on the uphill end of the coach was closed shut, and if there were now others aboard, we could not see them. We could not see much of anything. Even though the clouds had for the moment parted and some moon was out, the coach was dark. I could make out only vague outlines: the seats, the windows, and the dark movement of the land passing by the windows. I stayed down low to the floor with one eye peeking around the coach seats, focused toward the darkness up the aisle. The coach was starting to roll faster. We would need to work the brake or we could, and most surely would, get rolling too fast downhill, too fast out of control.

I whispered, "Need to get on that brake, Virgil."

Just as I finished speaking, the door opened. Virgil did not react by taking a shot, and neither did I. Virgil would never shoot into the dark. He would shoot only when he knew whom, or at least what, he was shooting. Regardless, whoever opened the door did not step into the door frame; the open door was just that, an open door, and whoever opened it remained — at least for the moment — off to the side. We continued to pick up speed. A breeze was now moving through the open doors as the coach leaned slightly on an eastward turn downhill.

"Who goes there?" a deep, raspy voice called out.

We knew that voice. The voice was that of Bloody Bob Brandice. Bob caught a piece of lead in his throat prior to going to prison in Huntsville.

"Virgil Cole."

There was a long pause before Bob replied. His voice was low and quiet.

"Virgil Cole?" Bob grumbled.

"That's right."

There was another long pause.

"Bullshit."

"No bullshit, Bob."

Bob paused again, even longer than the time before. He had heard Virgil say his name out loud, and this gave him pause.

"Virgil Cole," Bob said slowly. "I heard it was you. When I heard it was the great and mighty Virgil Cole, that you were the lawman aboard, I thought, well, if it ain't my lucky day."

"I wouldn't be too reliant on luck, Bob," Virgil said.

"Looked around for you for a spell, Cole, when I got out. Never laid eyes on ya," Bob said, "and now this."

"Now this," Virgil replied.

"Now this," Bob said again.

"Last I heard you was west in mining country, suckled up with some lilac whore."

Virgil did not reply.

Bob laughed, a raspy, snarly laugh.

"I'll be go to hell," Bob said.

"I don't believe you have a choice, Bob," Virgil said.

Virgil stood center aisle with his shoulders facing squarely toward the door.

There was a long silence, and Bob said slowly, "Fuckin' Virgil goddamn Cole."

"That's right," Virgil said, "and Everett Hitch."

Bob laughed again, this time a loud, booming, raspy laugh.

"What the fuck you two tamers doing?" Bob said. "I heard there was some law on this night train, but I'd'a never figured it'd be a couple a right-minded saddle tramps the likes of you two. But it goes to figure, lilac bubble-bath do-gooders would be sitting on velvet seats, 'specially you, Cole."

Virgil whispered to me, "Any second now."

37

Bob laughed loudly again. He was enjoying himself. I suppose this encounter had been a long time coming for Bob, considering Virgil was the one responsible for the lead in Bob's throat and his however many years spent in Huntsville.

"Yeah, you got soft," Bob said. "Probably eating cakes and candies, too."

Just like Virgil said he would, Bob stepped out quick. He managed to get a shot off, but Virgil shot him, twice. Bob dropped his rifle in the aisle and staggered back to the platform rail. He leaned on the rail like he was bellying up to the bar.

"You fuck," Bob said. "Aww . . ."

"Slow us down, Everett," Virgil said.

The wind was moving through the coach, and we were rolling pretty fast now. I thought about what Whip had said, about going too fast. I stepped out onto the downhill platform and turned the brake wheel. The brakes engaged, making a screeching, grinding sound, and sparks shot out from the undercoach. I let up some, maintaining a pressure that was firm but not too hard. The last thing we needed was for the chain to break. I looked back through the coach. Virgil was standing square in the aisle, facing Bob. Bob was still standing next to the platform rail. After a moment, the coach started to slow.

Virgil took a few steps toward Bob and stopped.

"What are you doing on this train?" Virgil said.

"I ain't on the train. Fact is, I'm in a goddamn coach with two holes in me 'cause you just shot me."

"You shot first."

"I did at that."

"You had a choice."

"I did at that," Bob said, "and a goddamn good choice I made. If I knowed for a fact it was you, you lilac son of a bitch, and Hitch I was shootin' at, I would'a took better aim! Fucking do-gooders, the both of ya."

We were now traveling slowly, but the wind was whipping through the coach. I stepped into the coach just behind Virgil.

"Hell, fuck," Bob said quietly. "Virgil Cole

and Everett Hitch."

Bob turned slightly, facing directly toward us. It looked as though he was shot high in the chest and high in the side. Which was consistent with Virgil's style and pattern, tight and high. Virgil always shot high on the body. As long as I had been with Virgil, I never saw him put a bullet in a man's gut.

Bob leaned over and spit. "Shit."

He was holding his side with his left hand just under his armpit. His other hand held on to the platform rail, and his body moved ever so slightly with the rhythmic side-to-side motion of the coach as we continued rolling.

"Y'all," Bob said, "are most likely teetotalers, too, I 'magine."

Bob moaned and leaned back on the rail. A blast of wind whipped through the coach, and the door between Bob and us slammed shut, and the remaining glass in the door shattered. In an instant Bob was no longer standing there. Virgil and I moved quickly up the aisle with guns ready. We opened the door and stepped onto the platform, but Bob was gone.

"Stop us, Everett," Virgil said. "Get us stopped."

We were still rolling pretty fast. I turned the brake wheel some more, and we started to slow again, but I had to take it easy.

"What the hell was he doing?" I said. "Don't make good sense, don't seem practical, Bob coming up this track, Virgil."

"Good sense 'n practical don't have nothing to do with Bloody Bob Brandice."

Virgil did not want to take any chances with Bloody Bob being on the loose. Since it was, in fact, Bloody Bob we'd encountered, Virgil didn't want to leave him to do more of what Virgil knew firsthand Bob was capable of doing.

"I guess the fact we'd been identified as being on this train and the fact there was a lone coach drifting down the track was good enough for Bob to start shooting," I said.

"That's right," Virgil said. "And if it just happened to be nuns or children he shot, so be it. Makes no difference to Bloody Bob who he shoots. If he didn't get me and he killed somebody else, he'd just put 'em on a spit and have 'em for late supper."

38

Virgil wanted Bob done. It seemed with the two high holes in his upper body Bob would not survive, but Virgil knew Bob was a tough man. Bob had survived more than a few deadly skirmishes, including a previous one with Virgil. Eleven years earlier outside of Amarillo, Virgil shot Bob in the neck.

"You think he was just coming after you, and that's that?"

Virgil shook his head.

"Bob's bloodthirsty," Virgil said. "Like a mountain lion. He knew what was south was of no interest to him. North proposed promise, proposed possibilities."

"Killing you being one of those posed possibilities."

"The other, getting to the kingpin, staying on the trail of the one-armed preacher, the conductor culprit who most likely left him. But Bob's a killer of the first order. He didn't know it was me in this coach, too dark to determine that for sure, but he didn't care."

Virgil picked up the rifle Bob had dropped on the floor.

"He didn't have a pistol. He'd have come at me with it if he did," Virgil said. "He just had this Henry rifle he dropped. This Henry and a big-size bone-handled knife. He's got his knife for sure."

It started raining again, not hard rain, but it was coming down. By the time I got the coach stopped, we were at least a quarter of a mile away from where Bob had dropped over the rail. I secured the brake wheel with the foot latch, and we stepped off the platform and into the falling rain.

"You go up that side of the track, I'll go up this side," Virgil said. "And Everett? I don't have to tell you, but I will anyway. With or without the Henry rifle, Bloody Bob Brandice is a slippery snake."

The rain started to pick up some as Virgil and I took off, walking up the track. It was sure enough dark out, but Virgil and I had plenty of experience in the dark, and we both had good night vision. The peripheral vision being the key, looking at everything as opposed to looking at something, was the best method for getting around in the dark.

Virgil moved up on the west, and I was on

the east. We stayed to the woods as we worked our way up the easement.

After about a hundred or so furlongs I could hear the Kiamichi to my right. It was a swift section of the river, and the moving water got louder as I kept walking. After a couple of hundred feet farther, a piece of the rapid river became visible and the water was crashing loud. I walked a bit farther and felt I was about to the place where Bob dropped off the coach platform.

I did not see any sign of Bob on or near the track. I kept walking, and the land I was walking on leveled out with the tracks. Still there was no sign of Bob. I figured by now I would see faint movement, ever so slight movement, and find Bob sprawled out on the track, dying.

I was sure I'd see that kind of movement I'd seen many times in the dark; movement with a little life left but waning, dying, like a wounded deer or Indian, or street gunman. On one hand, here in this life, but on the other, his life was slipping away, almost gone.

But Bob was nowhere to be seen. It started to rain hard again. The sound of the rushing river mixing with the rain made it hard for me to hear my footsteps. I stopped and turned around and turned around again, thinking I might see Bob, but saw nothing other than dark rain. I walked up and stepped over the east side rail and kept walking north. The railroad ties were slippery with the fresh rain on the oily timbers. I continued walking up the track. I looked over to see if I would see Virgil but saw nothing.

I kept walking, thinking I had to be past the spot where I would find Bob, when I stepped on something.

I stepped back quickly, not sure what I had stepped on. I looked down and could not see clearly, but I could tell it was Bob's beaded buckskin satchel, the parfleche pouch Emma had mentioned, but there was no sign of Bob.

I picked up the pouch, and when I did I saw movement out of the corner of my right eye, toward the river. I stepped over the rail and moved toward the woods, toward the direction of the movement. I looked back to the west side, looking for Virgil, but I did not see him. I walked toward the tree line next to the river, and the sound of the white water got louder as I got closer. The trees were thick. I thought I saw movement again but was not sure. Knowing Bob still had his knife, it most assuredly would not be a smart move on my part to walk into the trees. I backed up toward the track, and within a moment I heard.

"Everett."

I turned. It was Virgil coming down the track from the north. I walked toward him in the steady rain. He had his coat collar up and his hat snugged down low. Water was pouring off the brim.

"You see anything?" he said.

"I think he's in those woods there by the creek, but I don't know for sure. I found this."

I handed Virgil the parfleche pouch.

"Not much inside. I felt some cartridges, a whetstone, I think some jerky."

"As much as that goulash we ate in the Hungarian café at Dallas depot has worn off, I wouldn't eat that jerky," Virgil said. "Could be backstrap off his kinfolk."

I was not able to make out the expression on Virgil's face, but it was clear by his body language that he was not satisfied with the situation.

"We're not going in those woods," Virgil said.

Virgil stood and looked east toward the woods. He called out into the dark, rainy night.

"Bob Brandice! If you do not die in those woods, rest assured I will kill you!"

39

When we got back to the coach it was still raining hard, maybe even harder since we had left the place where we'd been looking for Bob. I was starting to feel the wet cold in my bones, and I know Virgil was feeling it, too. We had been waterlogged for hours, and I was hungry. I know Virgil was as hungry, too, but he would not say so. If food were an option or if dry and comfortable were an option, he'd cover the option, but there was no need to ponder the possibility of food or staying very dry. Thankfully, though, after we'd traveled for twenty minutes or so the rain started letting up, and we could see a piece of the moon.

"Looks like we might be leaving this rain behind."

"Does," Virgil said.

"Won't bother me none."

"That's good," Virgil said.

We coasted for a bit longer and came to a

tight canopy of trees that sheltered us from the sprinkling rain. When we cleared the tunnel of trees we were rolling pretty fast and were clearly on a wide sweep to the west.

"This has got to be the turn Whip was talking about," I said.

"Hold us up, Everett."

"What?"

"Slow her up."

I did as Virgil asked and turned the brake wheel, which made a low grinding noise as we slowed.

Virgil looked at me, cocked his head a bit.

"Smell that?"

I had not caught a whiff, but in the next second, I did.

"Smoke," I said.

"Let's stop."

I stopped the coach, and Virgil stepped off the platform. He walked down the dark track a ways, then stopped and stood still.

"Been plenty of lightning," I said. "Might be the woods struck up."

"Might be."

"Could be a homestead," I said. "Or Indians."

The rails in front of us turned and disappeared behind a wall of thick woods.

"Let me walk a bit," Virgil said. "Just follow me."

Virgil started walking down the track. I turned the brake wheel, freeing the coach, and very slowly began to roll. After maybe a hundred yards we entered into a tall rocky hillside that had been dynamited for the rails. Virgil was hard to see clearly in the darkness. He was walking about seventy-five feet in front of the coach, and when he got to the edge of the rocky hillside, he held up his arms, motioning for me to stop. I turned the wheel, and the coach started slowing. Virgil remained standing on the track, looking downhill as the coach came to a stop square in the middle of the dyna-mited hillside. I foot-latched the brake, stepped off the platform, and started down the track toward Virgil. As I got closer, I saw what he saw.

A quarter of a mile down the track was the fire. It was hard to tell exactly what was burning, but whatever it was, rain or no rain, it was burning and the flames were high. In the distance behind the fire and off toward the west a ways, there was a faint glow.

"Half Moon Junction," I said.

Virgil turned and looked back at me as I walked up.

"Maybe you can tell me for certain," Vir-

161

gil said, "but this dead hand here is Wood-fin, ain't it? One of Bragg's top gun hands. We had a run-in or two with him, did we not?"

I was fixed on the fire and the sight of the town, and I had not noticed the man lying directly in front of Virgil, between the rails.

I looked at the big bearded man with the white shirt covered in blood, and he was for certain who Virgil thought he was.

"That's him. That's Woodfin. Vince and him were Bragg's two backup bulls," I said. "Lying between the rails like this, he's obviously not one we shot."

"No, he ain't," Virgil said.

I leaned down a little closer, and when I did I could see under Woodfin's beard his throat was sliced open across his jawline, from ear to ear.

"Throat cut," I said.

"Handiwork of Bloody Bob, no doubt," Virgil said.

"Good of him to do some stall mucking."

"Is," Virgil said. "Reckon him and Wood-fin had a misunderstanding."

"Wonder what the outcome of an argument would have been?"

I looked back to Virgil. His attention was now on the distant flames ahead of us.

"That the coaches on fire, you think?" I said.

"Looks like it," Virgil said. "Hard to say for certain."

"Figure we'll know soon enough," I said.

"Figure we will."

"And Half Moon, just there."

"That it is," Virgil said.

40

We left the coach where it had stopped and walked on down the track toward the fire. With the recently slain bandits, Virgil and me had plenty of weaponry choices. I carried my Colt and two other long-barreled Colts. Virgil had the .44 Henry rifle Bob dropped in the aisle and a second Colt in his belt.

"Least with Bob shot up, gone, hopefully dead," I said, "and Woodfin cut like that, we have two less gunmen to deal with."

"We do," Virgil said.

"Vince is shot up, too," I said. "No telling how bad, how deep. Might be he's dead."

"Might well be," Virgil said.

"Ear shots are damn sure painful."

"They are."

"Hard to stop the bleeding," I said, "and the pressure on the brain."

"Don't know he's even got one."

"Well, if he don't bleed to death," I said,

"he'll most likely go crazier than he already is."

We continued walking, following the track toward the fire ahead and the halo of light from Half Moon Junction just beyond. There was no more rain now, and the moon was showing full in the sky as we made our way closer to the fire.

"That's the coaches burning for sure," I said.

"It is," Virgil said.

As we got closer we could see the fire was a single coach engulfed in flames, but the wood was nearly consumed and the flames were getting lower.

"The governor's car," I said. "The Pullman."

"Is," Virgil said.

"Let's hope him and his wife are not inside," I said.

"Yep," Virgil said. "Let's."

As we got closer we could see the other cars were safe.

"The Pullman's separated from the cars behind," Virgil said.

The other coaches were disconnected from the burning Pullman and were sitting fifty or so feet farther down the rail.

"Must have been disconnected on the move," I said.

Avoiding any possibility of being spotted by anyone, we skirted off the tracks, moved into the trees, and continued on closer to the burning Pullman and back section of the train. As we neared the coaches we could see there were lamps burning in the fifth and sixth car and the caboose, but there was no one moving about. We stopped, staying out of sight in the woods when we were parallel with the coaches. Even though the windows were fogged over, there was no movement inside the fifth and six coaches.

"Don't see nobody," I said.

"Ramp's out."

The stock car door was open and its boarding ramp was extended.

"Made off with our horses," I said.

"They did."

"Half Moon looks to be not but a quarter a mile there."

Virgil and I moved on a ways past the coaches, stepped out of the woods, and walked toward the caboose.

"Look here," I said.

There was a line of muddy footprints where passengers departed the coaches. The tracks tapered off to the south, toward Half Moon Junction.

The back door of the caboose was wide open. I looked in; there was nobody inside.

We moved on, looked inside the stock car, and as figured, all the horses, including Virgil's stud and my lazy roan, were gone. We walked through the sixth coach to see if there was anything significant to reckon with, but it was eerily empty; even the bodies of the first two that got killed, Redbeard and the fellow with the two Schofields, had disappeared. Virgil's cigar was still in the ashtray where he had left it when this whole rhubarb went down. He picked it up and flicked the ashes off with his finger. I produced a match from the matchbox the undertaker had placed in my coat and handed it to Virgil. Virgil dragged the tip of the match across the back of the seat and lit his cigar. After he got it going good he waved the match in the air and flicked it away with his middle finger.

"That was a good horse," Virgil said. "Good saddle, too." "It was," I said.

41

Virgil took a few deliberate puffs on his cigar and we moved on. Like the sixth coach, the fifth was empty, too. We walked back up the track a ways and looked closely at the remainder of the burning Pullman. The heat was intense and the light was bright. Virgil stayed back as I walked closer, looking into the fire of the fancy coach. I walked slowly around the coach, looking into the dancing flames.

"Don't see nobody in there, do you, Everett?" Virgil said. "No burnt-up people, no bones?"

I continued walking around the coach, looking into the fire.

"Nothing yet," I said as I walked back up the other side of the coach, looking closely into the smoky fire.

"Do not," I said. "Don't see any bones."

I looked back to Virgil holding the Henry rifle. The rifle's brass receiver was reflecting

168

the flames and glowing a brilliant golden orange against the darkness.

"I reckon the governor and his wife got out, and away," I said.

"Seems so," Virgil said.

"Yep," I said. "Somehow, some way."

I walked back to where Virgil was standing, smoking his cigar. He was looking off toward Half Moon Junction.

"Hard to figure all this," I said. "The governor and his wife, horses gone, the Pullman burning, the passengers, cars separated."

"Is," Virgil said.

"I figure the bandits took off and left the passengers to fend for themselves."

Virgil nodded, slowly smoking the cigar.

"You think they took the governor and his wife hostage?" I said.

Virgil shook his head.

"Don't think so," Virgil said. "Now they are back here away from us, don't think they'd have a need for 'em."

"No," I said. "Don't guess they would."

"Whether they are alive or not," Virgil said, "is another matter altogether."

"So what are you thinking?" I said.

"I'm thinking we do ourselves the necessity of getting over to this Half Moon Junction," Virgil said, pointing the Henry rifle in the direction of the town, "and figure out just what befell."

I nodded, and we started walking toward the town. We walked back past the other cars and past the caboose. A lamp was hanging on the back of the caboose, and as we passed it I noticed the engraving on the receiver of the Henry rifle Virgil was carrying.

"That yellow belly looks fancy," I said.

Virgil held up the Henry a bit.

"It is," Virgil said. "Got detailed engraving on it. Bunch of new scratches on the stock, and the front sight is busted off."

We continued walking and left the light from the caboose behind.

"Not Bloody Bob's rifle, that's a fact," Virgil said. "He stole it, I imagine. It's got a deck of cards and a riverboat engraved on it."

"Maybe he got it off some professional boat gambler," I said.

"The other side of the receiver has happy and sad masks," Virgil said. "Like you'd see displayed on tent shows."

"Maybe it belonged to a gambler," I said. "Who is a performer, a thespian or something."

"Might," Virgil said. "Just might."

I opened Bob's pouch and pulled out the

extra cartridges I'd previously felt were inside and handed them to Virgil as we walked.

"Here," I said. "What's left of the cartridges."

Virgil took the bullets and put them into his coat pocket as we continued making our way toward Half Moon Junction.

42

Half moon junction was painted in Gothic-style lettering on the north side of the water tank. The south side, the side I'd seen when we were passing through, traveling north, simply bore the symbol of its namesake, a painted half-moon. Virgil and I walked down the tracks, around the water tank, and crossed over the planks of the depot's wide loading dock. We stepped over another set of rails that tapered off to the west and made our way up the wet caliche road toward the streetlights of Half Moon.

The first sign of life was at an encampment on the east side of town at the edge of a small brook. There were several tents pitched around an open-sided teepee with a fire burning beneath it. A few miners were having a spirited game of blackjack in their underwear; their trousers and shirts were hanging near the fire to dry. Across from the brook was another encampment with rows of single tents, and somewhere within we could hear a man and a woman arguing about something. A short ways on, there was a lean-to shack set back off the road surrounded by a corral with a few scrawny goats and a donkey. There was a wagon-wide bridge over the brook, and on the other side was the start of the proper buildings of Half Moon Junction. We crossed over the bridge, and a young barefoot fellow wearing a China hat approached carrying a laundry sack. He looked to be part Chinese and maybe part Indian.

"Young fellow," Virgil said, stopping the young man's forward momentum.

"Yes," the young man said.

"You speak English?"

"Yes."

"Where would we find an officer of the law, sheriff, marshal, police?"

The young man nodded, smiling.

"Yes."

"Yes," Virgil said.

"Yes," the young man said, then hurried on over the bridge and into the tent encampment.

Virgil looked at me, smiled a bit, and said, "Yes."

We walked on. The rails that were running

westerly from the depot had a section of track that switched off into a big miners' yard with a covered loading facility on our right. Just past the miners' yard, there was a livery stable. The door was open, lamps were on. There were a number of horses standing in a lot next to the barn. Virgil walked next to the rail, looking at the horses in the lot, and when he got to the barn door, he looked inside. There were two young Indian men at the back of the barn, mucking stables. Virgil took a few steps inside and looked around. The Indians watched him for a moment and went back to work. Virgil walked down the center of the barn, looking at the horses in the stalls. When he got to the end he turned around and walked back to the door. As he figured, there was no sign of his chestnut or my lazy roan, but he was taking a look anyway, if for no other reason than just to provide himself an understanding of some sort.

We walked on up the street, and the next building we came to was a small church on the south side nestled between two big tents. A large woman opened the door as we walked by and threw out a basin of water. She turned to go back inside but stopped when she saw Virgil and me.

"Well, hey there, boys. How 'bout getting

a piece of Heaven with Betty Jean?"

Virgil looked up to the steeple. He glanced at me and looked back to Betty Jean. Betty Jean was no church lady, and obviously this church was no church. It had been converted into a brothel, and Betty Jean was most likely a member of the congregation.

"Come on in," Betty Jean said. "You can ring the bell."

Betty Jean's face was thick with face paint. She looked kind of like a harlequin queen on a deck of French playing cards, with wide, dark eyebrows and red lipstick that exceeded the borders of her lips. We could smell her strong perfume from where we were standing. If it were not for her behemoth breasts that were nearly falling out of the low-cut dress she was wearing, I would have thought she was a man.

"What kind of law is in this town, Betty Jean?" Virgil said.

She leaned on the doorjamb sort of manly-like and smiled, showing her big teeth smudged with lipstick.

"You're looking at it," Betty Jean said.

Another whore poked her head out the door from behind Betty Jean. She was a skinny woman with a large nose.

"Y'all with them others that come off that train that got all busted 'n burnt up?" She

175

looked at Betty Jean. "Are they?"

"We got some whiskey," Betty Jean said. "Why don't y'all come on in and let me and Laskowski here take good care of you."

"Where are the others that came off the busted train you're talking about," I said.

"A couple of 'em come in for service, but they done left," Laskowski, the skinny whore, said. "So why don't y'all come on in and confess with me and Betty Jean here."

Virgil tipped his hat and was already walking away when he said, "Evenin'."

I tipped my hat.

"Some other time, ladies," I said, and followed Virgil.

"Won't find no better," Betty Jean said as we moved on.

I caught up, getting in step with Virgil.

"There is something wrong there," I said.

"There is."

"Not being a religious person, but that just does not seem right."

"No," Virgil said. "It does not."

"If there is a trap door to hell," I said. "I reckon that might be it."

"No need to find out."

"I'm not sure I could even do it under those conditions."

"Not sure any conditions you'd even ever want to do it."

43

Pete's place was a small open-air saloon
with a thick board spread across two barrels. A nicely painted sign in front let us
know this was Pete's Place. Virgil and I
stepped up. Pete's Place was empty except
for an elderly bartender who was cleaning
an old single-shot twenty-gauge and two
Indians dressed in white men's clothes. The
Indians were drunk. One Indian was sitting
on the floor, asleep, with his head to the
wall. The other Indian was sitting in a chair,
glassy-eyed and staring straight ahead like
he'd been hypnotized.

The old fellow smiled and slid two small
glasses in front of us and was pouring before
I could say "Whiskey."

The old fellow poured us two generous
portions.

We drank, and he poured two more.

"You two with the group that got
stranded?"

"No," Virgil said.

"We are not, but we are looking for them," I said. "Some of them, anyway."

I slid back my coat and showed him the badge on my vest. Pete's eyes shifted back and forth between Virgil and me.

"You Pete?" I said.

"I am."

Virgil and I drank our second shot and Pete poured two more drinks.

"Hell of a thing that happened with the train," Pete said. "I looked up and them folks came traipsing through town like a bunch of tuckered cattle."

"You see any of them on horseback?" Virgil said.

"No, they was all on foot."

"Where are they now?" I said.

"I think some of them caught the last D and WV back to Denison, but I'm not for certain. There's three hotels here; some of 'em might be there. This joint was full of black coal faces for a few hours, and I was busy for a while with the shift change, so I don't rightly know."

"Who's in charge of this place, Pete?"

"I am."

"The town, Pete," I said. "Who's in charge of this town?"

"Oh. Officially, that'd be the Choctaw Nation," Pete said. "But Burton Berkeley is the constable-elect. I think he's a quarter Choctaw, but he don't look it."

"Where's the jail?" I asked.

"Just up the street, but he ain't never there, really. He's got a few deputies that might be there if they got somebody locked up. Only on rare occasions do they lock somebody up. Most everybody here in Half Moon is pretty scared of big Burton, and therefore they don't do much to get themselves arrested. Burton is tough, and miners for the most part are a hardworking, harmless sort."

"Where can we find him," Virgil said. "The constable, Burton Berkeley?"

"The Hotel Ark."

"And where might that be?" I asked.

"On Half Moon here." Pete pointed east. "Go past Quarter Moon Street, the next street you get to is Full Moon, turn right, and you'll come to Three Quarter Moon Street. That's this town: Quarter, Half, Three Quarter and Full, those are the streets. On the corner there of Full and Three Quarter is Hotel Ark and Saloon. That's his place. Most evenings that's where he is."

"He owns the place?" I asked.

"He does. He owns damn near the whole of Half Moon Junction."

44

We left Pete's place and walked up the south side of Half Moon Street past a busy card house, a bathhouse, and a grungy miners saloon where a bare-chested wrestling match was under way. We crossed to the north side at Quarter Moon Street and walked past dark alley passages between storefronts, with upstairs rooms where working women were practicing their trade. We turned right on Full Moon and made our way toward what was obviously the main part of town, passing a pool hall saloon with a sign advertising *Chuck-a-Luck, Faro, Roulette and Bowling.*

"Big place," I said.

"Is."

"Lot of people."

A bit farther ahead was a double-decker lavishly painted brothel, aptly named Over the Moon. A few ladies tried to sell us a piece on the walk just before we got to

Three Quarter Moon Street, but we declined and moved on.

"Whip was right," I said.

" 'Bout?"

"This town does seem like a place written about in the Bible where God got mad."

"Not shy of whores," Virgil said.

"Nope," I said, "it's not."

"They ain't a bit shy, neither."

"No, they're not."

We stopped on the corner under a lamp, where a swarm of bugs circled around the light as a mule team passed by, slowly pulling a long flatbed loaded with pipe. Staggering along following the flatbed was a short, round swamper. He was talking to himself.

"Half Moon Junction seems like an appropriate name for this wallow," I said.

"Does," Virgil said.

We crossed the street to the Hotel Ark on the corner of Full and Three Quarter. Hotel Ark was a big hotel, bigger than the Boston House in Appaloosa. From the outside it resembled its title; it was oddly constructed to look like a big ship, and the whole structure was without an inch of paint. The porch wrapped both sides of the building facing Full and Three Quarter Moon Street. It had crooked oak supports for porch posts and a thick rope for railing.

We entered the front door, and inside the foyer there was a stuffed pair of snarling black bears to greet us. The foyer set the stage for the main room. Inside, the place looked more like a hunting lodge than a hotel; the walls were covered with animal hides and taxidermy mounts, with as many male/female couplings of animal species as could be pulled together. There was a set of narrow stairs rising up behind the front desk with a mezzanine overlooking the main room. Behind a set of saloon doors next to the front desk, a piano was playing a snappy rendition of "Camptown Races." A woman's voice was doing a pretty good job of singing along with the piano. I thought about Widow Callico and Allie and their nightly mus-A-cal duo and was quite certain they did not sound near as good as the Hotel Ark duo. A big bald fellow was behind the front desk, folding pillow covers. He was young and had big bulging biceps.

"Evening, gentlemen," he said.

"How do," Virgil said.

"Fine, just fine," the big fellow said. "You from the train?"

"We are not," Virgil said.

"Need a room?" the big fellow said as he moved to the registry book sitting on the front desk next to a hen and drake mallard.

"No," Virgil said. "Looking for Constable Berkeley?"

"He's in the saloon, but unless you're a member or a guest of the hotel, that's off-limits, I'm afraid."

"What's your name, son?" Virgil said.

"Burns."

"Well, there's no reason to be afraid, Burns," Virgil said. "We're here on marshal business."

Virgil pulled back his lapel so the big fellow could see his silver star.

"Oh," Burns said. "Um . . . well. I suppose then it'd be okay for you to go right ahead on, Marshal."

"S'pose we will," Virgil said. "Much obliged."

Burns grinned a lopsided grin. Then he resumed folding pillow covers.

We walked across the wide room toward the saloon, where a pair of bobcats stood side by side on a twisting sweep of bleached-out juniper. Their backs were arched, and they looked ready to attack.

"Look damn near alive," I said.

"Odds are they're not," Virgil said as we pushed through the doors and into the saloon.

45

The saloon was small and cozy compared to the main room of the hotel. It was nicer, too, with velvet-covered chairs and paintings of ships and naked women. A big painting of Noah's Ark covered at least six feet of the wall behind the bar. A bartender with a twenty-past-eight mustache and wearing black satin armbands was standing in front of the painting with his head down, reading a newspaper. The piano player and a heavy-set chanteuse were set up in the center of the room, working the song louder than it needed to be worked, and somewhere, something smelled good.

"Food," I said.

Virgil nodded as he looked around the room.

"Fancy place," I said.

"It is."

We could tell right away this place catered to a more exclusive clientele. There were two separate couples at the bar: one couple at one end, and another couple at the other. The whores were goodlooking and acting like they were interested in what the men were saying. Sitting at a corner booth were two young men wearing expensive suits with bowlers and two older yet well-put-together whores.

"Members, I reckon."

"Guests, maybe," Virgil said.

For the moment, nobody in the place even paid us any attention.

"In respect to what we've seen of this town so far," I said. "Seems kind of civilized."

"Does," Virgil said. "For a whoring facility, it most assuredly does."

In the back, behind a set of half-closed curtains, we could see three women throwing darts, and behind them in the corner sat a few men at a card table, playing poker. One of the dart-throwing gals came from the back room and out to the bar. She was real pretty, and though she was a whore with a flower in her hair she could pass for someone proper, a teacher or a college student. She was young, straight-backed, with high cheekbones and pointed shoulders. She stopped when she saw Virgil and me.

"Oh!"

She walked over to us.

"Good evening, gentlemen," she said.

Only then did the bartender look up from his newspaper.

"Evening," we said.

"Have you two been helped?"

"Nope," Virgil said.

"Just walked in the door," I said.

"Well, nice of you to join us."

She smiled. Her teeth were straight and white. She pointed.

"Handsome pouch you got there, handsome," she said. "You're no Indian with that blond hair."

I followed her point to Bloody Bob's pouch I forgot was hanging from my shoulder and resting on my hip.

"Allow me to get you gentlemen something," she said.

She turned to the bar. Virgil interrupted her.

"We are looking for Burton," Virgil said. "Burton Berkeley."

She smiled sweetly.

"Um, okay, may I tell him who's calling."

"Sure. I'm Marshal Virgil Cole; this fellow here is my deputy, Everett Hitch."

"Oh, well, okay. Just one moment, Marshal, Deputy."

46

We watched as she walked back through the curtains and to the corner table where the men were playing poker. She leaned down and spoke to one of the men at the table. He turned and looked back at us. He looked to the others at the table, excused himself, and started walking toward Virgil and me. The piano player and the chanteuse started up another tune as Berkeley walked in our direction. Berkeley was a big man with big features, wearing an expensive suit. He had a thick head of curly hair slicked back with shiny oil. He came through the curtains and held out his hand.

"Burton Berkeley," he said.

Virgil did not take his hand. I interceded and shook hands with Berkeley. I showed him my badge.

"I'm Deputy Everett Hitch; this is Marshal Virgil Cole."

Virgil was looking through the curtains to

the men at the poker table. They were looking at us.

"Well, this has been quite an evening here
in Half Moon Junction," Berkeley said.
"Were you the lawmen on board?"

"We were," I said.

He shook his head. "How, how in the hell
did you get back to here?"

Virgil did not answer; he asked instead,
"Where's the governor?"

Berkeley looked back and forth between
Virgil and me.

"Well, he's safe, Marshal."

"He's not one of the fellows back there at
the table looking at us, is he?" Virgil said.

Berkeley turned, looking at the men in the
back room who were looking at us, and then
turned back to us, shaking his head.

"No," Berkeley said.

"Did he leave on the Denison?" Virgil said.

"No," Berkeley said. "He is here."

"At this hotel?"

"Yes."

"His wife with him?" Virgil asked.

Berkeley put his hands to his hips holding
back his suit coat.

"Yes, they retired. This is terrible. They
were obviously in shock and, well, with their
daughters in peril. Do you know anything
about them, their whereabouts?"

The piano player kicked into a loud section of his already noisy tune, which annoyed the hell out of Virgil but provided him the opportunity to ignore Berkeley's question. Virgil was not accustomed to, nor interested in sharing, details about anything to anyone, especially someone he just met with a white flower in his lapel.

"What about the other passengers on the train?" Virgil asked.

"Some, most, we were able to get on the Denison train back to Texas. There are a few I believe at the other hotels, wishing to depart tomorrow."

"What about the robbers," I said. "They had the horses from the stock car. Any sign of them?"

"No," Berkeley said. "I'm afraid not. It's my understanding when the coaches came to a halt, they told the passengers to wait until they were gone, out of sight, before anyone stepped off the train. That's my understanding, anyway. I have no idea where they are. They most likely moved quickly away from the fray, but I honestly have no idea. What with dealing with the governor and the rest, I'm sorry, I just do not know. We did look for them. I had a few of my deputies look around. We had their descriptions, but we came up with nothing.

There are a lot of men in this town."

"The two back there, staring at us," Virgil said. "That Lassiter and Hobbs?"

Berkeley turned, looking at the men. He turned back to Virgil and nodded slowly.

"Why, yes," Berkeley said. "As a matter of fact, they are. That's James Lassiter and Chester Hobbs."

47

We ate pork chops with pepper gravy, corn, and cat-head biscuits covered with molasses. The pretty whore with the straight back and pointed shoulders smiled at me as she picked up my empty plate. Virgil lit a fancy cigar Berkeley gave him, and we listened to Mr. Lassiter and Mr. Hobbs tell us about their account of the evening. With the exception of learning about the large dollar amount of money the governor was carrying, so far Lassiter and Hobbs' story coincided with what Emma and Abigail told us. Hobbs was wiry and angular, with thin hair and muttonchops. Lassiter was taller and handsome, with intense eyes. They both had gray hair and appeared to be close to sixty.

"We were en route for a business endeavor in the Indian Territories before we were tossed from the train," Lassiter said.

Hobbs twisted a napkin like he was trying

to get water out of it.

"It was a grueling walk back here," Hobbs said. "I can tell you that. God knows I've got the blisters to prove it."

Lassiter scoffed a bit.

"If it weren't for the mule team traveling down from the camps, we'd still be out there," Lassiter said.

"Yes, and thank God in Heaven," Hobbs said. "No telling what might have happened to us."

"No sooner than we got back," Lassiter said, "and I wired ahead, the governor and the others arrived. Just the goddamnedest thing."

"And thank God," Hobbs said. "But now the poor girls are missing. I pray for their safe return."

"What did you wire ahead?" Virgil said.

"Well," Lassiter said, "alerting the way stations of the situation, of course."

"The situation being?"

"Well, that we were being robbed," Lassiter said, "and to notify authorities."

"A heinous test of mettle all around," Hobbs said, "not to mention the extravagance of the robbery."

Virgil sat back in his chair, puffing on his cigar. He moved around some crumbs of biscuit on the table.

"You said a half a million dollars," Virgil said. "That is a lot of money."

Lassiter let out a whistle between his teeth. "Indeed it is, Marshal Cole," he said. "Indeed it is."

"It was," Hobbs said. "A business endeavor that simply went awry."

"Awry in the worst of ways," Lassiter said.

Hobbs bobbed his head, concurring with Lassiter.

"Hell of an ordeal," Hobbs said. "Hell of an ordeal."

"Was that the extent of your wire?" Virgil said.

Lassiter squinted at the question like he didn't like it.

"It was," Lassiter said.

Virgil took a pull on his cigar. He blew out the smoke, and it swirled under the lamp hanging over the table.

"You send a wire to anybody else?" Virgil said.

Lassiter looked at Hobbs and shook his head.

"Like who?" Lassiter said.

"Texas law officials?"

"Did not," Lassiter said.

"How come?"

"What do you mean?" Lassiter said.

"Just that," Virgil said.

Lassiter looked at Hobbs.

"Your governor was on the train. His life in danger," I said. "Just curious why you did not contact Texas Rangers or military."

"Or other members of the Texas government," Virgil said.

"There was no reason to alarm anyone," Lassiter said, "until we knew what we were dealing with."

"And now you know?" I said.

"Well, to some degree we do," Lassiter said. "Yes."

Virgil took another pull from his cigar and blew another roll of smoke across the table.

"How did this conductor fellow come to target the governor; you, Mr. Lassiter; and you, Mr. Hobbs?" Virgil said.

"What do you mean?" Lassiter said.

"Just that," Virgil said.

"He got into the Pullman with you," I said, "and ordered you to get your luggage down?"

Lassiter and Hobbs looked at each other and nodded in tandem.

Hobbs said, "That's right."

"Why?" Virgil said.

"Why?" Lassiter said.

"How did he know the governor had that amount of money on him?" I said.

"Well, I don't know," Hobbs said. "We

don't actually know."

Lassiter crossed his arms and frowned a bit.

"I suppose he did not know for certain," Lassiter said. "I mean, how could he have known?"

"That's what I'm trying to asscertin," Virgil said, then shook his head. "That ain't the word I meant. What is the word I'm looking for, Everett?"

"Ascertain."

"That's right," Virgil said. "That's what I'm trying to ascertain."

48

Berkeley came from the bar with a bottle of cognac and poured us a snort.

"I have arranged for a posse," Berkeley said. "They'll be gathering here at first light."

"Splendid," Hobbs said.

"This endeavor you were planning on in the territories," Virgil said. "What was the nature of this endeavor?"

"What do you mean?" Lassiter said defensively.

"What was the governor planning to do with that money?"

Hobbs and Lassiter looked at each other. Lassiter sat tall and said, "The territories will open; the land run will be taking place very soon."

"This much I know," Virgil said.

"We were providing resources for the city developments," Lassiter said.

"And how were those resources to be

distributed?" Virgil said.

"We provide the marshals to stake the claims, and the payment would be for their services," Hobbs said, "and in turn, we retain ownership."

"Ownership?" Virgil said.

"Yes," Lassiter said. "Essentially."

"Essentially," Virgil said, "what you were doing was buying Indian land or planning on buying Indian land with Texas money?"

Lassiter and Hobbs looked at each other like they didn't like the sound of what they heard.

"And whose idea was this?" Virgil pressed.

"Idea?" Hobbs said.

"Yep."

"The state of Texas was in surplus," Lassiter said, "and this, this land run, provided us, and the state, an opportunity."

"Everett, when we left Mexico, how long did it take us to get out of the state of Texas?" Virgil said without looking at me.

"Five days, altogether."

"Five days?"

"Yep," I said. "Five days by train."

Virgil smiled.

"And to think the state of Texas ain't big enough," Virgil said. "Now they want the Indian Territories."

Lassiter and Hobbs laughed.

" 'Provided us,' you say," Virgil said. "Are you, Mr. Hobbs, Mr. Lassiter, members of the legislation?"

They shook their heads together again.

"We are both attorneys," Lassiter said. "Law partners."

"So what was the nature of your involvement?"

"We had the contacts; we both have served as legal counsel for the Nations," Hobbs said. "The Five Civilized Tribes, and we had the relationships."

"That's right," Lassiter said.

"What was in it for you?"

"Mr. Cole," Lassiter said. "We are not on trial here, and we are as interested as yo—"

"Just answer the question, Mr. Lassiter," Virgil said politely.

Lassiter shook his head slightly and looked to Hobbs.

"We were just providing the contacts," Hobbs said. "The governor is our close friend, and this was an opportunity for all of us."

Virgil took a sip of the cognac and smiled. He puffed on his cigar for a moment while Hobbs and Lassiter just looked at him. Berkeley took a seat across the table from us, between Hobbs and Lassiter.

Virgil looked at his cigar and to Berkeley.

"Got a doctor in this town?" Virgil asked.

"Doctor?" Berkeley said. "Yes, we do. Well, I should say we did, but he has moved out to the camp, the miners' camp, for the time being. A lot of the men have been sick, so he's out there for now. There is a dentist here that has been doing doctoring in the interim. Doc Meyer."

"Where would we find Doc Meyer?"

Berkeley pointed.

"Right across Three Quarter Street here, just up a ways. If he's not there in his place, he's most likely at one of the gambling parlors down the street. He gambles a bit . . . a lot, actually."

Virgil stood up, and I did the same.

"Are you feeling bad?" Berkeley said.

" 'Bout some things," Virgil said.

"Not the food, I hope?"

"No, food was good. Fact, that's some of the best food we've had in a long time," Virgil said. "Don't you think, Everett?"

"I do."

Berkeley smiled as he scooted back the chair he was sitting in and stood up.

"Well, good, then."

Berkeley retrieved two keys from his pocket and handed one to me and one to Virgil.

"Got you gents a room here if you want.

When you come back, just talk to Burns here at the desk, he can get you some hot water. There is a tub at the end of your hall, second floor."

"Muchas gracias," Virgil said.

49

We crossed the street to the south side and walked east. There was less commotion, fewer folks moving about in the streets than there were when we had entered Hotel Ark.

"You think those lawyers got something to do with this, Virgil?"

Virgil worked on his cigar for a moment, thinking as we walked.

"Don't know."

"But maybe?"

"They looked at each other an awful lot," Virgil said.

"They did."

"There was some knowing by somebody about something for this ball to drop like it did," Virgil said.

"Seems probable," I said.

"More than probable."

"What are you thinking?"

"Don't know," Virgil said. "But Bloody Bob Brandice and that one-arm conductor fellow didn't stumble into that Pullman car by chance."

"What about the governor?"

"Hard to say."

We walked on. I moved up on the board-walk. Virgil stayed walking in the street.

"Constable Berkeley seems like an okay hand for a whore handler."

"Big boy," Virgil said.

"Serves up some good food."

"Does," Virgil said.

"His whores are good-looking."

"They were."

We walked on a ways farther, looking for Doc Meyer's office.

"How much do you think it'd cost for that pretty whore with the baking-soda teeth and the flower in her hair?" I said.

"More than you got."

"Here we go," I said.

We came to a narrow two-story structure with a *Dentist Office* sign on the door. Virgil was standing in the street, looking up.

"Lamp burning," Virgil said.

I knocked on the door. We waited for a moment, but no one stirred. Virgil stepped back into the street a bit more, looking up to the upstairs windows. I knocked again and looked back to Virgil.

He shook his head.

I knocked again, harder this time. I heard some bedsprings squeak, followed by a man's voice.

"Hold on, just a goddamn minute, hold on . . ."

Through the wavy sugar-glass window of the door, light and shadow of a lamp coming down the stairs at the back of the office stretched and turned.

A man's shadow grew huge against the back wall of the stairwell as he descended the steps. After he got to the bottom step he started talking loudly as he approached the door.

"Don't you got no better sense than to bother me at this time of night! The cost is double this time of night, just so you know, goddamn double!"

50

He opened the door. He was tall, wearing an old worn-out silk paisley robe and floppy night slippers. He was most likely in his forties, but his slouchy body looked more like sixty. He was unshaven, his hair stuck out in every direction, and he reeked of alcohol.

"What's the goddamn problem?"

I looked back to Virgil. Virgil stepped up on the boardwalk next to me.

"You Doc Meyer?" Virgil said.

"No," Doc Meyer said, "I'm the goddamn tooth fairy! What do you want?"

"I'm Marshal Virgil Cole; this is my deputy, Everett Hitch."

"You got a toothache? You hurt?"

"We are looking for a wounded man," I said. "We want to know if he came to you tonight, if you've seen him, treated him."

"I treat a lot of people! This here is a community of ignorant goddamn miners getting hurt every day. Now, I was asleep, and if you don't mind, I'd like to go back to it!"

He started to close the door, but I stopped it with my foot.

"Recently, in the last few hours?" I said. "A bullet might have clipped the side of his head, maybe his ear."

Doc Meyer looked down at my foot, and his shoulders sagged. He scratched his scalp and yawned with his mouth open wide. He made a high-pitched yawn noise and said, "What's in it for me?"

"You will have an opportunity to go back to sleep," I said.

"Otherwise Everett will come in there and have to knock you around a bit," Virgil said politely. "He don't want to, but he'll put a knot in your ass if you don't cooperate."

Doc Meyer reacted like a skunk sprayed him in the face. He held up his lantern, looking at Virgil. We could see his face clearer now. His nose and cheeks was a spiderweb of broken blood vessels, and his eyes were bloodshot. He looked Virgil up and down like he was looking at a painting in a museum. He shook his head and opened the door.

"Oh, good goddamn, no rest for the wicked, no goddamn rest . . . come in, officers, come on in. The only thing worse than card cheats is goddamn lawmen."

Virgil looked at me and smiled, and we followed him inside. Doc Meyer dragged his slippers across the floor as he ambled back to a cluttered desk next to his dentist chair. He set the lantern on a stack of books and flopped down in his squeaky chair behind his desk. There was a skull sitting on the desk with a silver tooth that caught a piece of light when Doc Meyer turned up the gas on the lantern. He leaned over and opened the bottom desk drawer and pulled out a whiskey bottle. He bit the cork, spit it on the desk, and took a swig. He took a second swig before leaning over and picking up a white piece of cloth from a small trash canister. He unfolded the cloth and laid it on the desk next to the lantern. Inside the cloth were pieces of bloody flesh. For effect, he pointed at the pieces of the flesh with a scalpel. He figured since we were providing him some unpleasantness he would return the favor and give us a bloody little show.

"That's all that was left of his helix, anti-helical fold, and concha."

Doc Meyer leaned back in his chair, holding the scalpel between the thumb and first finger of his hand, smiling at us with a liquored-up look on his face.

"The bottom part, the external auditory meatus, antitragus, and lobe, he got to keep, though I'm certain his hearing will be impaired in that ear. Something tells me, though, his well-being is of no goddamn concern of yours."

"How long ago was he here?" I said.

"Two hours," Doc Meyer said, "give or take."

"Do you know if he is still here," I said, "in Half Moon?"

"I have no idea."

"Who was he with?" Virgil said.

Doc Meyer took another swig off the whiskey bottle. He belched and swiveled the palm of his hand over the bottle top to remove his saliva and offered us a pull. We declined.

"There were three other miscreants with him," Doc Meyer said. "I was walking up to my office here when they arrived. They were kind of like the two of you, rather obnoxious and demanding."

"Mounted?" Virgil said.

Doc Meyer shook his head.

"I did not see any horses, no."

Doc Meyer folded the ear pieces back up in the cloth and held it above the trash canister.

"Shall I dispose of these pieces, or were you thinking souvenir?"

"We appreciate your time," I said.

Doc Meyer leaned to his side slightly and released gas as he opened his hand and let the cloth drop to the trash.

"Good of you to stop by," he said as I followed Virgil out the door.

51

We stood on the boardwalk in front of Doc Meyer's office. Virgil puffed on his cigar, thinking. A buckboard came around the corner from the east and stopped. Two tired-looking miners jumped from the bed, grabbed their gear, and entered a boarding-house. The buckboard moved on west and turned north at the corner of Full Moon Street.

"What do you allow, Everett?"

"Vince and the others did not stable the horses with the livery, that much we know . . . could be long gone."

Virgil glanced back through the office window as Doc Meyer turned out his desk lamp and we started up the boardwalk toward Hotel Ark.

"But," I said, "they don't feel any threat from this town."

"No, don't think they do."

"And on pure speculation, I don't think

they hightailed it out tonight, either."

"Don't?"

"I don't."

"You wouldn't?"

"Nope. Don't think I would, considering the circumstances."

"Circumstances being?"

"First circumstance being they lost some of their hands tonight. That being the case, fellows of this ilk got no way of dealing with those kinds of feelings, other than drinking and busting a nut."

"That's right."

"Next circumstance, they would not be expecting us here in Half Moon Junction, so they won't be skittish."

"No, they won't," Virgil said.

"Far as they know, we are near a hundred miles from here."

"That's right."

"Don't think they would have the gall or stupidity to check in to a hotel, though."

"But maybe," Virgil said.

"Next circumstance is, they got money."

"They do."

"If they stayed," I said, "I think bedding down with whores would be their most astute move."

"Seems prospect," Virgil said.

"Don't you imagine?"

"I do," Virgil said. "That'd be my summation as well, considering the circumstances."

A mangy cur stepped out of the shadows from between two buildings in front of us and stopped. He looked at us for a moment and moved on slowly across the street. He sniffed at something, then disappeared behind a rotted section of siding on a blacksmith's shop. We continued walking until we got to the corner of Full and Three Quarter Moon and stopped.

"They might have picketed the horses outside of town, hidden in a stand of trees or someplace," I said, "and come back in on foot."

"Sounds right," Virgil said. "Come back, gamble a bit, buy a piece for the evening."

"Probably too lazy, though, considering," I said. "Been a wearying day for those boys, with all the commotion they've had to go through. First, the expectant excitement of the robbery, followed by the shooting and friends dying off. Vince having his helix and concha pieces wrapped in a napkin and sitting at the bottom of a trash bucket in the drunk dentist's office. They're going to be in need of some comfort, some mothering, a basic hankering for food, drink, and women. Plus, they got dollars and dimes they stole from the people on the train

212

burning a hole in the bottom of their pocket."

Bugs were circling the gas lantern again near where we stood across from Hotel Ark on the southeast corner of Full and Three Quarter Moon Streets. Virgil stood with his thumbs in his vest pockets puffing on his cigar, thinking. He pulled out his pocket watch and looked at the time. He looked back to the south and to the north.

"We got four blocks with alleys," he said. "I'll look around the backside outskirts, all the way around. You do the center alleys. We meet back here, thirty minutes."

I looked at my watch.

"We see something," Virgil said. "We come back here. Put together a go-to-it plan."

52

I walked south on Full Moon Street and came to a single-story building on my left with an opening between it and the two-story building next to it. I moved through the opening and walked toward the rear of the buildings. When I got to the back of the buildings I started walking the narrow turns of the alley passage. A few lamps were burning, but for the most part it was dark. Right away, I came upon three horses stalled in a small pen that backed up to a surveying company. Straightaway I could tell they were not our horses. All three were big plow horses. I walked around the pen and came to an empty side alley that connected to Half Moon Street. I walked the narrow alley path to the street and looked around. The street was empty except for the mangy cur Virgil and I had seen before. He was startled to see me. He stopped, looked at me, and walked off slow-like. In a moment, he was gone into the shadows. I turned and came back through the side alley.

Sitting at the top of a dark stairwell, a woman with her back to me was smoking a cigarette. She did not see me as I turned and started back to the east. Up ahead of me, a horse blew and a hoof pawed at the ground. I moved up slowly, and somewhere ahead of me in the shadows, a man coughed.

I stopped, stayed back, listened for a moment, and moved on slowly around the corner. He coughed again. The sound of the cough was coming from inside the outhouse. Whoever was inside had a lamp. There was light streaking out through the cracks between the boards. The dust the horse was pawing up drifted through the shafts of light as I waited. After a moment, the door opened and an old man came out carrying the lamp. He had a thick book under his arm that looked like a Bible.

I thought to myself, *There might be an inkling of sanctimony in Half Moon Junction after all.* He walked slowly up a set of stairs and ducked inside a rickety tenement quarters, closing the door behind him. I moved on and came to the horse I had heard pawing and blowing. It was a lonesome old gray horse that was trying to loosen up the ground he was standing on. I scratched his

215

nose for a second and kept walking until I came to an opening between two buildings that led me out to Quarter Moon Street.

It was late enough of the evening now; there was no one moving about. I crossed the empty street and walked through a dark divide between two small houses. After about thirty feet I cleared the narrow passage between the houses and found myself on the rear section of buildings that faced both Half and Three Quarter Moon Street.

As I walked on, the buildings started to thin out, and after a short ways I was on the backside of the livery stable just shy of the miners' yard. I turned and walked between the livery stable and a Chinese laundry, where steam rose from the back half of the building. The Chinese were inside working, talking loudly, as I made my way past their shop and back to Half Moon Street. I heard a pop, followed by another pop. I heard a third pop and realized the sound was a muffled gunshot. The sound came from the west. I started running west on Half Moon Street, past the whorehouse church and past Pete's Place. When I got to the corner of Quarter Moon Street, a young man wearing underwear came running out from between two buildings and headed in my direction. He was bleeding. He had a gun in his hand

and was looking back over his shoulder as
he was on the run. He did not realize he
was running directly at me in the dark
street. I stood stock-still and pointed my
long-barrel Colt at him.

"Stop," I said.

When he saw me he raised his pistol at
me, and I shot him.

He staggered and tried to shoot again, and
I shot him again. He dropped his gun,
walked a half-circle, and fell to his knees.
He stayed on his knees for a moment, looking around. He moaned and toppled over
onto his side. I moved quickly up to the
boardwalk and into the shadows. I reloaded
and with my back to the boards of a dry-
goods store moved toward the opening
where the young man had come running
out to the street. I looked around the corner
of the dry-goods store and could not see
anything but dark.

"That you, Everett?" Virgil called from the
alley.

"It is."

"You shoot the fellow in his undergarments?"

"I did."

"Coming to ya!" Virgil said.

I stepped off the boardwalk, looking down
the dark alley. A sharp, short, high-pitched

whistle rang out, followed by a "Get up," and looming out of the dark came Virgil, riding Cortez at a quick pace toward me. He had my bony dark-headed roan and two other horses in tow.

53

"You're cinched, swing up!" Virgil said.

"Where are the others?" I said as I swung up on the back of the roan.

"Drunk," Virgil said. "Commingling with a wild bunch of whores, but if they heard the shots, they're getting their wits about 'em . . . this way."

Virgil and I took off south at a clip. Virgil rode fast, pulling one horse, and I was behind him, pulling the other. We quickly skirted around and came up on the backside of the west end of town. Virgil slowed and pulled up short behind an outbuilding and dismounted. He pointed to the backside of a white house.

"That house there," Virgil said. "They're in the front parlor, don't appear they heard nothing."

I dismounted. We tied the horses behind the outbuilding and moved closer on foot.

"I came to the end of the street," Virgil

said. "Heard music. I stayed in the dark, got up on the porch and looked inside. They were dancing, singing. One of the women was sawing on a fiddle, another beating a piano. The windows were fogged over. Men singing, but all I could see was the whores doing the music and dancing about naked."

"Just like we figured," I said.

"Is," Virgil said. "Didn't see men, though. Then I got a glimpse of the back of a man sitting on a sofa between two whores. He had a white bandage wrapped around his head."

"Vince."

"Damn straight Vince; not anybody else wrapped up like that."

"You didn't see any others?"

Virgil shook his head.

"Just Vince, but I heard the others. They are in there," Virgil said. "I got off the porch, walked to the back of the building, but I did not see the horses. I thought, like we talked about, they must have hobbled, or picketed somewhere. Then I heard a horse flapping his lips. I followed the sound, walked around that water shed there, and on the backside found the horses. They were saddled, loose cinches, and had their bridles hanging over their saddles."

"You figured you'd just get them."

"I did. I could hardly hear the music from there, but they were still carrying on. I figured since it was dark and them boys being occupied with the whores, I'd move off with the horses."

A big wagon pulled by six mules passed behind us. We watched until it moved on past us.

"I gathered up the horses," Virgil said, "walked off, back that way. I was halfway down the alley, headed toward the street, but was interrupted by the bandito in his undergarments with his quick-draw rig strapped on his hip."

"He followed you?"

"No. He was there in the alley, retching up a gullet of turned whiskey. He looked up as I was walking by, wiping his mouth. He looked at the horses. It took him a moment to figure out one of the horses was a horse he'd previously been riding. He stepped back, quick-like, and asked me what I was doing. I told him I was taking my horse, taking my deputy's horse, too, and while I was at it, taking his horse and one other to boot. He told me if I took another step he'd have to shoot me. I took another step. He pulled, and I shot him in the collarbone. He took off like a pheasant. I was between him and the whores' place, so he went through the alley there toward where you were. I would have shot him again, but I had my hands full with the horses. He shot two wild shots at me as he was on the run down the alley. A moment or two later, you shot him."

We moved up near the clothesline behind the whorehouse, where the horses had been picketed. We found a secure place and kept watch on the backside of the whorehouse.

"Don't see anybody," I said.

"Front parlor is where they are."

"Maybe they're putting the pieces together," I said. "Just moving slow."

"Might be. The undergarment fellow was firmly liquored up. No doubt they're all a flush lot."

"They can't see where the horses were picketed from where they are in the house there," I said.

"No, they can't."

"Dumb of them."

"It was," Virgil said.

"Pussy will do that to a man."

"It will."

"Make a man do dumb things."

"It does."

"Like what they have done here tonight."

"Yep," Virgil said.

"Mix it with sour mash and whatever smidgen of smarts they had left, slips

222

sideways, right out of the saddle."

"Lookie here?" Virgil pointed.

A door opened from the front parlor. There was now light spilling into the back room. We could hear the music from the parlor and could see someone moving inside.

"Sounds like they're still at it," I said.

"Does."

"They didn't hear the shots."

"Don't seem so," Virgil said.

"They got no idea."

"Nope."

"Unless it's a trap."

Virgil shook his head.

"No," Virgil said. "They got no seesaw for that."

The back door opened.

"Here we go," Virgil said.

A strong-looking, smaller man stepped out onto the porch.

54

He staggered as he fumbled with the buttons below the buckle of his gun-belt then positioned himself next to the porch rail and relieved himself. Like the other young man I shot dead in the street, he was wearing his underwear, hat, boots and hip rig. He swayed a bit as he went about his business off the side of the porch. He looked down, watching himself, then jerked his head up, looked about at nothing in particular, and hollered.

"Rex! You fuck!"

He looked back down for a moment. Then he turned a bit, looking about, and took an unsteady step. He stabilized and continued to empty himself.

". . . the fuck you go, boy?"

He looked down again, watching himself some more. Then looked up again, looking about.

"Rex!"

He finished relieving himself and put his instrument away. He swayed and leaned on the rail with both of his arms. He looked to his left.

"Rex! The fuck!"

He looked right.

"Boy! Where the fuck you go?"

He took a step back and a step over. He walked down the steps of the porch. He pulled up on his leather rig, snugging it up, and took a few wobbly steps away from the white house and stopped. He turned and turned again.

"Hey! You drunk fucker! Where'd you go!"

He looked toward the watershed.

"He's gonna come," Virgil said.

He did just that. He started walking toward the shed. We waited, and after a moment we heard him laugh as he got closer.

"Boy?"

He walked around the shed. I let him get a step past me, and I snatched him. I gathered him up quick and got his arms behind his back. Virgil took his pistol. He tried to resist. Virgil told him to settle, but he didn't. Virgil slapped him hard a few times, and he went slack in my arms. I pulled him over, propped him up on the back wall of the shed. Virgil lodged his handkerchief into his mouth.

"I'll get some rope," I said.

In short order we snugged his hands behind his back, pigged them with a half-hitch strain to his feet, and left him curled up in the shed.

We made sure he was breathing good. Then Virgil and I moved up quick on the white house before Vince and the other bandit could grow curious. They were still singing and playing music as we commenced with our plan.

"I'll come in the front door," Virgil said. "Same time you come in from the back room into the parlor."

We heard loud laughter followed by another tune being kicked up and sawed on a fiddle.

"Watch me," Virgil said. "Once I'm up front, we count ten."

"Okay."

I stood next to the back porch and watched Virgil walk through the narrow opening between the white house and the building next door. When Virgil got to the front he looked back to me. He raised his arm and dropped it, signaling me.

I started counting to myself as I stepped over the railing and entered the back-room door. Thousand one . . . thousand two . . . thousand three . . . thousand four . . .

I stayed out of view of the half-open door leading into the front parlor . . . thousand five . . . thousand six . . . thousand seven . . . thousand eight . . . thousand nine . . . I pushed open the door and entered the parlor at the exact time Virgil came through the front.

"Nobody move!" Virgil shouted.

A big bald fellow sitting next to a whore at the piano got to his pistol kind of fast, and I shot him. The women screamed. He fumbled with his pistol like he was still trying to get a shot off, and I shot him two more times. He fell back onto the piano keys, making a dull thumping tune, and dropped to the floor between the bench and the piano pedals.

Vince was caught with his left arm around one whore and his right around the other. He jerked his right arm free and froze with his hand on the grip of his Colt.

"Don't do it, Vince!" Virgil said.

Vince looked back and forth between Virgil and me.

"Quiet!" Virgil yelped to the ladies.

The women stopped whimpering.

"Far as I know, Vince, you've not killed anybody," Virgil said.

Vince kept his hand on the handle of his pistol, looking back and forth between Virgil and me.

"Serve some time, live to an old age. Talk about the time you lost part of your ear on the rail north of Half Moon Junction, or you can end it right here, getting killed by me, or Everett, or both of us."

Vince kept looking back and forth between Virgil and me.

"Rex is dead," Virgil said. "The other hand is bundled up like a bale of alfalfa in the water shed."

The bandage wrapped around Vince's head was showing a spot of red.

"Be good to get you to the jailhouse," Virgil said. "Lock you up. 'Course, it's your call."

Vince knew he was done up, and he did not like it. Not one bit. If there was betting going on, I would put money on him doing something stupid, but his cowardliness got the best of him. He removed his hand from his pistol and hung his arm back over the shoulder of the woman on his right. He let his bandaged head go back and rest on the top of the sofa. I moved to him and removed the Colt from his belt. I handed the pistol to Virgil and gathered Vince by the buttons of his long johns and jerked him to his feet.

55

We woke up Constable Berkeley. He came to the jailhouse with one of his deputies, J. B. Larson, a young fellow with a big wad of tobacco in his mouth, and they got the place opened up for us. The jailhouse was a two-room structure with an office on one side and two cells on the other. Thick double doors that remained wide open divided the office and cells. We got Vince and the smaller bandit locked up, each in his own cell.

I walked back in the front door from taking care of the horses, and Virgil was still sitting in a cane-back chair in front of Vince's cell with the Henry rifle resting in his lap. He was doing the same thing he was doing when I had stepped out, questioning Vince. Deputy Larson was asleep in a corner chair, and Berkeley was yawning wide as he stirred a pot of boiling coffee.

I walked over behind the main desk and

took a seat in what looked like a comfortable chair, but when I sat on the cushion I felt Bob's parfleche pouch under my butt. I freed the long strap from my shoulder, put the pouch on the desk, and let my butt settle into the cushioned seat. I put my leg over the edge of the desk and seriously thought about sleep. Vince and Virgil were both visible from where I was sitting.

Vince was sitting on the bunk with his elbows resting on his knees, looking at the floor. I could tell he was tired of Virgil's questioning. Before I had stepped out, Vince had told Virgil everything he knew about the Yankee, and what he said pretty much matched what Dean had told us.

"So why did the Yankee target you?"

"What do you mean?"

"You were in Wichita Falls, playing Seven-Up at the Bluebell Pool Palace and the Yankee asked you to be a part of this robbery?"

"It came up I was a train hand. I told him I worked as a brakeman. I worked for a couple of different railways, Union Pacific being the main line, but got laid off after the air brakes took over."

Virgil looked at me and back to Vince.

"George Westinghouse."

"That's right," Vince said disgustingly

230

with his Irish brogue. "The Yankee said he had a job and he needed somebody that was familiar with trains."

"Why was it you set the Pullman on fire?"

"I didn't."

"Who did?"

"The other fellow."

"Who?"

"I never met him before."

"But you met him tonight?"

Vince nodded.

"He was?"

"Bob Brandice. He got on, boarded with the Yankee. Bob's a mean son of a bitch."

"Why?"

"Why?" Vince said. "He's a mean son of a bitch. That is why."

"Why'd he set the Pullman on fire?"

"He threw a damn lantern. The fire kicked off quick."

"Why?"

Vince shook his head.

"He was mad I would not stop the coaches from rolling backward."

"Why was he mad?"

"When I knew we had you and Everett to deal with, I was not about to go back looking for the Yankee who double-crossed us. But when it came out, when I said your name, when I said Virgil Cole, Bob got angry. He insisted we stop."

"And you wouldn't."

"Hell, no, I wouldn't."

"Why?"

"So I would not have to see you or Everett Hitch. Hell, it would be all right with me if I never saw the two of you ever again, including right now."

Virgil looked at me and smiled.

56

Berkeley pulled the coffeepot from the stove. He poured cups and handed them around. The first cups he passed through the bars to Vince and the other prisoner. They both looked at the coffee like it might be poisoned.

"Just coffee, boys," Berkeley said.

Berkeley poured more cups. He gave one to Virgil, then me. He kicked the chair where Larson was sleeping. Larson looked about, wondering what happened, and Berkeley handed him a cup.

"Nap's over," Berkeley said.

Virgil sipped on his coffee for a moment, then continued questioning Vince.

"So, Brandice wanted to stop, why?"

"He wanted to come after you."

"He told you that?" Virgil said.

"Oh, yeah, he did," Vince said. "He damn sure did. He said he had bloody plans for you. Not Hitch."

Vince looked over to me and back to Virgil.

"Just you. He said he was going to cut you into pieces. He went into detail how he would go about it, too. He's an animal, and judging from what I saw, he was not just whistling a waltz."

Virgil looked at me and smiled a bit and looked back to Vince.

Vince continued, "He told me to brake the cars from rolling backward or else. I said, or else what? And he came at me like a bit dog. He cocked his rifle, but big Woodfin was fast. He grabbed the rifle and hit him so hard he went down in a clump."

I was looking at Virgil. He looked to me, then back to Vince.

Vince was looking at the floor.

"And Woodfin?"

Vince stayed looking at the floor for a moment before lifting his eyes back to Virgil.

"I told Woodfin to keep an eye on him. I had Rex, big Butch, and Eddie here" — Vince pointed to the smaller fellow in the cell next to him — "working the brakes in the other cars. We was rolling for a good long while, and after some time I came back to the Pullman. Woodfin had Bob at gunpoint, by the uphill door. When I came back in through the door, Woodfin looked to me, and when he did, Bob, real fast-like, spun around on Woodfin and in a second had a knife to Woodfin's throat. I went for my Colt, but Bob said he'd cut Woodfin if I touched the Colt. Woodfin still had Bob's Henry rifle in his hands. Bob told Woodfin to let go of the rifle. But instead of letting go of the rifle, Woodfin just slung the rifle out the door, and when he did Bob cut Woodfin's throat," Vince paused looking at Virgil. "He just cut Woodfin's throat. I never seen anything like that, just cut his god-damn throat and flipped him off the rail. I went for my Colt, and when I did Bob slung the conductor's lantern at me. I shot, but I don't think I hit him. Next thing I knew, he was off and the Pullman was on fire. He's a mean son of a bitch."

"Then what?"

"I told the governor to get his wife and get into the back car. That is exactly what happened, and within a short time the cars started to go real slow. I disconnected the Pullman, and after a few moments we were stopped, just stopped."

"Then what?"

"I told the governor, all the people, to stay put in the cars. Give us time to get going, and then they could do what they needed to do."

Virgil looked at Vince, who was now looking at Virgil, nodding.

"I'm telling the truth."

Virgil stood up to close the heavy doors
between the cell and the office.

"Ask the governor, he'll tell you."

I figured Vince was telling the truth, and
so did Virgil, but for whatever reason Vince
felt his routine was deserving of some
sympathy or acknowledgment, but Virgil
was not about to oblige Vince in any way.
Virgil just closed the doors.

"That's the truth!" Vince said as the doors
closed with a thud.

57

Virgil set the stock of the Henry rifle on the floor and leaned the barrel on the edge of the desk.

"That sounds right," Berkeley said. "What he was saying is pretty much what the governor said. At least in respect to how the fire started, anyway."

"Might well be," Virgil said. "Hard to say what is what with boys like Vince. With a lifetime of lying, they don't know when they're even doing it."

Virgil walked to the stove and poured some more coffee into his cup.

"There is a cigar there for you, Marshal," Berkeley said.

"Box on the desk."

"Don't mind if I do."

Virgil set his coffee down and got a cigar from the box. He got a match from a narrow porcelain cup and dragged the tip across the underside of the desk. He got the fire going good, picked up his coffee and walked to the open door, and looked out into the street. He leaned on the doorjamb and took a sip of coffee.

There were two wingback chairs opposite the desk where I was sitting. Berkeley poured himself some more coffee and sat in one of the chairs. He blew on his coffee before he took a sip.

"Your Indian pouch?" Berkeley asked motioning to Bob's pouch on the desk.

I picked it up and looked at it some.

"Naw."

I dropped it back to the desk.

"Belonged to the mean son of a bitch Vince was talking about."

Berkeley blew on his coffee some more and took a sip.

I picked up the pouch again and looked at its handiwork. It was sure enough Indian-made — it had fringe, a few bear claws and rattlesnake tails dangling from the sides. The long waist strap was made of tightly woven deer sinew. I opened the pouch and dumped the contents on the desk.

"Whetstone, coin sack, comb, jerky," I said.

I tossed the comb and jerky in the trash and picked up the small leather coin sack with a brass snap. I opened it. Inside, there was a single silver dollar, two Indian heads, and a folded-up piece of paper. I opened the paper. It was a newspaper article. I leaned over and turned up the desk lantern. I read the caption out loud:

DATELINE HUNTSVILLE.
CONVICTS ESCAPE.

Virgil turned, looked at me. I waved the article in the air.

"A keepsake, no doubt . . . from Bob's pouch here."

"Must be exploits accounted."

Virgil took a sip of coffee.

"Read me the clipping."

I leaned into the light and read.

58

Prison guards killed as Two Convicts Escape Huntsville. Murderer and Criminal Mastermind Break Out of Jail in Huntsville, TEX, March 1.

Years ago on the Sweetwater Ranch, now part of the infamous XIT Ranch, ranch foreman Jay Christopher Wood and his wife, Sharon, were brutally stabbed to death by Robert Brandice. Brandice was tracked down by Sweetwater's law counsel, Virgil Cole.

"Law counsel?" Virgil said as he moved from the door and sat in the chair next to Berkeley, "That's a new one. We were hired guns."

"Least you got your name in the paper," I said, and continued reading.

Brandice was eventually apprehended by Cole after a shoot-out that left Brandice on his deathbed. Brandice was subsequently found guilty and sentenced to hang, but his sentence was reduced to life, considering Brandice's fragile condition.

"Fragile?" Virgil scoffed. "Fragile like a Chicago mill saw."

Eleven years later, Brandice and his cell mate, John Wellington, walked out the front door of Huntsville Prison at seven o'clock this evening dressed as prison guards. The uniforms they were wearing belong to Huntsville guards Cameron Thomson and Gary Dempsey. Both Thomson and Dempsey had worked at the prison for twenty-plus years and were revered and respected senior employees of Huntsville. Thomson and Dempsey were found under the bunk in Brandice's cell. Both had been tied up and stabbed to death. A homemade knife was later found at the scene. Brandice's cellmate, Wellington, was serving a sentence of sixty-five years for second-degree murder and masterminding an embezzlement scheme that nearly brought down the Texas banking industry, leaving one person dead. Wellington had been incarcerated for two years prior to this escape. Wellington lost an arm while operating a steam lathe during his incarceration in Huntsville. Both men are considered extremely dangerous. Sheriff Daniel McGinley called for a posse just after midnight. He divided the men into four groups to scour the territories within a radius of the penitentiary. Sheriff McGinley offered a $1,000 reward for each of the men. Men at Large: Robert Boulder Brandice, forty-six. Brandice is described as a lean man, medium height, with long hair and beard. He has a history of violence and has been in and out of jail many times. John Bishop Wellington, fifty-five. Wellington is European; however, his nationality unknown. He's tall, well mannered, speaks several languages fluently, and was reported to be an experienced Shakespearean performer.

I looked at Virgil. He put his cigar between his teeth, set his coffee on the desk, and picked up the Henry rifle.

"Thespian, huh," Virgil said.

Virgil slid the Henry rifle under the light on the desk and pointed to three small letters engraved on top of the receiver near the rear sight.

Berkeley and I leaned in for a closer look.

"JBW," Virgil said. "Not that it does us

any good knowing who he is, but at least we got us a handle on the mysterious Yankee. John Bishop Wellington."

I continued reading the remainder of the article to myself but stopped and looked up at Virgil.

"There's more here, Virgil. This part provides us some good."

Virgil looked at me; I continued.

Wellington's crime gained the state's attention when three prominent Texas attorneys — Stephen Humphrey, William Mills, and James Lassiter — were also indicted after the ill-fated embezzlement scheme went awry. Charges were eventually dropped on the three due to the lack of state's evidence. Many believe Wellington was the scapegoat for the others, who were heavy with counsel.

I looked at Virgil, Virgil looked at Berkeley, and Berkeley looked at me.

"Attorney James Lassiter," I said. "Huh, wonder if that is the same Lassiter who's dreaming about aforementioneds and abrogate absentions in the Hotel Ark about right now?"

59

After the hard rain, a low mist was rolling in across the dark streets of Half Moon Junction. The air was dense and damp. We left the horses hitched in front of the jailhouse and walked the short distance up the street toward the Hotel Ark. For some reason it wasn't until we were on the move that I realized how big Berkeley was. He was almost a foot taller than me, and moving at a quick pace like we were, his long strides were hard to keep up with.

"So this escaped convict, John Bishop Wellington," Berkeley said. "You think this is his plan?"

"Don't know," Virgil said.

"What about Mr. Hobbs?" Berkeley said. "Do you believe there is a cooperation between the men, that they were in on this together, Hobbs, Lassiter, and this Wellington?"

"Don't know for sure, either," Virgil said.

"Figure we'll find out soon enough."

"I have to say, Marshal, I was not remotely leery of Lassiter and Hobbs," Berkeley said. "Frankly never crossed my mind they could be behind something like this, never. I considered them to be caring and intelligent."

"Money makes smart men do stupid things," Virgil said.

"Especially a half-million dollars," I said.

"Especially," Virgil said.

"I believed them, based on their relationship with the governor and their prominence, their credentials."

"Bigger the credentials, bigger the prospect you'll find a rat or possum at the bottom of the barrel," Virgil said.

"What about the governor?" I said. "You think he had a dog in this hunt?"

"Be a fool if he did," Berkeley said.

"Well, he is a Texan," I said.

"That he is," Berkeley said.

"And a politician," I said.

"Questionable combination," Virgil said, "but having his family and the Pinkerton agents along, I'd say he was set up."

"I can tell you, he was in bad shape when we got him and his wife into the hotel room. White as paper. He just collapsed in a corner chair, closed his eyes as if it were a bad dream."

"How do you want to go about this?" I said. "Rousing Lassiter up?"

Virgil stopped at the bottom of the steps before entering Hotel Ark and looked at Berkeley.

"Which room is Lassiter's?" Virgil said.

"Second floor, top of the stairs on the right, first door on the east."

"And Hobbs?"

"His room is just to the other side of the stairwell, west side. Stairs split the two rooms."

"What about the governor?" I asked.

Berkeley pointed up.

"Got one room on the third floor. Governor and his wife are there," Berkeley said.

Virgil looked at me.

"You go through Hobbs' door. I'll go through Lassiter's at the same time. No polite knocking or knob turning; needs to be a surprise."

"I'll be right there with you," Berkeley said, "in case you need backup."

We started to move.

"One thing," Berkeley said as he pulled a gold-plated watch from his vest pocket and flipped open the lid. "It's late." He looked at his watch. "Or I should say early."

"They should be sound asleep," I said.

"They should," Berkeley said as he slipped the watch back into his pocket, "but I want you to know, they both got trim . . . So if you would, please be mindful of the merchandise."

Virgil nodded slightly with his eye on me, and we entered the hotel.

60

We walked into the hotel, moving quietly
past the pair of black bears that guarded
the entrance, and into the main room. A
single lamp was burning on a belayed
wagon-wheel chandelier hanging low in the
middle of the room. Big Burns stepped out
of his small room behind the desk, yawning.

"Need something, Mr. Berkeley?"

Berkeley put his finger to his lips for
Burns to be quiet.

Burns looked back and forth between the
three of us. Berkeley got close to him.

"Seen anybody come or go?"

Burns shook his head.

"No, sir."

"Stay put," Berkeley said. "Make no
noise."

Burns nodded, looking at the three of us.

Berkeley retrieved a small cut-glass finger
lantern from a low cupboard behind the
desk and lit the wick. Once he got the flame

going good, we followed him past the bobcats and walked very quietly up the steps to the second floor.

When we got to the second floor, Berkeley pointed to each of the rooms, identifying first Lassiter's room and then Hobbs' room. Then he stepped back, placing his back to the wall at the top of the staircase. I positioned myself with my Colt in front of Hobbs' door. Virgil leaned the Henry rifle on the wall behind him, drew his bone handle, and got in front of Lassiter's door. Berkeley pulled out a .38 Smith & Wesson Lemon Squeezer from his belt and nodded that he was ready.

I kept my eye on Virgil.

Virgil looked at me and dropped a sharp nod of his chin.

I moved fast, my shoulder hit Hobbs' door hard, and in an instant I was in the room. Hobbs was flat on his back, lying naked in the center of the bed. The pretty whore we'd met earlier in the evening was riding him. She had a steady diagonal lope working that was causing Hobbs some toe curling, but she stopped and looked at me as if I was there to borrow some flour or sugar. Hobbs raised his head up like a turtle on its back. What hair he had on his head was pointing in every direction, and his face was beet red.

"Wh-what . . . What's the meaning of this?" Hobbs said.

The whore stayed atop of Hobbs, looking at me. A skilled equestrian awaiting instruction.

"Off," I said.

She responded quickly. She pulled back and slung one leg over him. Hobbs grabbed the crumpled bedding and covered his privates. The whore stayed on her knees, looking at me.

I picked up a crocheted blanket at the foot of the bed and tossed it to her.

"Who do you think you are?" Hobbs said.

"You know who I am, Mr. Hobbs."

"Damn right I do, and you have no business coming here."

"Stop talking," I said. "I'm gonna let you get your trousers on. You'll have plenty of time for talking, rest assured."

Hobbs groveled, "Now, see here."

I raised my Colt a little more toward the center of his eyes, and he stopped talking and shook his head.

"Oh, for the love of God," Hobbs said. "Rose, get me my unders and trousers."

Without wrapping herself in the blanket, Rose walked to the corner chair like she had a book on top of her head and retrieved Hobbs' underwear and trousers. She walked back to the bed and handed Hobbs his clothing.

"Everett," I heard Virgil call out from the hall, "you got Hobbs?"

"I do!"

Virgil stepped into the room, Colt in one hand, the Henry rifle in the other. Berkeley was a step behind him.

"Lassiter flew the coop."

61

"Where'd he go?" Virgil said to Hobbs.

"What?" Hobbs said, looking over his shoulder at Virgil as he pulled on his trousers. "I don't know what you mean."

Virgil looked at me.

"The woman in the room with Lassiter said he told her to stay put till he came back. Said he left as soon as they got upstairs, over an hour ago."

Virgil looked back to Hobbs.

"Where did he go?"

"He left?" Hobbs said. "I don't know. I have no idea. Why?"

Virgil stayed focused on Hobbs but spoke to Berkeley, who was standing behind him.

"Mr. Berkeley, I need you to get our horses out front. The chestnut and the roan; leave the other two."

"Will do," Berkeley said, and left the room quick.

Rose picked up the blanket and moved

near to me as Virgil walked around the bed and faced Hobbs.

"Tell me about Wellington?"

"Who?"

"I don't got time for you to dally with my demeanor."

"Dally with your . . ."

Hobbs shook his head.

"I do not know what you are talking about."

"Read the back end of that clippin', Everett," Virgil said without looking in my direction.

I pulled the article from my vest pocket, opened it, and read it out loud.

Wellington's crime gained the state's attention when three prominent Texas attorneys — Stephen Humphrey, William Mills, and James Lassiter — were also indicted after the ill-fated embezzlement scheme went awry. Charges were eventually dropped on the three due to the lack of state's evidence. Many believe Wellington was the scapegoat for the others, who were heavy with counsel.

I looked up at Virgil. Virgil was looking at Hobbs.

"Lassiter and you are partners, law partners."

"Our companies merged less than a year ago."

"What about Wellington and the trial?"

"I was on a big case in New York during that brouhaha. By the time I had returned it was old news. Being an attorney is a nefarious business, and there is often a thin line between right and wrong, Mr. Cole. I never gave the banking trial involving this Wellington a thought. We firms are always caught in the middle between good and evil."

"Stealing money ain't in the middle."

Hobbs stood up from the bed.

"I never knew this Wellington."

Hobbs limped slightly to the corner and sat in a chair, where his shoes were on the floor in front of him.

"Wouldn't know Wellington if he hit me in the face."

"Who had the relationship with the governor?" Virgil asked.

"You mean who was the idiot who encouraged the governor to invest in the territorial lands, putting him and his family's lives at stake?"

Hobbs shook his head as he picked up a sock from inside his shoe. He crossed his leg and put the sock on his foot.

"That would be me, Mr. Cole; that would be me."

Hobbs picked up his other sock.

"I have known the governor for a long time. We went to college together. I introduced James and the territorial idea to him. That was me; hell, I introduced him to his wife."

"Lassiter?" Virgil said. "How long you known him?"

Hobbs shook his other sock and put it on.

"Long time, not closely; however, not until our firms merged and we began working together did I get to know James intimately, evidently not intimately enough."

Hobbs slowly turned his attention from Virgil to the floor.

"You believe this is James' doing, I take it?"

"And yours," Virgil said. "You're his partner."

Hobbs shook his head slowly, not so much as an answer to Virgil's pointed inquiry but rather to the realization of something he had not suspected.

"It just can't be . . ." Hobbs said.

62

Hobbs worked his right foot into his shoe and sat back, looking at Virgil, with his elbows resting on the arms of the chair. He slowly shook his head from side to side.

"I know nothing about any of this," Hobbs said. "Absolutely nothing."

Virgil looked at him steadily.

"Who hired the Pinkerton agents?"

Hobbs raised his hand like a schoolboy.

"Afraid that, too, was my personal blunder," Hobbs said. "What now, Marshal?"

"Tell me about Lassiter."

"What would you like to know?"

"What you know."

"Well . . . he's one hell of an attorney. Not married. Divorced. I think. No children that I know of . . . this the type of information you're interested in?"

"He in trouble?"

"Not that I know of."

"Owe people money."

Hobbs shook his head.

"I don't think so. If so, I have no knowledge of such."

Rose was standing close to me. The blanket was draped loosely off her shoulders, barely covering her breasts, and was open down the side, revealing the curves of her naked body.

"You can go," I whispered to her.

"Oh, no," she said a little too loudly. "I'm enjoying this."

Virgil looked at Rose. Then me. Then he looked back to Hobbs.

"Maybe he's in debt, I don't know," Hobbs said. "He's a gambler. He gambles a great deal, that I know, cards, the races, everything. He's a big spender, too."

"On what?"

Hobbs shook his head. "Expensive taste, fine stuff, horses, carriages, clothes, women, everything, guns. I don't know."

"Guns?"

"He has a huge collection. Civil War and beyond. Works on guns in his spare time, repairing them, engraving them. A fine craftsman — exquisite, actually. Gives them as gifts. He's a generous man. He gave me a fancy Derringer."

Virgil turned the receiver of the Henry rifle in his hands so Hobbs could view the engraving clearly.

"Like this?"

Hobbs reached over his shoulder and retrieved a pair of spectacles from the breast pocket of his jacket hanging on the back of the chair. He put them on and looked at the engraving on the rifle and his eyes narrowed. He frowned for a brief moment and removed his spectacles. He looked up at Virgil with a steady gaze.

"Yes," Hobbs said, "like that."

Berkeley bounded up the stairs and came to the doorway out of breath. His big hands held on to each side of the doorjamb.

"Son of a bitch stole my black," Berkeley said.

He took a big breath.

"After supper he asked me if I was a horseman. We got into a discussion about bloodlines," Berkeley said. "Like a fool, I showed him my prizewinner. My Thoroughbred. He was in a corral next to the hotel here."

Berkeley took another big breath.

"But not anymore," Berkeley said. "The son of a bitch."

"Mr. Berkeley?" a voice called sternly from the hall. "What on earth is happening here? What is with all the commotion?"

Berkeley turned. A man stepped up be-

258

hind him. He was older, medium height, lean, with intense eyes and a groomed goatee.

"Governor, sir," Berkeley said. "Um, we have a situation here."

"What sort of situation?" the governor said sharply.

The governor looked into the room past Berkeley, to Hobbs sitting in the corner chair wearing one shoe.

"Chet?" the governor said. "What's happening?"

The governor moved swiftly past Berkeley and came into the room.

"What's the situation . . . ?"

Rose took an abrupt step back, stepping on the blanket, and it dropped to the floor, leaving her standing buck naked.

The governor looked to Rose, then to Virgil, then to me, then back to Hobbs.

"What in the hell is going on here?" he said.

63

After we searched the whole of Half Moon Junction and found no sign of Lassiter or anyone who might have seen him, the governor, Hobbs, Berkeley, Virgil, and I collected in the main room of Hotel Ark just as the sun was coming up. Burns came in from the saloon with a pot of coffee and set it on the front desk next to the pair of mounted mallards.

"Anything else, Mr. Berkeley?" Burns said.

"No," Berkeley said. "Thank you, Burns."

Burns went back into his room behind the desk and closed the door. The governor had not said much to us since he had previously entered Hobbs' room. What little he did have to say let Virgil and me know right away he was not part of the unfolding plot of thievery.

The governor was angry with Hobbs, and at the moment was pacing. Not just a little bit angry but a lot. His knuckles were on his hips, holding back the flaps of his jacket, as he moved back and forth in front of Hobbs. Hobbs was seated in a tall-backed chair next to the bobcats. Virgil and I stood leaning on each side of the foyer arches. The black bears were behind us, just inside the hotel's entrance. Berkeley perched on a stool by the reception desk. A single shaft of morning sun peeked through one of the windows and lit up the hen and drake mallards sitting on the reception desk like a theater spotlight. After a wave of uncomfortable silence, the governor spoke.

"My God, Chester," the governor said.

Hobbs looked at him, but the governor did not look at Hobbs.

"How could you?" the governor said. "Are you mad?"

Hobbs said nothing.

"How in the hell could you have dragged me and my family into this?"

Hobbs looked at the floor and shook his head.

"I asked you if you evaluated the security of the situation," the governor said, "and you assured me this was a sound business proposition and we'd be safe! My girls, my wife! My God! I trusted you!"

The governor stopped talking for a moment and paced quietly, trying to let off some steam. Following a bandy of turns, he stopped and looked at Virgil.

"And for what?" the governor said. "They did not even get the money they were after!"

"What?" Hobbs said as he looked up from the floor. "Well, where is it?"

The governor turned on Hobbs like a badger and slapped him so hard blood instantly came to his nose.

"My daughters have been abducted!"

Hobbs grabbed his bleeding nose and just looked at the governor.

"God knows what will come of this, and you have the audacity to ask: Where's the money!"

The governor stood over Hobbs with his fists clenched at his sides — as if Hobbs would even think of retaliating — but Hobbs just remained seated, looking up at the governor as his nose bled.

"Why did you ask me about where I was carrying the money?" the governor said.

"What?"

"Goddamn you, Chet! Why? You asked me more than once. Why?"

Hobbs looked down at the floor again, and blood dripped off his chin onto his shirt.

"Lassiter wanted to know," Hobbs said. "I thought for security, I'm sorry —"

"Sorry? Damn right you're sorry!"

"I was the one who got the Pinkerton agents," Hobbs said.

"Yes! You are the one who got the Pinkerton agents! You got the Pinkerton agents killed!"

The governor jerked a handkerchief from his pocket and slung it at Hobbs.

"Goddamn you, Chet," he said.

64

The governor was sure enough angry and certainly distraught. He was doing his best to remain composed, but he was not doing a very good job of it. He resumed pacing but avoided looking at Hobbs. He spoke to Virgil and me as he moved.

"Even with the Pinkertons on guard, I was not so stupid to carry that amount of money in my possession," the governor said. "Or in the freight safe with guards. God knows how many payrolls have been absconded from train safes."

Continuing shafts of sun slanted across the room as Half Moon Junction was waking up. Outside, a skinner hawed a team of mules as they rounded the corner of the hotel and drove north up the street. After a moment more of pacing, the governor stopped in front of the snarling bobcats and turned to face Virgil and me.

"So," he said, "what now?"

Virgil looked at me.

"Lassiter showed his hand," I said.

"He did," Virgil said.

"Didn't have to."

"No," Virgil said, "he didn't."

"Article just mentioned him," I said, "didn't convict him."

"He convicted himself."

We thought about that for a moment.

"Something spooked him," Virgil said.

"That would be you, Marshal," Hobbs said as he removed the handkerchief from his bleeding nose. "You scared the hell out of him when you were asking us all those questions."

"He said that?" I asked.

"No," Hobbs said, shaking his head, "not in words, anyway. He did say he thought the questions were unnecessary and insensitive, but in retrospect, I realize he was seriously disconcerted after your inquisition."

"Disconcerted to the point he took my goddamn horse," Berkeley said.

"Lassiter planned this with this thief Wellington," the governor said. "The whole devious plot. Most likely intending on returning to the firm, keeping his profile."

"Not now," Virgil said.

"Nope," I said. "Don't think Texas will be part of his itinerary," I said, "no time soon, anyway."

"He's got one of two options. He'll get as far away as possible or he goes after Wellington, and the money he thinks Wellington has," Virgil said.

"Wellington was vicious with his demands, and Lassiter was rattled, or he seemed rattled," Hobbs said. "Do you think Wellington double-crossed him?"

"Lassiter thinks, or I would assume he thinks, Wellington has the money," the governor said.

"That's right," Virgil said.

"And Wellington," I said, "since he had your case, Governor, thought he was in possession of the money."

Virgil pushed up on the brim of his hat a slight bit.

"There's one thing for certain now, though," Virgil said. "Now he knows he's not in possession of it."

"Might try and go after it," I said.

"Might," Virgil said.

The front door opened and a skinny young boy with coal dust on his hands and face and a head full of shaggy blond hair hurried in. He stopped by the black bears in the foyer and looked up at Virgil and me standing in the entrance to the main room of the hotel.

"Mr. Berkeley," the boy said.

Berkeley got off the stool to have a look at the towheaded boy.

"What is it, Charlie?"

Charlie took a deep breath.

"Sam told me to fetch you right away!" Charlie said. "Said it was important! It's got something to do with the governor's daughters!"

65

The sun felt warm on my face. It was a new day, and sleep apparently was not an option, at least for the foreseeable future. Virgil and I had been in many sleep-deprived situations before, situations in which we had to operate on gumption and get-go, and this was shaping up to be one of those very situations. We walked down the street, heading to meet Sam and figure out what important information young Charlie was talking about regarding Abigail and Emma. The air was crisp, and there was not a cloud in the morning sky as Virgil, Berkeley, Hobbs, the governor, and I followed Charlie as he hurried ahead in front of us. Virgil and I lagged behind, out of earshot of the others.

"What do you allow, Virgil?"

"Hard to speculate."

I didn't say anything else as we continued walking.

"You?" Virgil said.

"Don't know," I said. "Been sort of expectant about it."

"Sort of?"

"More than sort of."

We walked on for a bit.

"I saw it right off," Virgil said.

"What?"

"Feelings," Virgil said. "The feelings that sprung up between the two of you. You and Emma. Short time as it was, I saw it."

We walked a bit more.

"Like you surmised," I said. "After we disconnected from the first coach, there was not a damn thing we could do about the fact Emma and Abigail were headed north and we were headed south but I've not for an extended moment stopped thinking about them, Virgil."

"Nope," Virgil said. "Me neither."

"I hope to hell they are alive."

Virgil rested his hand on my shoulder.

"Me too, Everett," Virgil said. "Me too."

Up ahead, the governor looked back to Berkeley.

"Just where is the boy headed, Mr. Berkeley?" the governor said. "Where is this Sam?"

"At the depot, sir," Berkeley said. "Sam is the Half Moon Junction stationmaster."

We walked by the tent encampments as

we neared the depot. I did not need the aroma of coffee and bacon cooking to remind me I was getting hungry again. Just before we passed the encampment I heard the sound of a locomotive building up steam followed by two blasts of the engine's whistle. When we cleared the last tent I saw the engine coming down the track. It was a Yard Goat, a heavy duty 0-6-0 locomotive, used for moving cars around switchyards. It was engineered by a burly man with his hairy arm hanging out the window.

"That Sam?" Hobbs said.

Berkeley shook his head.

"No, that's Uncle Ted, Sam's uncle in the Yard Goat," Berkeley said. "Looks like he's getting the track cleared."

The Goat was connected to the coaches that had been left on the track and was in the process of pulling them into the switch-yard.

Berkeley pointed to a little man walking next to the Yard Goat.

"That's Sam there," Berkeley said.

Sam switched the rails, and the Yard Goat whistle blasted two shorts and moved the cars slowly off the main track onto a side rail that dead-ended in the switchyard.

Sam said something to Uncle Ted and gestured up the track to the north. Uncle

Ted nodded, saying something back, and throttled the Goat into the yard. Sam walked down the track toward the depot with his hands in the front pockets of his overalls.

As we neared the depot, the Yard Goat stomped past us, moving the coaches onto the dead-end section of track behind the water tower. Just below the Yard Goat's window was a skillfully drawn chiaroscuro of a muscled horse running at a full gallop. Under the painting was the single word: *Ironhorse.*

When the coaches passed, Sam saw us walking toward the depot, and only then was it apparent Sam was in fact a woman dressed like a man. She wore a man's shirt under her bib overalls and had a bowler hat snugged down low on her head.

We arrived at the porch of the depot at the same time as Sam. Sam's skin was dark from the sun, and her eyes were sapphire blue.

"Burton," Sam said.

"Sam," Berkeley said. "This is the governor, Mr. Hobbs, Marshal Cole, Deputy Hitch. Charlie here said you had some information?"

"Charlie, go on and help Uncle Ted with them cars."

"Okay, Sam," Charlie said.

Charlie scampered off the depot steps and ran toward the Ironhorse.

"What is it, Sam?" Berkeley said.

"Yes, please," the governor said. "The boy said you have information about my daughters?"

Sam removed her bowler, revealing her close-cropped blond hair, and narrowed her eyes thoughtfully, looking at the governor.

"Yes, sir, Governor, sir," she said. "Let me show you."

66

Sam opened the door of the depot and ushered us in with a slight swing of her hat.

"After you," she said.

We entered, and Sam hurried past us, and we followed her across the long, narrow corridor of the depot.

"Last night we received a wire alertin' us the Fort Smith Express out of Paris was off schedule," Sam said. "When Jenny, our telegraph operator, opened up this mornin', she got a number of messages right quick about what happened on the track last night."

We entered a small glassed-in corner office overlooking the track, where a young woman sat at a telegraph desk.

"This here is Jenny," Sam said. "Anythin' else come in, dear?"

"No, nothing," Jenny said as she swiveled around in her chair from the desk.

Jenny was smaller than Sam. She, too,

wore men's clothes: breeches, a bowler, and a pin-striped shirt under a corduroy vest. Jenny opened the top drawer, took out a telegram, and handed it to Sam.

"This wire we received," Sam said. "Addressed to you, sir."

Sam handed the telegram to the governor.

"I sent Charlie to fetch you right away," Sam said, "first thing when Jenny received it."

The governor read the telegram. His eyes narrowed. He read the note again and looked to Jenny.

"You're certain this is correct," the governor said.

"Yes, sir, it's correct, sir," Jenny said. "It's the message that was sent."

Jenny spoke quickly with crisp, precise diction.

The governor looked at Sam.

"Jenny knows telegraphin' beyond her years," Sam said. "Her daddy was a telegrapher, taught her enough and then some. She's good with code 'n everythin' comes through here, Choctaw, Chickasaw, Cherokee, heck, Greek —"

"Marshal?" the governor said.

He handed the telegram to Virgil.

"Sometimes wires get changed when repeaters are not in line," Jenny said, "or if

274

notes have to be retransmitted over long distances by other operators, or if someone is a novice on the key, but that wire is from just up the rail at the top of the Kiamichi. I know that operator."

Virgil looked up at me and back to the telegram. He reread the message and handed it to me.

"Up the rail, top of the Kiamichi?" Virgil said. "Where are you talking about, Jenny?"

"As far as I can tell, the transmission came from Tall Water Falls."

I read the note and looked at the governor. He sat slowly into an armchair next to the desk. He was doing his best to maintain his composure. He gazed out the window toward the iron rails tapering off in the distance and shook his head slowly from side to side.

"For God's sake," Hobbs said. "What in God's name has happened? What are we dealing with?"

The governor took the note from my hand and handed it to Hobbs. Hobbs read the telegram and looked at the governor with a shocked expression on his face.

67

"Ransom! dear God! The gall!" Hobbs said. "What more? This is madness, absolute madness."

The governor took the telegram from Hobbs. Then he leaned over in the chair, rested his elbows on the arms of the chair, and stared at the telegram.

"What did you mean," Virgil said, "as far as you could tell this telegram was from Tall Water Falls?"

"The telegram could come from anywhere in the loop," Sam said.

Jenny nodded.

"Yes, but as I previously mentioned, I know that operator; there are two of them at the depot. That operator is from Tall Water Falls. I don't know the operator personally, but I know that fist. That is Ernest C.'s fist."

"Fist?" Hobbs said.

"The operator's key pattern," I said.

"Every operator has a fist," Jenny said. "A signature way of keying. We all key a distinct style. Though that wire is cryptic, that is Ernest C. from Tall Water Falls, no doubt about it . . . But . . ."

"But what? Something wrong?" I said. "You curious about something?"

Jenny looked at me then looked to the governor.

"Ernest C. didn't provide a sine or confirmation to the wire," Jenny said. "Sine is an operator's signature."

"Which is unusual," Sam added.

"It is," Jenny said. "Normally all railroad- and depot-dispatched transmissions are retyped in complete with sine. That way depot communications maintain a high degree of accuracy for zero confusion and safety. Right after I received this wire I replied with a received confirmation but got nothing back. With the Express not arriving in Tall Water Falls and everything that has happened this morning, compounded with the nature of this note, I knew something was wrong."

"What are you saying?" the governor said.

"I believe Ernest C. is under watch or something of that nature," Jenny said.

"So there is no telling where the note really came from?" I said.

"There is not," Jenny said.

"Have you had any other communication with Tall Water Falls?" Virgil asked.

Jenny shook her head and said, "No. The last contact we had was prior to this note, and that was last night, right before I closed."

"Which was what?" Virgil asked.

"I received word the Express out of Paris did not arrive at the scheduled time in Tall Water Falls," Jenny said.

"You tell anybody about this?" Virgil said. "Last night?"

"Pardon?"

"When you got that news about the Express, you tell anybody else?"

"I left and alerted Sam right away," Jenny said.

"Nobody else?" Virgil said.

"No," Jenny said. "Well . . . except when I was closing the office there was a man who came just as I was leaving, asking about the next express to Fort Smith."

Virgil looked at me, then back to Jenny.

"Tall man," Virgil said. "Silver hair?"

Jenny looked back and forth between Virgil and me and said, "Why, yes. He was a tall man, silver hair."

68

Virgil looked to the governor, who was looking at Hobbs.

"Goddamn Lassiter," the governor said.

"What did you tell him?" Virgil said.

"I told him I was not certain when the next northbound would come through."

"You tell him why?" Virgil said.

"You mean did I explain to him why I was uncertain?"

"Yes."

Jenny thought for a moment.

"Well, I believe I said because there was trouble with tonight's Express not arriving in Tall Water Falls. I told him he would have to check today for the next scheduled train, but that was it."

"He ask you anything else?" Virgil said.

"No, sir."

"He send a wire himself?" I asked.

"No," Jenny said. "He did not."

"The son of a bitch liar," Hobbs said. "He

told me he wired to alert the authorities."

"Yep," I said. "Told us that, too."

Virgil looked to Sam.

"You said you got a number of messages about what happened on the track?" Virgil said.

Sam crammed her hands into her front pockets. She looked to the clock on the wall for a moment before she looked back to Virgil.

"Yes, sir," Sam said. "We got us a bad situation here, Marshal."

Sam fidgeted a bit, looking at Virgil and the governor.

"Go on," Virgil said.

"Them telegraph lines started buzzin' with everything goin' on," Sam said. "From every direction. Jenny?"

"The Express not arriving in Tall Water Falls," Jenny said, "started the normal, or I should say necessary, transmissions for a situation like this."

"We've never had nothing like this happen, ever," Sam said.

"Section gangs already figured out a lot about what happened last night," Jenny said. "First, the main terminal stations in both — Paris to the south, and Division City to the north — were alerted of the situation so the train and the schedules would be put on hold."

"There was one Southbound Express already en route out of Fort Smith," Sam continued, "but it was delayed until the foul cars are removed. Section gangs were dispatched to survey and report their findin's first thing this mornin'."

"Which were?" I said.

Sam shook her head.

"Well, last night there was some serious bad business I can tell you," Sam said. "Nobody would have ever expected nothin' like what has happened here. Some of it I 'spect you already know about. Some of it I 'spect you don't."

Sam stopped talking and looked to the governor.

"Go ahead," the governor said.

Virgil offered a short nod.

"There was a robbery on the evenin' Express out of Paris, which resulted in folks gettin' killed. All along the track, from the top of the rise here at Half Moon all the way up through the woods of the Kiamichi, there have been a number of men found dead. We found these cars here with the burnt Pullman, and at the top of the rise, north of town here, we found another coach and a body of a man with his throat cut on

the track. Along with the dead, Standley
Station, the next way station up, also found
an abandoned coach on the track. That car
was full of passengers."

69

Sam stopped talking. She looked at Jenny and bit her lip. Then looked to the governor.

"That it?" Virgil said.

Sam shook her head.

"No, sir. Next up. Crystal Creek gang found the engine and first coach stalled out."

Sam swallowed hard.

"Apparently, where the engine was stopped on the track just north of Crystal Creek, riders showed up."

"Riders?" Virgil said.

"The pickup riders," I said.

"No doubt," Virgil said.

"Evidently, they stayed diligent heading north," I said.

"Evidently, they did," Virgil said. "Go on, Sam."

"All this was a wire from Crystal Creek . . . which also said shots were fired and two women were pulled from the coach," Sam said.

The governor looked out the window, then looked to the floor.

"Where's the engine now?" I said.

"The section gang is removing the engine and coach from the main line to a set out on the wye track," Sam said. "Never seen or heard nothin' like this, ever."

The governor remained looking at the floor.

"That it?" Virgil said.

"Yes," Sam said. "Well, other than the scheduled South Express from Fort Smith had to stop in Division City and wait. Once the track is clear it will get on its way down. I figure them stranded passengers will board the Express when it's up and runnin' again."

"Nothing else from Tall Water Falls' section gang?" Virgil asked.

"Nothing," Jenny said. "Just this, this telegram, but nothing else."

Virgil looked to the governor and pointed to the telegram the governor was holding in his hand.

"Need to reply," Virgil said.

The governor looked at the telegram and nodded.

The telegram was for certain cryptic but clear enough to understand.

TO: The Great Governor of Texas — exchange engendered upon payment, 500K. Promptly comply for instructions or swift terminus will be guaranteed. "So wise so young, they say do never live long." — RICHARD III

Jenny pulled up the chair and sat at the desk in front of the key and readied herself. The governor looked to Virgil, thinking for a moment about what to say.

"Um . . . how about, 'Compliance agreed . . . Describe how, when, and where you wish to proceed'?"

Jenny held a steady gaze on the governor before looking to Virgil.

Virgil looked to me.

"Sounds right," I said.

Jenny got a nod from the governor and scribbled the message on a piece of paper.

" 'Compliance agreed,' " Jenny said as she wrote. " 'Describe how, when, and where you wish to proceed.' "

Jenny looked to Virgil and he glanced up to the clock.

"Yes," the governor said as he slowly got to his feet. "Send that."

Jenny quickly pounded out the message on the key. She sat back in her chair and looked up at the clock on the wall. The time was half past seven o'clock. Jenny turned her chair sideways at the desk. She looked to the governor and Virgil before turning her attention back to the sounder sitting on the desk. All of us in the room looked to the sounder and waited.

70

Uncle Ted and the Ironhorse continued working, clearing the track. The big engine towed the burnt Pullman into the yard, making the windows of the telegraph office rattle. It was now a quarter past eight o'clock. The sounder sitting on the desk in front of Jenny had remained silent, and we had heard nothing back from Richard III. There had been no activity at all on the line since Jenny sent the wire to Ernest C. in Tall Water Falls. Virgil sat in the corner of the office with his hat down over his eyes, the governor was pacing slowly back and forth in the corridor of the depot where Berkeley and Hobbs sat half asleep on a bench, and I stood looking out the window, watching Sam walking next to the Ironhorse. I turned from the window and sat in a chair next to the desk. Jenny looked up from a book she was reading about Egyptian pyramids and smiled. For a girl who fancied herself as a man, she was attractive. Her skin was the opposite of Sam's weathered complexion; Jenny was honey-colored and smooth. She looked as though she had never spent a day in the sun.

I looked at the connections on the key, relay, and sounder that were sitting on the telegraph desk in front of her.

"Everything been working good here, Jenny?"

"It has," she said. "It's all old as the hills, belonged to my father, but it's J. H. Bunnell and Company equipment and works better than most of the new stuff."

"Batteries are good?"

"They are," Jenny said. "The whole series circuit from Paris to Fort Smith has been very reliable, no problems."

The governor poked his head into the office.

"Marshal, Deputy?" the governor said.

Virgil lifted his hat from his eyes.

"I need to let my wife know what's happening."

"We'll be right here," Virgil said.

The governor gazed at the sounder sitting on the desk.

"I'll walk with you," Hobbs said as he got to his feet.

The governor glanced back to Hobbs and

looked to Virgil.

"Marshal," he said, "if this madman responds, and I pray to God in Heaven he does, I implore you and your deputy might provide the necessary backbone and tactical maneuvers and whatever Lord knows what else might be needed for this exchange to be successful."

Virgil looked at me.

"I will pay you handsomely," the governor said.

"No," Virgil said.

"No?"

"No," Virgil said as he got to his feet.

The governor was at a loss for words.

"Won't be any need for your handsome pay. My deputy and me are territorial marshals. Wards of Congress. Federal government pays us, and providing we are still alive when each payday comes around, we get paid regularly."

"It's what we do," I said.

"It is," Virgil said.

"Then you will do it?"

"Sure."

"Good."

"Of course, we'll need you to supply the necessary wherewithal for the exchange."

The governor took a step toward Virgil.

"In that freight car out there," he said,

pointing out the window to the section of coaches now on the dead-end track behind the water tower, "you'll find two crates addressed to the University of Kansas, Department of Epidemic Research. Each is marked boldly with warnings — caution, handle with care, deadly bacteria, hazardous materials, skull and crossbones stenciled on them — that sort of thing. Inside each, you will find two hundred and fifty thousand dollars in thousand-dollar bills. I want to make sure we give that son of a bitch that money, all of it, and get my daughters back."

With that, the governor turned and walked off down the long depot corridor, and Hobbs followed.

Uncle Ted let out two long whistle blasts from the Ironhorse, and the windows of the telegraph office started vibrating again as the big engine moved away from the burnt-out Pullman and powered back onto the main track. Sam closed the switchgear behind Uncle Ted and walked back toward the depot beside the Ironhorse as it started building steam and heading north. Sam looked up to Uncle Ted and said something. Uncle Ted nodded and gave her a thumbs-up. The Ironhorse thumped loudly as it got closer to the depot. When the big engine passed the telegraph office, Uncle Ted gave a slight wave to Jenny and stomped on by up the track. After the loud rumbling of the Ironhorse passed and the vibration stopped, Jenny sat up like she had a fish on the line, and I heard what she heard, the clicking of the sounder.

71

The governor rushed back to the depot with Hobbs, and Jenny read the telegram:

Sundown tomorrow, tethered under a red-bud tree next to the last switch in the south mountain pass, you will find a mule. Fill the mule's panniers, then set the mule free. Ample time is provided for your swift rouncey to make the pass by tomorrow night.

"Rouncey?" Hobbs said, interrupting Jenny. "What in God's name is he talking about?"

"Rouncey," Berkeley said, "is a horse. He's talking about a horse."

"There's more," Jenny said.

"Go on, Jenny, please," the governor said.

Jenny nodded and continued:

When the freight is received, the operator

will provide instructions where to locate progenies. Traveling north past the switch or trailing the mule (which would provide only levity) will prompt expiration of merchandise.

— RICHARD III

Jenny looked up at us.

"That's it," Jenny said. "No sine on this, either, but this note was pounded by Ernest C. from Tall Water Falls for sure."

"Richard the Third. Levity. Good Lord," Hobbs said. "Expiration of merchandise. A mule? My God. Absolute madness."

"Hell, that's at least sixty miles from here," Berkeley said. "He's giving you what is left of today and all day tomorrow to travel sixty miles up rough country. Be hard pressed to get there by nightfall tomorrow if you left right now."

"That's true," Sam said. "The pass he's talking about is five and a half miles past Crystal Creek. Ten miles this side of Tall Water Falls."

"From what we've seen of this line, most likely not an easy ride, either," I said.

"I'd say not," Sam said.

"Hell, no, that is what I am saying," Berkeley said. "It is not."

"It's rough, rocky," Sam said.

293

"Especially if you follow the tracks all the way up," Berkeley said.

"There is a trail that is straighter, but that's rough, too," Sam said. "Not really traveled much anymore, not since the rail."

"The last section was where Mr. Hobbs and Lassiter picked up the ride from the teamster coming down from the Half Moon mining camps to get here. That is a straight shot," Berkeley said, "but above that, going north, it's just hell, bad road."

"What is the terrain up there?" Virgil asked.

"At the pass?" Sam said.

"Yes," Virgil said.

"Steep up on both sides," Sam said. "Damn near straight up."

"A mule?" Hobbs said. "What in God's name is this man thinking?"

"Smart," I said.

"Is," Virgil said.

"Like a homing pigeon," Berkeley said.

"Yep," Virgil said.

"And in this case, most likely just as hard to follow," Berkeley said. "Not to mention it'll be dark."

"I don't understand," Hobbs said.

"Mules are used like that," I said. "We used mules in the service to carry mail and supplies. It's common. Mule can cover

294

rough terrain, too. Most likely, like Sam is saying here, what we are dealing with is straight up. That's what he means by 'levity.' He thinks it'd be humorous for us to try and follow a sure-footed mule. Unless a horse has been raised in rough country, they can't do it. Best of riders, best of horses, couldn't follow."

"You know any outfits up there with working mules? Mining, farming, timber, cattle?" Virgil said, looking between Berkeley and Sam. "Know anyone up there?"

"Don't," Sam said.

Berkeley shook his head.

"No, can't say I do, either," Berkeley said.

"There were mines up there," Sam said, "but no more."

"Except for the depot towns, it's sparse country up through there," Berkeley said.

"Maybe there is no mule," the governor said. "Or muleteer. Might it not be a ploy with an ambush intended?"

"Could," Virgil said, "but doubtful."

"Why?" the governor said.

"No reason to concoct it," Virgil said.

Jenny raised her hand politely.

"Yes, Jenny," Virgil said.

"Something was different," Jenny said as she looked at the sounder sitting on the desk.

"What's different?" Sam said.

"The attracting and releasing armature on the upper and lower stops was weak."

"Weak?" Virgil said.

"The signal's weak?" Sam asked.

"Um, yes. Odd, though," Jenny said. "The first wire we got from Ernest C. was, as I said, from the Tall Water Falls depot, but this wire signal is weaker than the signal I normally get from Tall Water Falls."

"What are you saying, Jenny?" the governor said.

"I think Ernest C. is someplace else, at another location now."

72

"Sam, this last switch, in the south mountain pass this telegram's referring to," Virgil asked. "Where is this, exactly?"

"Let me show you," Sam said.

Sam moved to a large map on the wall next to the desk. The map was detailed and colorful but faded. It showed the river and townships along the winding St. Louis & San Fran route, from Paris to Fort Smith.

Sam pointed.

"Here we are here," she said, "at Half Moon, and this is where the pass is here, and the last switch the wire is referring to is here."

"How many telegraph terminals are there in Tall Water Falls?" I asked.

"One at the depot and another in town, at the Western Union office," Jenny said.

"Do you correspond with the Western Union?" I asked.

"Every now and then," Jenny said. "But

mainly our correspondence is with the depot."

"Does it seem like this wire might have been transmitted from that Western Union office?" I asked.

"I'm not completely sure," Jenny said. "But I don't think so. I think it is from someplace, a weaker location."

"Are there remote terminals on the line for service and repair?" Virgil asked.

"There are, but I don't actually know where," Jenny said and looked to Sam. "Do you?"

Sam shook her head with the corners of her mouth turned down.

"No," Sam said. "Hard enough for me to keep up with all the train cars I have to push and pull around here. You'd have to ask one of the telegraph superintendents, or linemen."

"Regardless," Hobbs said, "it's imperative these demands are taken seriously, is it not?"

I looked to Virgil, who was looking at the map.

"This Richard the Third, not wanting us past the switch, is operating from Tall Water Falls, or somewhere near Tall Water Falls," I said.

"That sounds right," Virgil said.

Virgil moved closer to the map, looking it over.

"What is all this in here?" Virgil said.

Virgil pointed to a spot on the map above the pass where a bunch of *X* marks appeared across what looked to be a mountain ridge.

"That's the Division City mines," Sam said. "Or what is left of them."

"The mines recently shut down," Berkeley said. "The companies moved and are operating the fields down this way now, toward Half Moon."

"What kind of telegraph activity is there in Division City?" Virgil asked.

"Gosh, quite a lot," Jenny said. "Well, there are a number of telegraph offices there. Division City is a big place with a good number of businesses and factories there."

"What about these mines?" Virgil asked. "Are there telegraph offices in the mines?"

"There were," Jenny said. "There used to be a lot of activity from the mines, but like Mr. Berkeley was saying, they shut down."

Virgil stood looking at the map with his arms crossed over the buttons of his vest.

"Marshal," the governor asked. "What are you thinking?"

Virgil moved a little closer to the map and

made a circle with his finger in an area around where the pass switch was located.

"They're operating from somewhere in this area," Virgil said.

"Which means this crazy man could be anywhere near there?" Hobbs said.

Virgil pointed to the X's marking the mines.

"You say these mines near Tall Water Falls," Virgil said, "are called the Division City mines?"

"They are. Even though those mines appear closer to Tall Water Falls here on the map," Berkeley said. "There is a mountain ridge there, and those mines are accessed from Division City way."

"Unless you're a mule," I said.

73

Virgil turned from the map and looked at me. He nodded slowly and turned his attention back to the map. He looked closely at the X's marking the mines.

"Mr. Hobbs?" Virgil said.

"Marshal," Hobbs said.

"You said you and Lassiter had contacts, relationships, up here in the territories, right?"

Virgil turned from the map and faced Hobbs.

"Yes," Hobbs said. "That is correct."

"What kind of counsel?"

"We were agents," Hobbs said.

"What kind of agents?"

"Cattle operations, mostly, leasing."

"Leasing?"

"Yes, when the eastern beef prices and demand soared, the cattle drives north out of Texas required sustenance leasing for Chisholm, Goodnight-Loving, the Great

Western Trail, and the like."

"Those trails run through the western part of the territories," I said. "Cheyenne, Arapaho reservations."

"That's right," Hobbs said, "and the Cherokee outlet to the north."

"What about mining?" Virgil said. "Were you agents to mining operations, too?"

"I didn't, no."

"Lassiter?"

"Lassiter I believe did handle leasing for mining, yes."

"You believe?"

Hobbs looked at the governor.

"Yes," Hobbs said.

"Do you know where?" Virgil said.

"That I don't know," Hobbs said. "Could be the part you're looking at there on the map for all I know. I believe the mining is in the eastern part of the territories."

Hobbs looked to Berkeley.

"I don't know all that happens border to border, but I'm pretty sure that is right," Berkeley said.

"You know of any particular outfit Lassiter was counsel, agent with?" Virgil said.

"No," Hobbs said. "I suppose there could be some way to find out. There must be records of such dealings, something that could show us the history."

Virgil shook his head and looked back to the map.

"No time for that," I said.

"I take it, Marshal," the governor said, "you think it probable they, whomever we are dealing with, are operating from one of these mining locations?"

"Everett?" Virgil said.

"Given the circumstances," I said, "I'd say more than probable."

74

Virgil moved to the window, and looked north up the track.

"Where would we find one of these telegraph lineman or superintendents?" Virgil said.

"The superintendents are never," Sam said, "or hardly ever, through here. They operate out of the north and south terminals."

"The lineman are stationed on each end, too," Jenny said.

"There are two of 'em," Sam said. "LeFlore brothers. They pretty much live on the line, all up and down it."

"LeFlore? They Choctaw?" I asked.

"They are," Jenny said. "I, I grew up with them."

"They wouldn't happen to be here now, would they?" Virgil asked. "In Half Moon Junction?"

"Nope," Sam said, looking at Jenny. "We

don't know where they are."

"Jimmy John works out of Division City and his brother Buck's out of Paris, but like Sam said they live on the line," Jenny said.

"Know 'em, Berkeley?" Virgil said. "These LeFlores?"

"Can't say I do, no."

Virgil looked back to the map.

"Do you know if there is still a telegraph line through to the mines?" Virgil asked.

"Got no idea," Sam said.

"I can try and contact Jimmy John," Jenny said. "See if he responds."

"No, please," the governor said. "Those kind of notions are too risky."

"Sure," Jenny said. "I understand, sir."

Virgil stood looking at the map for a moment before he looked to Jenny.

"Jenny, Sam said you know Choctaw," Virgil said. "That right?"

"She sure does," Sam said. "Like I tol' ya."

Virgil motioned to the key sitting in front of Jenny.

"You wire in Choctaw?" Virgil said.

"I can."

"Do the other operators?"

Jenny shook her head.

"No, not anymore. Other operators can code out Choctaw, and on occasion they do, but they are just relaying letters in the notes; they don't actually know the language. I do. My daddy was half Choctaw. He taught the language to me. I grew up with it."

"The linemen use it at all? The LeFlores, do they communicate with it? Do you communicate with it?"

"When they have something to say between them they don't want anyone else to know, they do," Sam said, looking at Jenny.

"Like I said, none of the other operators know Choctaw; the superintendents don't know it. Just me and Buck and Jimmy John. Every so often Choctaws wishing to communicate by wire use it, but that's all."

"For the most part, Choctaws don't mess with the wire," Sam said. "Choctaw are a superstitious lot. Leave voice on the wire to nowhere bad, they say."

Jenny offered a wry turn of her lips. "That's right."

"Regardless, whatever it is you are thinking, Marshal," the governor said, "we don't have time to waste. Please prepare. Let's do this, pay attention to these demands to the letter."

"We will do," Virgil said. "First, tell me something you and your daughters share, like a secret or some such?"

"What?" the governor said. "I don't understand."

"I want to make sure we hear from them,"
Virgil said. "I want to know of their safety
before we do anything. What's their favorite
something or other, song, time of year,
color? Something we can wire for them to
answer."

"Yes, that's a good idea," Hobbs said.

The governor looked out the window,
thinking.

75

Richard III wrote back and straightaway confirmed two important facts. The first being that plum pudding was sure enough the answer to the governor's inquiry, and the second was that the telegraph signal was still most certainly weak. The governor sat in the chair next to the desk. He pinched at the bridge of his nose with his thumb and forefinger.

"I suppose this provides us the necessary conclusion for you to get under way, Marshal?"

"Does," Virgil said.

Virgil turned, looking out the window north up the rail.

"What about that?" Virgil said.

He looked back to me as he pointed up the track.

In the far distance at the top of the incline north of town, we could see the smoke from the Ironhorse as it came over the rise and started down the grade toward the depot.

I knew what Virgil was thinking.

"That Yard Goat got tender enough to travel between the water stations, Sam?" I said.

"Sure," Sam said. "Well, of course, it depends."

"On what?" Virgil asked.

"The load it's pulling," Sam said. "On its own, no problem, though. Won't do too much too long; it's only got a sloped back twenty-five-hundred-gallon tender."

"Meaning?" Virgil said.

"Regular tenders for main engines are thirty-five hundred gallons; some are even bigger," Sam said.

"So more than likely it would?" Virgil said. "Long as it's not too heavy?"

"That's right, long as it's not too heavy."

Virgil looked out the window behind us and pointed to the stock car sitting in the switchyard near the water tower.

"Let's say the Ironhorse pulls that stock car there with some horses," Virgil said.

"Don't see why not," Sam said. "It's got smaller drive wheels, ya know, so you ain't gonna go fast like a regular running engine, but it will sure enough move."

"Faster than a horse, though," Virgil said.

"Covering distance," Sam said. "You bet,

faster than a horse."

Virgil turned back looking north, watching the Ironhorse getting closer.

"Not gonna snug that mule to a redbud tree tomorrow early, Everett," Virgil said.

"No," I said, "they won't."

"They'll do that late afternoon."

"What are you thinking," the governor said, "in regard to the locomotive?"

"We try and contact the lineman, LeFlore, to show us the line's in, figure what is active and what is not active. We go up tonight in the Ironhorse. They won't be expecting us to be getting up there in that short amount of time. We find out where they are hiding out, surprise them."

"No," the governor said. "I want the money delivered, and I want my daughters to be returned to me. I'm sure you can understand my concern, Marshal?"

"Understand your concern completely, but there is no guarantee, money or no money, he will honor this arrangement."

"Agreed," Hobbs said. "This man is mad. A goddamn mule? I tell you, simply mad. And there is absolutely no knowing what he might be capable of."

The governor stared at Virgil with a contemplative expression and started pacing again. His hands were behind his back this time, like an officer's. He made three turns across the floor of the telegraph office before he spoke up.

"What would be your move, your strategy, in this scenario?" the governor said.

"Just what I said, get to the lineman Le-Flore. He will know what lines are active and what lines are not."

76

The governor worked his way back and forth in the office some more. He was looking down at the floor, thinking as he paced.

"What if you don't find them?" the governor said.

"Don't find 'em," Virgil said, "we come back before nightfall and load the mule."

Virgil looked at me.

"Worth a try," I said.

The governor paced a few more times before he stopped and looked to Virgil.

"Okay," he said.

"We don't find them," Virgil said, "we pack the mule, send it on its way."

"Without question you do," the governor said. "I do not want to be reeling from tragedy for monetary concerns. I care not about the money, Marshal, make no mistake about that, not one iota. If my daughters' lives were not in danger it would of course be a different situation, but frankly it is not a different situation."

"Understood," Virgil said. "Jenny, these LeFlore brothers, they got no beef, no odds with each other? They get along with each other all right?"

Jenny nodded.

"I've known them my whole life; they're close. Jimmy John is a bit of a renegade, but they both are hard workers and do their job."

"Good," Virgil said. "I want to craft a note. Contact Buck LeFlore to the south. You said he was in the Paris office, right?"

"He works out of the Paris office. He's there sometimes. I can try to reach him."

"Good," Virgil said. "Try to wire Buck in the Paris office. Have him contact his brother north in Division City. We will let the communication be between them, all in Choctaw. That way there is no connection to this office and the LeFlore north, in Division City."

"Splendid idea," Hobbs said.

"Okay," Jenny said.

"Good," Virgil said.

The governor nodded, looking at Virgil with some resolve.

"Sam?" Virgil said.

He pointed to the mines on the map.

"Can the Ironhorse get us up to here by

morning?"

"Before then, if we get you going."

"Good," Virgil said. "Gives us time to locate them. If we don't get to LeFlore for some reason, we'll look on our own. We don't find them by mid-afternoon, we come back to the switch location and load the mule. Everett?"

"Sounds right," I said. "That Ironhorse in good working order, Sam?"

"It is," Sam said.

"What do we need to do to get going?" Virgil said. Sam pointed up the track.

"Soon as Uncle Ted gets back from removing the last foul car," Sam said, "just need to load the tender and get the stock car hooked up."

"That it?" Virgil said.

"Is," Sam said. "But we don't have a regular fireman. Charlie and me help out Uncle Ted here in the yard. You'll just need somebody to shovel coal on the trip is all. I suppose, push comes to shove, I can do the shovelin' for you."

As Uncle Ted and the Ironhorse got close to the Half Moon Junction depot, the engine blasted one long whistle. Smoke was billowing from its stack as it thumped back down the track pulling the coach Virgil and I had abandoned on the rise north of town.

The coach was the last foul car to be removed from the track. The next abandoned car north, with Whip, the undertaker, the grieving widow, the Apache woman, and the others, had been removed by the Standley Station section gang. The engine and first coach was in the process of being towed off by the Crystal Creek section gang, leaving the track open for travel.

The windows of the telegraph office rattled again as Uncle Ted, with his hairy arm hanging out the window of the Iron-horse, throttled the engine off the main track and rumbled to a stop in the switch-yard behind the water tower.

"God help us," the governor said.

77

A half-hour passed and there had been no response from Buck LeFlore. Jenny did receive a wire notifying us the Southbound Express was up and running again and on the move down the track en route to Paris. Sam told us she would have a better idea of where we would pass the Southbound Express once we were ready to leave, but she thought we would most likely have to use a pass track midway between Half Moon Junction and Standley Station somewhere around five and six o'clock.

In short order, Uncle Ted and Sam got the Ironhorse tender filled up with coal from the coal tower, Virgil retrieved the money from the crates in the freight car and transferred the loot to the stock coach, and I fetched the four horses from the jail.

It was half past noon when I walked the horses down to where Virgil was now standing with the governor and Hobbs in the switchyard with Sam and little Charlie. They were watching Uncle Ted maneuvering the Ironhorse.

Uncle Ted pulled the whistle cord, and three short loud blasts spooked the horses as the Ironhorse backed toward the stock coach.

I turned the horses away from the engine noise, circling them, getting their feet back solid under them, when I saw Berkeley walking toward me carrying a large carpet bag and wearing denim trousers and a barn coat.

"I'm your shoveler," Berkeley said.

He reached out and took two of the horses' leads.

"Packed us some rations, too."

"Good of you," I said.

"Least I can do."

"Hard to know how this will play out."

"One way or another, it will."

"It will, indeed," I said.

We crossed a dead-end set of rails just as the automatic coupler of the Ironhorse docked with the coupler on the stock car. Sam stepped up between the tender and the stock coach and connected the glad-hand coupler on the air line as we neared with the horses.

"Got us a fireman," I said.

Everyone turned and looked at Berkeley.

"Don't look so surprised," Berkeley said. "Contrary to what makes perfect sense, I'm no stranger to hard work. Besides, you have a train station to manage, Sam."

"Suit yourself," Sam said.

She moved to the side of the stock car and uncleated the rope from the block-and-tackle system that lowered and raised the ramp.

"I don't think Uncle Ted has bathed in six, maybe seven, years!" Sam said.

We lowered the ramp, and I got the two other horses familiar with getting up into the car and coming out of the car. The stud Cortez and the roan were knowledgeable train travelers and had no problem with the ramp, but the other two needed some encouraging. I loaded each horse a number of times and after a few smooth up and downs, making sure they felt comfortable, I removed their saddles and tack, set up the mangers with hay, and secured them in their stalls for the journey.

Uncle Ted got the Ironhorse and stock car onto the main track and let out three short whistles. He backed the tender under the water tank, where Sam and Charlie awaited. Sam swung out the spigot arm over the tender.

"Go ahead on, Charlie!" Sam said.

"Okay, Sam," Charlie said.

Charlie jerked down on the chain and started filling the tender with water.

78

I entered the side door of the depot and crossed the corridor to the telegraph office where Virgil was standing with the governor and Hobbs next to Jenny's desk. When I entered the office, Virgil looked to me and shook his head slightly.

"No word from LeFlore?" I said.

Jenny looked at me and shook her head.

"Nope," Virgil said.

"Reckon we go at it on our own," I said.

Virgil nodded.

"That's right," he said.

"Just follow the line toward the camps," I said.

"Yep," Virgil said. "See where it leads us."

The governor had his hands behind his back again and a troubled look on his face. He started shaking his head from side to side. I spoke up before he had a chance to say anything.

"Sir, if I may?"

The governor looked at me.

"Deputy."

"Virgil and I have been doing law work together for over twenty years. There's nobody better at law work than the man standing right there. Time and time again we have been in situations that have required every kind of can-do there is and we will do our very best to find your daughters and save them."

The governor looked at Virgil and me for a long silent moment.

"I will, of course, be anxious and waiting. If the circumstances were different and my wife were not with me, I would of course go with you."

"Me, too," Hobbs said.

"Shut up, Chet," the governor said.

The governor didn't even look at Hobbs.

"Just . . ."

The governor stopped talking and looked to Virgil.

"I don't know what else to say or do," he said.

"There is nothing to say," Virgil said. "As far as the doing goes, it's like Everett said. We are gonna do everything we can to get your girls back safe and sound."

"Thank you, Marshal," the governor said.

He sat down in the chair by the desk.

"Thank you . . ."

Outside I saw Sam raise the spigot and say something to Charlie. Charlie hollered back and then ran toward the depot.

Uncle Ted pulled the cable, and two long whistle blasts rang out. Steam built, the brakes were released, and the Ironhorse moved away from the water tower and chugged slowly toward the depot.

Charlie ran ahead of the Ironhorse to the depot, hurried up the steps, and came through the front door breathing hard.

"Excuse me," Charlie said. "Sam told me to tell you it's time to go!"

79

Sam stood on the depot porch next to Charlie as Virgil and I stepped up onto the Ironhorse with Uncle Ted and Berkeley. Berkeley was sweating. He was already dirty with soot from coaling up the Ironhorse to traverse out of the switchyard and onto the main track.

Virgil and I had been introduced to Uncle Ted from afar, but this was my first up-close-and-personal look at him.

"Here we go," Uncle Ted said.

Uncle Ted grinned. He was a big man. His arms and neck were covered with curly grayish red hairs, and he had a thick gray-and-red beard, but when he took off his cap and scratched his head there wasn't one hair, red or gray, on top of his scalp. Even though he had a permanent smile on his face and exuded friendliness, Uncle Ted looked and smelled just as Sam said, as though he had not bathed in six or seven years. If it weren't for the fact we needed to be alert, and to some degree cautious, I would be in the stalls with the horses. But the fact remained: we were on a mission with peculiar and dangerous circumstances, and readiness was important.

Virgil stayed on the Ironhorse step and looked back to Sam.

"What time will we get up there, you figure?" Virgil asked.

Sam looked at her conductor's watch.

"Well, like I tol' Uncle Ted, you have to take the pass between here and Standley Station for the Southbound Express by five. Once they pass, and you stay a steady pace, make all the drops, you should get to Crystal Creek, by, oh, daylight," Sam said. "There is a turnaround wye there on the north side of Crystal Creek. You get to that wye and switch off there. Give you plenty of time to get your horses unloaded and ride up to the pass south of Tall Water Falls."

"The other engine with the car that got stopped and ran dry, past Crystal Creek," Virgil said. "Where did that end up when it was removed from the track?"

"Good question. I don't know for sure; the wire didn't say. I would hope, and I would figure, they got it to the yard and did not leave it sitting on the wye. If the engine

324

and car are left on the wye, Uncle Ted will just have to maneuver them off the track until he gets the Ironhorse around."

"I reckon we will cross that bridge when we get to it."

"That's right, best you can do is do what you have to do," Sam said. "Worst case is you can't get the engine and car off the wye for some reason, and in that case, you'd have to back out of there."

"There are worst cases," Virgil said. "There always are, just got to be prepared."

"Sure, anyways, I tol' Uncle Ted what to do."

"She tells me everything to do," Uncle Ted said. "Stop, go, pass, sit, you name it. Hell, I can't remember the last time I even did something on my own."

"Main damn thing is, you make the pass like I say, Uncle Ted, or you'll blow ol' Ironhorse here and all y'all to smithereens."

"Goddamn, child, I got schedules running in my blood. I was runnin' comin's 'n goin's for Robert E. Lee before you was off the teat!"

"Yeah, and look where you ended up, lost the war and puttering around on a Yard Goat in Half Moon Junction," Sam said. "Just get off the track by five, then, once you get up to the Crystal Creek depot to the wye, you'll be good to go."

"See what I told ya?" Uncle Ted said.

Virgil looked north and nodded as if he could actually see Crystal Creek.

"All right, then," Virgil said. "Let's get going."

"Good luck, Marshal," Sam said.

I thought for sure Virgil would tell Sam the same thing he told the yard hand Whip and many others through the years, about how luck involved skill, but he just tipped his hat to Sam.

"Much obliged, Sam."

I guess for once Virgil was thinking perhaps a little luck might not be such a bad thing.

80

Uncle Ted let off the brake, moved the Johnson bar forward, pulled back on the throttle. The Ironhorse shuddered as it built up combustion in the boiler.

"Here we go, boys," Uncle Ted said. "Here we go."

Billowy white clouds of steam escaped from the drain cocks on the cylinders wafting across the depot steps. Uncle Ted pulled the whistle cord twice, letting out two long blasts, and the big engine started to chug. After a moment we were rumbling slowly away from the depot. I looked in the window of the office and saw the faces of Hobbs, Jenny, and the governor watching as we moved off up the track.

Sam tipped her bowler and put her arm around Charlie's shoulder. Charlie waved enthusiastically.

As we got going faster, Uncle Ted's odor drifted away with the wind, and for the moment all I could smell was the burning of the coal.

Virgil settled in on the off side of the cab. He lit a cigar he got from Berkeley and watched the scenery pass by. I settled on the engineer's side and found myself a place to sit on the front of the tender. I took off my coat, rolled it up, and made myself a seat. I got as comfortable as I could possibly be under the circumstances and even found a place to rest my head.

Uncle Ted was inching up the throttle as Berkeley was feeding the boiler with coal, and we were starting to move pretty fast.

I looked back to Half Moon Junction as we moved up the incline, and it wasn't long before the town was no longer in sight.

We made our way through the dynamited cut where Virgil and I left the coach and around the wide bend as the Ironhorse thundered strongly up through the quartz hills covered with oaks, pinions, and junipers.

Again, like the day before, we traveled the winding rail heading up the Kiamichi. When it got close to five in the afternoon we slowed on a long, flat stretch and stopped just past a red-painted switch target. Berkeley got out, made the switch and Uncle Ted throttled the Ironhorse off the main track and stopped on the pass where a stand of elm shrubs divided the pass lane from the main line. We waited for about thirty minutes before we saw it coming. The Southbound Express came upon us fast, and within a moment it passed with a short blast of its whistle and was gone.

Berkeley again switched the track, and within a few moments we were back on the main rail and heading north. Uncle Ted gave the Ironhorse some throttle, we picked up steam, and in no time we were on our way, running strong.

The late-afternoon sun pushed through faraway copper clouds, prompting rich shades of deep purple, red, and orange. I saw some doves heading south, and I wondered about the day, the month, the time of year, and I wondered when the weather was going to turn and start getting cold.

81

When I woke up it was dark out. The Ironhorse was pulling away from a water drop.
Berkeley returned from across the top of
the slope-back tender and into the cab.
There was a lantern burning in the cab, and
up ahead there was light shining on the trees
passing by from the engine's mantled oil
headlight that brightly illuminated the track
ahead. Uncle Ted increased the throttle, and
the Ironhorse built up speed. The cab
glowed a bright golden yellow color as
Berkeley opened the firebox and shoveled a
scoop of coal into the boiler.

"Where are we?"

Uncle Ted turned and looked at me.

"I'll be damn," Berkeley said. "You're
awake. Marshal said you was the only
person he knew that could fall asleep in a
fistfight."

I looked at Virgil. His chin was on his
chest, and he was asleep.

"Said the blackbird to the crow," I said.

I got up slowly to my feet and stretched.

"This is the stop before Standley Station," Berkeley said as he shoveled another scoop from the tender and into the firebox.

"We got a ways to go," Uncle Ted said, "but we are ahead of schedule."

Berkeley took out a canteen from his carpetbag and handed it to me.

"Gracias," I said.

"Got some hardtack, jerky, cat-heads, cans of beans, peaches, if you're hungry," Berkeley said.

I stretched some of the stiffness from my shoulders and back and drank some water from the canteen. I leaned out the cab and saw a small cabin pass by as the Ironhorse slowly built up speed. There was an aqueduct behind the cabin that trailed off into the woods toward the Kiamichi, but in a moment we were past it and there was nothing but trees.

"We been moving fast," Uncle Ted said.

"We have," Berkeley said.

"The old Ironhorse has got good goddamn giddyup," Uncle Ted said as he patted the throttle lever like a house cat.

"I believe we will be to Crystal Creek way before what Sam figured," Berkeley said.

"Little woman ain't so smart as she thinks

she is," Uncle Ted said affectionately, with a raspy chuckle in his voice.

"Like to hear you say that to her face," Berkeley said.

"Not on your life," Uncle Ted said. "Not on your goddamn life."

"Give this old blackbird a drink, Everett," Virgil said.

The three of us looked at Virgil as he lifted his chin from his chest and yawned real wide.

"You say we're ahead of schedule?" Virgil said.

I handed Virgil the canteen.

"That's what they say," I said.

"We are," Uncle Ted said.

"It's because there has never been a fireman quite as capable as me," Berkeley said.

He posed like a boxer.

"Never been one that smelled as good as you," Uncle Ted said, "or who was a pimp with a fancy whorehouse, I'll give you that."

"I'll have you know, I'm no pimp," Berkeley said. "I'm simply the entertainment supplier for mining executives."

"Pink paint on a pigsty," Uncle Ted said.

Virgil grinned a bit and took a drink from the canteen. He swirled the water around in his mouth, spit it off the side, and got to his feet.

"So how long do you think it will be before we get up to Crystal Creek?" Virgil asked.

"Way I have it figured is we should be there before Sam said for sure," Uncle Ted said. "We have been running good and we didn't have to wait for the Southbound at the pass too long, so I'd say before five in the morning for sure."

"Good," Virgil said.

"That is, providing we don't have no problems along the way."

"And the next drop is Standley Station, you say?"

"It is," Berkeley said.

"And how long will it be before we get to there?" Virgil said. "Standley Station?"

"Two hours, maybe less," Uncle Ted said.

Virgil took a big drink from the canteen and looked out at the trees slowly passing by.

"Figure this is about the place where we looked for Brandice," I said, "or not far from it."

Virgil leaned out and looked back behind us. He turned and looked ahead of us.

"Ted," Virgil said.

"Sir?"

"Let's us stop at Standley Station, get off,

333

move around a bit, check on the horses and such."

"You got it," Uncle Ted said.

82

The Standley Station water tower was like most of the towers on the St. Louis and Frisco line; an aqueduct fed the water from the Kiamichi River. The tower stood about one hundred yards south of the small depot ahead. The depot was situated behind thickets of evergreens, making the building difficult to see clearly, but there were lamps burning, lighting up the depot steps and the train track in front. Two men stepped off the depot porch and looked down the rail in our direction. They started walking toward us as Berkeley finished filling the tender and raised the spigot back to its upright position on the water tank. Uncle Ted eased the Ironhorse forward as the men walked toward us, shielding their eyes from the bright headlamp on the front of the engine. One man was tall and heavyset, and the other was older and hunched over slightly. Uncle Ted poked his head out the window as we closed in on the two men.

"Evenin', gents!" Uncle Ted called out.

He spoke loudly over the noise of the Ironhorse as he continued to ease us on up toward the depot.

The older man spoke up with a shout: "Who are you?"

"Theodore A. Thibodaux is the name!" Uncle Ted hollered, "I'm the hog head of this Yard Goat. We are outta Half Moon Junction."

"Half Moon Junction?" the old man said.

"That's right," Uncle Ted shouted back.

"What are you doing up here?" said the heavyset man.

"We don't have any Goat on the schedule out of Half Moon!" the older man shouted.

The two men turned back the direction we were rolling and walked beside the Ironhorse as it crept north toward the depot.

"We ain't on no schedule!" Uncle Ted said.

"So what are you doing here, then?" the heavyset man asked.

"We're just passin' through," said Uncle Ted.

"Passin' through to where?"

"Got some unfinished business to take care of up ahead," Uncle Ted said.

"What kind of business?" the old man said.

Uncle Ted looked to Virgil.

"These boys are nosier than my ex-wife, God rest her soul," Uncle Ted said.

Virgil stepped to the edge of the tender behind Uncle Ted and showed the men his badge.

"Marshaling business."

"Marshaling business?" the big man said loudly.

"What sort of marshaling business?" the old man said.

"This about last night?" the heavyset man said.

"I'll be asking the questions," Virgil said. "Once we get on up to the depot, you can answer what I might need to know."

The heavyset man said something to the older man, who nodded his head. He spoke back to Virgil as if what Virgil said was a question that needed an answer.

"All right," the heavyset man said.

Uncle Ted grinned, tucked his head back inside the cab, and moved the Ironhorse up to the front of the depot as the two men walked along beside us.

83

The depot at Standley Station was small but sturdy. A rustically constructed building made of stacked stones and debarked post oaks with thick wooden shingles. Behind the depot was a small house, and behind the house was a narrow street with what looked to be about ten structures. There was some lamps burning inside a few of the buildings, but there wasn't anybody moving about. Sitting on a dead-end track was the single coach Virgil and I had disconnected from the night previous and left on the rail five miles south of Standley Station.

Uncle Ted stopped the Ironhorse directly in front of the depot and set the brake.

I followed Virgil as he climbed down the steps of the engine and onto the porch of the depot, where the two men waited.

"Fellows," Virgil said politely. "Who's the railroad man in charge of this depot?"

"I am," the older man said. "I'm Stationmaster Wesley Crowsdale. I'm also the minister here in Standley Station. This is my son, Wesley Junior. He's the section gang foreman and part-time stationmaster."

"This is Deputy Marshal Everett Hitch, and I'm Marshal Virgil Cole," Virgil said.

Virgil made little eye contact with the men as he moved past them and peered into the windows of the depot. Virgil turned back and looked to Berkeley, who was climbing down from the Ironhorse.

"This is Burton Berkeley," Virgil said. "Constable of Half Moon Junction."

I moved past Wesley Senior as he looked to his son. The name Burton Berkeley added a slight narrow-eyed reaction and a frown from the old minister.

"We have heard of you, Mr. Berkeley," said Wesley Senior.

"If what you heard was unfavorable, minister sir," Berkeley said, "I assure you it no more true than our mother's continence."

I smiled to myself as I looked into the window of the depot. I glanced back to Wesley Junior and Wesley Senior, who was unsure as to what Berkeley meant, or even how to react.

"Mr. Berkeley, would you see to our horses?" Virgil said.

"Sure thing," Berkeley said.

I moved to the south edge of the depot, where there was a desk placed in front of a corner window. Sitting on the desk was the key, relay, and sounder.

"What can we do to help you, Deputy, Marshal?" Wesley Junior said.

"Who's the operator here?" I said.

"The both of us," Wesley Senior said.

"Were one of you on the key last night?"

"I was," Wesley Junior said.

"Does the telegraph line have any other connection into the town here?" I asked.

"No," Wesley Junior said, shaking his head, "this is the only terminal we got here in Standley Station."

"Were you here when the Northbound Express came through?" Virgil asked.

"I was," Wesley Junior said. "What was left of it. It was just the hog and one wagon, that was it. Didn't so much as even slow down, just come barreling through. A man was on the ladder just behind the tender and another man was on the back platform of the wagon. Damnedest thing I've ever seen."

"You contact north to Tall Water Falls?" I asked.

"I did," Wesley Junior said, "I got on the key right away and notified Tall Water Falls as to what I saw."

"They contact you back," I asked.

"They did, and then later they wired the hog and wagon did not show up."

"You had any contact with them since?" Virgil asked.

"No. Just from Crystal Creek, that's the next station up before Tall Water Falls. Crystal Creek wired this morning, they found the hog and wagon just north of them. It barreled through there, too, but seems the steamer went dry. The Crystal Creek section gang found the hog and coach this morning."

Virgil lit a cigar and walked to the north end of the porch and pointed to the coach sitting on the team rail next to the depot.

"The folks that was in that car, did they get on the South-bound Express that came through here out of Division City a while back?"

"Matter a fact, they did," Wesley Junior said.

"All of them?" Virgil said.

"Yes, sir."

Virgil looked back inside the window of the depot as he walked to the edge of the building and looked down the street toward the town.

"And where are the dead?" Virgil said.

"You know about that?" Wesley Junior said.

Virgil just looked at Wesley Junior, with his cigar secured in the corner of his mouth.

Wesley Junior looked back and forth between Virgil and me and pointed.

"In that buckboard over there across the tracks by the river," he said. "Good and down wind."

Virgil removed one of the lanterns hanging from the porch pole.

"Let's us go have a look-see."

84

The rapids of the Kiamichi grew louder as we walked across the tracks toward where the buckboard was sitting near the river.

"Me and my section boys had the duty of cleanup this morning," Wesley Junior said.

As we got close to the buckboard, I caught the slight odor of dead.

"We're all ex-Army," Wesley Junior said. "Seen a lot of dead, used to it, but still it was a hell of a thing to have happen, here on the Kiamichi."

Wesley Junior threw back a tarp covering the dead gunmen stacked between the rails of the buckboard.

"I tried to get the conductor of the South-bound Express to load them, take them and the car down to South Division in Paris, but they was too far behind. Paris dispatch said other arrangements would be made," Wesley Junior said. "They best hurry, otherwise I'm gonna need to bury them."

Virgil held up the lantern, and we looked at the bodies. They weren't exactly stacked real neat, and it was kind of hard to tell where one man started and another man ended, but I looked at them all closely.

"Don't see no buckskin," I said.

"Nope, don't," Virgil said.

"Buckskin?"

"One of them was shot up near here," I said. "Not sure if he made it or not."

Wesley Junior looked out into the dark and said, "You think he might be out there?"

"Hard to say."

"Was he mounted?" Wesley Junior said.

"No," I said.

"Why do you ask?" Virgil said.

"A horse was stolen from here. Nothing like that happens here — hell, a horse apple falling out a tree is the normal news around here, not a horse getting stolen," Wesley Junior said. "But still might be your buckskin fellow who done it. Thing is, though, another horse was left in its place. It was rode hard, real nice horse, well, it was a nice horse, but it was left in bad shape, damn near dead I think."

"Lassiter," I said.

Virgil nodded.

"Where did this happen, Wesley?" Virgil asked.

"Horse taken belonged to a logger named Gobble Greene. A mean SOB who lives on the end of town there. Whoever stole his horse is lucky Gobble was not around, 'cause Gobble Greene ain't nobody to mess with."

Virgil held the lantern up and looked at Wesley Junior.

"Take us there," Virgil said.

"Sure thing," Wesley Junior said.

He threw the tarp back over the top of the dead men and started back toward the tracks, and Virgil and I followed.

"Everett," Virgil said, "might be a good idea to get Berkeley."

When we crossed back over the tracks, we walked behind the stock car. The ramp was down, and Berkeley was inside with the horses. I moved to the opening of the car.

"Berkeley," I said.

"Yo," Berkeley said.

He came to the opening with a pitchfork in his hand.

"Come on," I said. "Got a set of circumstances that more than likely concerns you."

"That doesn't sound good."

"Didn't when it was spelled out, either."

Berkeley came down the ramp and we caught up with Virgil and Wesley Junior

walking in the street that entered the town
of Standley Station.

85

The little town was quiet. Even the beer saloon that looked like the type of joint to never close its doors was shut tight and locked up. We continued walking in silence. Virgil puffed on his cigar, leaving a trail of smoke in the damp evening air as we made our way to the end of the street.

"Where we going?" Berkeley said.

"We're going to see a fellow named Gobble Greene who got his horse stolen and had another horse left in its place," Virgil said.

When we got to the end of the street where a crooked shack was built next to a corral, Berkeley stopped walking.

"Goddamn," Berkeley said.

Standing backed into the corner of Gobble Greene's corral was a big black horse with his head hanging low. Berkeley knew right away this was his horse.

"Let me get Gobble out," Wesley Junior

said. "Last thing I'm sure you want is for him to go unloading buckshot."

Wesley Junior knocked on Gobble Greene's door.

"Gobble? It's Wesley Junior."

There was no reply from inside.

"Gobble!"

After a long silence, he answered.

"What?" Gobble said from inside.

"It's Wesley Junior. Got some folks here who need to visit with you!"

The door opened, and Gobble stood barefoot in his undergarments, holding a side-by-side.

"Who, about what?" Gobble said in a deep voice.

For some reason I pictured Gobble Greene would be a crusty old man, but Gobble was young. We could not see his face clearly, but overall Gobble looked like a Roman sculpture of a warrior. He had muscles on top of muscles and a head of curly thick hair.

"These men are lawmen, investigating the train mishap."

"What do you want with me?" Gobble said.

"When did this horse thieving take place?" Virgil asked.

Gobble took a few steps toward us and

into the light of our lantern. His face was as rugged as his shape, with a heavy brow, high cheekbones, and deep-set eyes.

"Midday sometime," Gobble said. "Not sure the time, was not here, got back here near dark, my horse was gone and this horse here was here."

Gobble moved toward the corral.

"This black breed horse," Gobble said.

When we got closer to the corral with the lantern we could see the Thoroughbred was in bad shape. His body was covered in dried salt sweat; his head hung low and his eyes were closed. There was dried blood in the corners of his mouth, and there were cuts on his face and neck. Open blisters behind his withers were still bleeding where the saddle rubbed him raw, and he was holding his left rear hoof off the ground.

"Need to just leave him to be for now," Gobble said. "Through hell he's been, breathing rough, run out, maybe. If he makes it through the night I'll clean him up, see what's left . . . right now he can drink if he feels like it, eat if he feels like it, but he needs to be just left alone."

"The son of a bitch," Berkeley said quietly. "The son of a bitch."

86

We left Berkeley's black breed with Gobble Greene in Standley Station and set off again in the Ironhorse steaming north up the winding rail. Gobble told us his horse was a big dun gelding with a dark mane and tail. And if we happened to find him, he'd like to have him back.

"I'm a bad judge of character," Berkeley said.

Berkeley shoveled a load of coal into the firebox.

"Like I told you, I never saw Lassiter's color," Berkeley said. "You damn sure did, Virgil. You saw it."

"Goes with the territory of being a lawman," Virgil said.

"Well, hell, I'm a lawman, too," Berkeley said. "Don't forget I'm the constable-elect of Half Moon Junction."

"You're a pimp," Virgil said, "who happens to be a constable."

Uncle Ted laughed and slapped his knee.

Berkeley stopped shoveling and looked at Virgil.

"Course," Virgil said, "with all that shoveling, you don't smell like a pimp no more."

Virgil took a final pull on his stubby cigar and flicked it out of the cab. He looked at Berkeley without an inkling of a smile, but Berkeley knew he was being ribbed.

Berkeley looked at me and Virgil and smiled.

"Well, hell," Berkeley said. "Anyway, I did not see it coming, Virgil."

Virgil didn't much care for having friends like most men do. I suppose I was Virgil's friend. Friendship, however, was not something Virgil was much concerned with. Virgil tolerated some men but avoided most. I could tell, however, Virgil genuinely liked Berkeley. He knew how much Berkeley cared for his horse, too. The relationship between a man and his horse Virgil understood well. Virgil knew that what had happened to the black Thoroughbred had deeply offended Berkeley. And it prompted Virgil to provide something he was not accustomed to providing: friendship.

"Double-dealing's one thing," Virgil said. "Stealing money is another. Stealing a man's horse is altogether another. But riding a horse into the ground . . ."

Virgil shook his head.

"That's 'bout as low as a man can go."

Berkeley stood tall, looking at Virgil.

"It is," Berkeley said. "It damn sure is."

Berkeley shoveled a few more scoops of coal, closed the door on the firebox, and we traveled for a while in silence. The air was cooling off some as the Ironhorse continued to climb in elevation. After a while, Berkeley set his carpetbag in the center of the cab and opened it, showing us what was inside.

"Help yourself there, gentlemen."

"Don't mind if I do," Uncle Ted said.

Uncle Ted fished himself out a piece of jerky and a wedge of hardtack.

I got out some jerky from the bag and handed a piece to Virgil, a piece to Berkeley, and got some for myself.

"Got nothing other than water in there for the whistle?" Virgil said.

"A good pimp always provides," Berkeley said.

He pulled out a full bottle of whiskey from the bottom of the bag and handed it to Virgil. Virgil twisted out the cork and took a drink. He handed the bottle to me. I took a drink and handed the bottle to Uncle Ted.

"No, thanks," Uncle Ted said. "I only partake when I know I can get took."

I handed the bottle to Berkeley, and he took a swig.

"So, this mining business?" Berkeley said. "What do you figure, Virgil? Do you think Lassiter and Wellington had a place near here? A meeting place of some sort?"

Virgil nodded slowly.

"Hard to know what to speculate," Virgil said. "What do you allow, Everett?"

"Well, what we do know for certain," I said. "Like Hobbs said, Lassiter has a history with the mines. Lassiter also believes the money is with Wellington."

Virgil nodded.

"And he knows the Northbound Express did not make Tall Water Falls," Virgil said. "Now he is in route, destination or no destination, but I believe as we are hunching on, that there is a destination."

"Lassiter don't know about the ransom demands, though," Berkeley said as he passed the bottle again. "At least I don't think there is any way for him to know."

"That's right," Virgil said. "Be hard for him to know that."

"I'd say there is some place," I said. "Some backup place for a rendezvous."

"Rendezvous!" Uncle Ted said, "I like that. Rendezvous . . . That's French."

87

It was starting to get light out as we pulled into Crystal Creek. The water tower at Crystal Creek was situated like the one at Standley Station, about one hundred yards south of the depot. After Berkeley filled the tender with water, Uncle Ted eased the Ironhorse up to the depot and stopped. There were no lamps burning, and the depot appeared to be empty.

The Crystal Creek depot was built more like the Greek Revival structure of the depot in Half Moon Junction, a long brick building with a mansard roof that extended over a wraparound porch. A lathed balustrade between columns supported the porch ceiling made of pressed metal that was picking up hints of metallic light from the glistening waters of the Kiamichi.

"You want me to pull up to the wye Sam was talking about, Marshal Cole?" Uncle Ted asked.

"I figure so," Virgil said.

Uncle Ted moved the Johnson bar forward and the Ironhorse chugged slowly toward the wye north of town. We traveled a ways and crossed over a trestle north of town, passing over a creek that married with the Kiamichi River running by the depot.

"I'll get the switch," Berkeley said.

He climbed down from the engine hustling his big frame forward toward the switch.

Berkeley threw the switch and Uncle Ted eased the Ironhorse off the main rail and onto the wye section of track that curved off to the west behind a large wall of pine trees separating us from the main line.

"One thing you got going for you," Uncle Ted said.

"That being?" Virgil said.

Uncle Ted pointed to the engine and first coach sitting off in the dark at the far end of the westward swing of the wye.

"There's the down pony over there. We got plenty of room to back up and get back on the track heading forwardly south."

"That's good," Virgil said.

"It is," said Uncle Ted. "Might as well get us going that direction now, don't you think?"

"I do," Virgil said.

Uncle Ted moved the engine along the half-moon curve of the wye and throttled down to a stop short of the west switch. He looked back to Berkeley and pointed to the switch in front of us. Berkeley waved, nodding, and moved ahead of us and made the switch. Uncle Ted urged the engine forward and stopped. He looked back, watching Berkeley. Berkeley threw the switch again, and we backed up with our stock car now pointing to the north. Uncle Ted backed up shy of the main line, stopped the Ironhorse, and set the brake.

"This is it," Uncle Ted said.

"Good," Virgil said. "I reckon we shut this thing down until it's time to return."

"You got it," Uncle Ted said. "Just so you know, if we go completely cold it will take three hours to fire back up, maybe longer."

"How long will it take to get going again if you keep the fire stoked?" Virgil asked.

"Hour, tops."

"You got enough coal to keep us warm?"

"Do if you don't leave me here till winter."

"Then let's keep the fire burning."

"Will do."

Uncle Ted set about putting the Ironhorse into the biding pattern. He turned off the air jammer, shut down the hydrostatic lubricator, the whining dynamo, and finally closed the turret valve, cutting the supply to the injectors. He opened the door on the firebox, shoveled in more scoops of coal, and began moving the coals around, banking the fire.

"I'll keep us warm," Uncle Ted said. "Be as cozy as a concubine's kitty when you return."

The Ironhorse coughed a few final pounding chugs. The boiler shot out puffs of steam, and the big engine went silent. My ears felt like they were full of water from listening to the noisy locomotive. The only remaining noise was the cooling iron popping and the crackling from the fire inside the firebox. Virgil and I stepped out of the cab and climbed down from the Ironhorse.

"Virgil," I said.

Virgil looked at me and followed my look to a dark stand of trees about thirty yards away, next to the river.

Virgil saw what I saw.

"Rider," Virgil said.

"Is."

Virgil slowly pulled back the lever and cocked the Henry rifle.

There was no movement from inside the trees, but there was without doubt someone there, sitting on a horse, watching us.

88

Though there were dense, dark patches of shade along the river where the rider was, sunshine made an appearance on the spikelet tops of the tall bluestem grass that stood between the river and us.

Berkeley walked up from the west switch.

"In the trees, just behind you," I said. "Caballero."

"Not Lassiter," Berkeley said without looking behind him in some obvious move. Berkeley turned slowly. "Surely not Lassiter."

The rider edged his mount out of the trees and started walking slowly toward us.

"Here he comes," I said.

We watched.

He was on a tall muscled bay horse with a bosal-style hackamore. The rider worked the bay around a patch of low boulders and walked toward us. He was a dark man wearing a denim coat and a sombrero that sat low, just above his eyes. He continued coming closer.

He stopped about twenty feet from us.

"Virgil Cole?" the rider said.

Virgil took a short step forward.

"You?"

"LeFlore," he said.

Then he swung his leg over the saddle and slid to the ground with athletic poise.

"Jimmy John LeFlore."

He walked toward us, and his bay followed. Jimmy John was a handsome Choctaw. He had a thin mustache and chin whiskers. He was tall, lean, and tough-looking. He wore his trousers tucked into tall rugged boots, and he carried no gun, at least no gun that could be seen. He stopped about ten feet from us.

"My deputy, Everett Hitch, Constable Burton Berkeley."

Jimmy John looked at me, Berkeley, and back to Virgil.

"You need some help of some kind?" Jimmy John said.

He spoke clearly with an educated quality to his voice and no hint of Choctaw tongue.

"We do," Virgil said.

"What do you need?"

"Need you to help us find some people."

Jimmy John's horse turned and pulled at

some grass.

The saddle was a well-worn, heavy-duty working rig with large saddlebags. A slim scabbarded short bow with arrows hung between the front cinch and fender. A long length of wire was coiled like a rope that draped from the pommel. A pair of pole climbing spikes and a ratchet lever come-a-long hung from behind the cantle. Leather straps tied off all types of telegraph line odds and ends, but they were all secured so as not to make noise.

"Who?"

"Two women, they are being held for ransom."

Jimmy John took a single step closer.

"Who has them for ransom, and why?"

"Jenny in Half Moon Junction said you would be the only one who could help us," I said.

The name Jenny seemed to change Jimmy John's demeanor. He tipped his hat back on his forehead and came a step closer.

"How can I help you?"

"I understand the Division City mines used to have wire service, is that correct?" Virgil said.

"That is correct."

"Is the line still there?"

"It is."

"Is it operational?"

"The line still exists, it's in the loop," Jimmy John said, "but the mines, the businesses are gone."

"So, if the line is still there," Virgil said, "there is a possibility for one of them to wire?"

Jimmy John looked at Berkeley. Then at me. Then at Virgil.

"There is," Jimmy John said. "Why?"

89

Jimmy John was by all means knowing and understanding of white man's culture and craft but remained stoic and reserved as if he were not part of its fabric. His countenance seemed that of the patient eagle.

"We got reason to believe the ransom wire came from the Division City mining camps," Virgil said.

"What makes you think that?" Jimmy John said.

"The father of the women being held hostage received a wire, a ransom demand, back in Half Moon Junction. According to Jenny, the signal was weak," I said. "Weak, but was for sure pounded by the Tall Water Falls operator. Jenny feels the operator is not in Tall Water. Says the telegram came from someplace else altogether."

"Jenny say which Tall Water Falls operator?"

"Ernest," I said. "Ernest C."

Jimmy John looked at me and nodded very slowly.

"The ransom note spelled out the demands, which provided us a radius," Virgil said.

Jimmy John looked off toward the river, thinking before he responded.

"A radius?" Jimmy John said. "From where an exchange would take place?"

"That's right," Virgil said. "Part of the exchange, anyway."

"The money part?" Jimmy John said.

Virgil nodded and pointed up the track.

"The last pass switch in the south mountain pass," Virgil said. "Want the ransom strapped on a pack mule."

"Mule takes it from the pass switch to the mines?"

"That's right," Virgil said.

"Smart," Jimmy John said.

Jimmy John turned back to his horse, opened the saddlebag, and pulled out a wide leather-bound book.

"Tough route up through," Jimmy John said. "Hard to follow a mule."

"Know any *arrieros,*" Virgil said. "Any muleteers operating in these parts?"

"Don't," Jimmy John said. "There were many of them years ago. All the mines had working mules when they were operating, but I've not seen any of them, not for a while."

Jimmy John moved toward us and opened the book he got from his bag. He turned the pages until he found what he was looking for. He got down on one knee with the book opened up for us to see.

"Here are the mining camps," Jimmy John said, pointing to a spot on the page of the book. "Or what used to be the camps. Here is the main telegraph line along the rail, and this here is the south pass switch you are talking about. The line runs through this valley and across the top through here, connecting to the mines here."

"Did all the mines connect to the telegraph line?" I asked.

"They did when they were operational. They had just one operator that traveled between them with the relay, key, and sounder. I took care of the main line only. Each mine had a station, though. When one station was not operating, that station had a cutout that kept the telegraph loop closed."

"Did they just close the cutout when they shut down operations?" Virgil asked.

"That's right."

"Is there any way to determine if one of these telegraph lines is still operable?"

"A man should be able to do that," Jimmy

John said. "Need to test the current, one by one, of each line that drops into the camps to determine who is connected and who is not."

Jimmy John stood, turned back to his bay, and returned the book to the saddlebag.

"You being that man," Virgil said.

Jimmy John looked back to Virgil as he tied the flap on his saddlebag.

"Nobody else," Jimmy John said.

"We got the better part of the day to look for them," Virgil said.

"How long a ride do you figure it is to the pass from here?"

Jimmy John turned back to face Virgil. "The road into the mines runs to Division City, not toward the tracks. Riding along the rail would take three and a half, four hours," he said. "I have a short cut, get us there in two and a half. But it will take time to check each line."

"You can do this?" Virgil asked.

Jimmy John looked at Berkeley, me, and back to Virgil. "I can."

"Could get tricky," Virgil said.

"It could," he said, nodding his sombrero slightly, "or it will?"

"Most likely will."

"Most things do."

"They do," Virgil said.

"Take a bad lot to hold women for money."

"They are."

"How many?"

"Don't know," Virgil said. "A few, maybe a few more." Virgil nodded to the bow and arrows packed on the side of Jimmy John's bay. "You shot anything besides rabbits with that stick 'n string?"

"Man does what a man has to do," Jimmy John said.

"You packing anything with a primer?"

Jimmy John pulled back the flap of his denim coat, revealing a shoulder-high holster with a pearl-handled pistol sticking out.

"Not afraid of using that?"

"I'm not afraid of anything," Jimmy John said.

"So you will do it?"

"Sure," Jimmy John said. "Can't have somebody stealing wire service, it just wouldn't be right."

90

We lowered the ramp from the stock car and one by one got the horses out. We walked them around in slow figure eights across an open patch of grass covering the middle ground of the wye track before walking them to the river so they could drink. We gave them some hay. Then some feed. After they got comfortable and situated we got them saddled. Uncle Ted served us up some coffee he brewed over a patch of coals inside the firebox, and we took off.

Virgil figured we'd make a pass through the town of Crystal Creek on our way out. He wanted to be sure we didn't see any sign of the getaway horses, or Gobble Greene's dun that Lassiter absconded with. Or anything in general that might be out of the ordinary before we set out for the camps.

Virgil, Berkeley, Jimmy John, and I walked the horses through Crystal Creek as the town was waking up. I pulled the extra horse, which had the money packed on its back inside an oilcloth bedroll, tied behind the cantle. Crystal Creek was a sleepy little place, bigger than Standley Station but not by much. We saw only a few folks moving about as we walked down the short street. We passed through a bunch of chickens picking over dried grass. A big Cochin rooster with a bright red comb perched on a short gate watched as we passed by. When we got to the end of the street and it was obvious there was nothing that registered out of place, Virgil turned to Jimmy John.

"Let's get."

Without a word, and without the benefit of the stirrup, Jimmy John swung up on his horse and was on the move.

"That was an unnecessary display of" — Berkeley grunted as he climbed slowly into the saddle — "something, don't you think?"

Virgil grinned a bit.

We mounted up and trailed Jimmy John north out of town toward a tall grass meadow surrounded by a wall of loblolly pines.

At the edge of the meadow Jimmy John entered the forest between two huge pines and we followed. The sun slanted through the trees making what was left of the morning dew on the pine-needle floor shine a little.

We followed a deer trail paralleling the river for close to an hour and crossed the river at a wide beaver ford and started up a steep grade on the other side. When we got to the top of the high ridge, Jimmy John stopped and turned back, looking at us. When we all were close to him, he pointed down. A hazy fog was slowly crawling up through the valley below.

"There is the rail," Jimmy John said.

A quarter-mile away the rail cut through the valley along where the fog was coming in.

"The south pass switch is just down there," Jimmy John said, pointing, "and Tall Water Falls is just around the other side of that mountain over there."

He turned and pointed to the west.

"If it were clear you could see Division City over there. The mines are just ahead, beyond that next rise. It will take us an hour to get over there, and just on the other side is the telegraph line."

"So we'll be coming down on top of them?" I asked. "Behind the mining camps?"

"We will. The mines are all lined up side by side on a straight road about a quarter of a mile apart. The wire is above them on this side. The mining camps and the coal road are on the other side, below. That is how the mines shipped out what they'd harvested, on that road. The coal was loaded onto big wagons and shipped west to Division City." Jimmy John pulled at some pine needles from a branch that lay just in reach. He looked up and back behind us. "It's going to get bad."

Jimmy John moved on, and we followed.

We rode down the rocky north face, and when we got to the bottom we crossed a stream lined with sumac. When we started back up the other side, the fog was starting to get heavier.

I rode just behind Jimmy John as we worked our way through a forest of cypress, elm, and cedar. Jimmy John looked back to me. We rode a ways.

"Little Jenny was my fiancée," Jimmy John said.

Jimmy John offered a slight glance back to me.

"That right?" I said.

"Yes."

Silence.

"Well, she is a lovely young lady," I said. "Smart, too."

Jimmy John nudged the bay around a wide

evergreen.

We rode in silence for a while longer. I looked back to Virgil and Berkeley, who were out of earshot. I could see their horses clearly but their top half was hazy with fog.

"At one time," Jimmy John said. "Been a while now. Years. We had a future in front of us."

Silence. We rode a bit farther.

"Things change," he said.

"They do," I said.

We skirted west around a watery rock bluff covered with wax myrtle and yellow pimpernel, and when we got to the other side, two whitetails, a buck and a doe, scooted out of some thickets to our right. They leaped once, twice, and with the third leap they were out of sight.

We rode for a while longer before Jimmy John stopped and looked back to Virgil and Berkeley. We waited, and as soon as they were close, he spoke.

"Just up here a ways," Jimmy John said, pointing, "is the top of this rise, and just on the other side is the telegraph line. That way" — he pointed to the west — "is the farthest of the mines and the road out to Division City. Each operation has a pole above with a service line dropping down below to the mine offices. The only way to determine if the line is active or not is to check at the top of each pole that drops into each of the separate camps."

"How far down is each camp from where you check the line?" Virgil asked.

"About a quarter of a mile," Jimmy John said, "give or take. When we get to the top of this rise up ahead here, we'll follow the line to the west. Start there and work our way back toward the track, toward the main line."

"How much time is needed to get down to the pass switch from up here where the line runs?" Virgil said.

"Well, like I said, there is no road past the east end mine. It's not a real long ride, but it's rough and it takes longer than the way we rode in. There is a long rock bluff between the lines and the track we have to go around."

I looked to Virgil.

Virgil nodded.

"Hence the mule," I said.

91

The telegraph poles were creosote-soaked oak and stood more than twenty feet tall. Some were crooked and some were fairly straight. Jimmy John moved ahead a ways, and we rode under the line for about twenty minutes, heading west.

Berkeley nudged his horse up near me.

"This line is not that old," Berkeley said.

I looked up overhead through the growing mist as we rode. I could see the line and the insulators at the top of the poles. They did look new, and the telegraph wire that ran between the poles was taut and didn't appear to be much weathered.

"The mines weren't up here that long," Berkeley said. "They just moved south when the rail to Denison came to Half Moon last year. Move more coal faster. Fatter pay. Bigger business south to Texas."

"Texas," I said.

"Yes, great big Texas."

"That it is . . ."

"Taller grass, fatter cattle . . ." Berkeley said.

When we got to the farthest west section of the line, Jimmy John turned his bay around to face Virgil, who was riding in front of Berkeley and me. Virgil stopped Cortez, and we stopped behind Virgil.

"I will start here and work my way back," Jimmy John said, pointing to the pole just behind him.

Virgil had both of his hands draped over the horn of his saddle, looking up at the pole.

"If I find one of the lines is active, what will you do?" Jimmy John said.

"We'll figure us a plan and get right in the middle of it," Virgil said.

Jimmy John just looked at Virgil for a moment and offered a short nod. He swiveled his bay around, moved on down the line, and stopped close to the last pole. Jimmy John turned sideways in his saddle and faced the pole. He untied one of the pole climbing spikes from his saddle and slipped it under the sole of his boot. The bay stood stock-still as Jimmy John wedged his boot, pushing the spikes underneath it into the pole, and fixed the leather straps of the spike tight over the top of his boot. After he got one spike on, he strapped on the other. He pulled a wide braided belt with clasps on each end from his saddlebag. He pulled back his coat and clipped the belt to metal rings that were attached to his trouser belt on each side of his hip. This was most certainly a routine the horse and rider were accustomed to doing. He opened another bag and took out a leather-covered box with a strap.

"What is that box?" Berkeley asked.

"Galvanometer," Jimmy John said as he lifted his sombrero, slid the strap of the box over his head, and replaced his hat.

Berkeley looked at me.

"Measures the flow of the electric charge on the wire," Jimmy John said as he pointed up to the telegraph line. "Tells me who is home and who is not."

Jimmy John placed first one foot followed by his other foot on each side of the pole. He unfastened one side of the belt, passed it around the pole, and refastened it to the metal loop on his trouser belt. Without saying another word, he lifted himself off the saddle and was on the pole.

With the aid of the belt we watched Jimmy John climb swiftly up.

"I don't think that boy is altogether normal," Berkeley said.

When Jimmy John got up to the wire, he leaned back into the braided belt like he was sitting in a comfortable armchair and opened the leather-covered box that was hanging from his neck. From the box he took out two wires with what appeared to be brass clamps on each end. He connected the two wires to the telegraph line, one on the line going in and one on the line coming out, and looked at the box in his hand. He wiggled the wires connected on the line, making sure he had good contact, and looked at the box again. He wiggled the wires again. Then he looked down to us and shook his head.

"Nope," he said. "Nothing on this one."

Jimmy John undid the brass connectors from the wire and climbed down the pole. Within a moment he was sitting back sideways in his saddle aboard his trusty bay, which had not moved one step.

Jimmy John disconnected one side of the belt from his hip and pulled it around, freeing it from the post. He swung one leg over the saddle, straddling the bay, and with his spiked boots hanging free of the stirrups he moved the bay at a quick pace down the line and we followed.

By the time Jimmy John had checked the next line that dropped into the second camp, the fog was so thick we could barely see him at the top of the pole.

He checked three more lines and found nothing, and after he climbed down from the fourth pole, the fog that had turned into a mist, then finally became a steady drizzle.

The wire checking took some time. It was getting on in the afternoon by the time we got to the halfway point and Jimmy John got to the top of the fifth pole. I figured if Jimmy John's judgment of distance to the pass switch was correct and if we were going to deliver the wherewithal to the mule before sundown, we didn't have too much time left. I pulled out my watch and it was half past three. I turned to Virgil, and before I could say anything Jimmy John said, "Hombres?"

We looked up to Jimmy John.

"This hobby horse has a hickory dick," he said.

92

The air was thick, and our sound was contained. The volume of our voices and movement didn't carry too much. Being up on the wooded ridge in the dense wet haze was like being inside a big tent with a low ceiling. The drizzle thinned out the fog some, but our visibility was still limited to not more than about forty feet.

"What are you thinking, Virgil?" Berkeley said.

Virgil turned and spoke to Jimmy John: "You have any idea what the lay of the land is with the mining camp?"

"Been a while since I was in any of these camps, but the layout's pretty much the same."

"Being?" Virgil said.

"The mining takes place across the road."

"At the bottom of this rise here?" I asked.

Jimmy John nodded. "Don't remember this particular camp exactly, but I think the miners had bunk quarters that were along the road."

"This side or the other?" Virgil asked.

"On this side," Jimmy John said. "Mess hut, too."

"Tents?" I asked.

"Yes, wood walls, canvas roof," Jimmy John said, "makeshift as they were, I'd say more than likely they're not there anymore, but don't know."

"What about the offices?" Virgil asked.

"Across the road were the mining offices. Shacks really, and tool sheds. Best I can remember."

"Good and downhill here?" Virgil asked.

"Steep, you mean?" Jimmy John asked.

Virgil nodded.

"Is," Jimmy John said.

"Don't want to ride in there," Virgil said.

"Don't want to leave our horses uphill, either," I said.

"No, we don't," Virgil said.

"That road down there. The way out is that way, west, toward Division City, right?" Virgil asked Jimmy John.

"It is."

"What does the road do in this direction," Virgil said, pointing east.

"It dead-ends," Jimmy John said.

"And this ridge we are on here," Virgil

said, pointing east. "Where these telegraph posts are?"

"If we stayed on this ridge we are on here," Jimmy John said, "following the poles, it gradually drops to the road. There are two more mines before the road. The telegraph line crosses the road there, and there are three small mines on the other side of the road, but the road itself just dead-ends there."

"So if we stayed riding in this easterly direction on the ridge it levels with the road?" I said.

Jimmy John nodded. "It does, about half-mile or so."

"But here" — I pointed north downhill to the camp where we located the telegraph connection — "it's steep."

"It is," Jimmy John said. "Real steep, all the way east right before the road and there it levels off."

Virgil thought for a minute.

"In the event we need to gaff 'n get gaited, the last thing we want to do is have to climb up a steep goddamn hill to get to our horses," Virgil said. "Figure we get the animals close toward the bottom, go that way toward the dead end of the road."

"That'd be closest to the tracks, too," Berkeley said.

"That's right," Virgil said, "that way, if we get into this mining camp situation, find out we need to configure things differently, we will be closest to the mule proposition. 'Course, we stay shy of the road, get the animals sequestered. Work our way up back to the mine, staying to the trees. Everett?"

"Sounds right."

"Gents?" Virgil asked.

Berkeley nodded. Jimmy John nodded.

"All right, then."

We moved off and rode our horses atop the ridge through the drizzling haze, heading east.

93

We rode past the next line dropping into a camp and continued on for about another quarter-mile before Jimmy John stopped and turned his bay slightly around to face us.

"The road is not too far ahead," Jimmy John said. "We could ride for about four more poles, but not any farther."

"Good. When we get there to the fourth pole, we'll drop off the ridge to the right and find us a good place to leave the animals."

Jimmy John nodded and led us on.

My lazy roan was doing pretty well for a flatland horse of poor conditioning. I moved him up a bit and sidled up next to Virgil and Berkeley as we rode on following Jimmy John.

"You given any detailed thought to what you was saying just now?" I said.

"About if we have to configure things differently?" Virgil said.

"Yep, like if this don't pan out like what we are hedging on?" I said.

"Like if the girls are not here?" Virgil said.

"That, or worse."

"Or nobody is here?" he said.

"That and all the other various possibilities," I said.

"Various possibilities that might not provide us fortuitous circumstances?"

"Yes," I said.

"No," Virgil said. "I ain't."

Jimmy John's bay shied, took a step to the side, and the other horses reacted a bit. Jimmy John looked back to us. He turned the bay quick and moved to us, stopping us.

"Horse," he said with a hushed voice as he pointed ahead of us into the fog.

"You sure?" Virgil said quietly.

Jimmy John patted the side of his bay's head and looked around back over his shoulder. "There, that way." Jimmy John pointed again. "I heard it blow, even. It's a ways ahead. Not sure. Could be one, could be many."

Virgil looked around, and just behind us, to our right was a wash sloping south off from the ridge. He pointed to it, turned Cortez toward it, and we followed. The eroded section of the hillside dropped us below the ridge to a flat piece of ground, where Virgil dismounted. Berkeley, Jimmy John, and I did the same, pulled up to a halt and dismounted. Virgil tied off Cortez. We followed suit and tied off our mounts.

"Jimmy John," Virgil said quietly. "Ready that stick 'n string."

Jimmy John nodded and pulled his short bow from the side of his bay.

Virgil took out the Henry rifle from his scabbard and looked to Berkeley and me.

"Avoid gunfire on a have-to basis. 'Course, we find ourselves in a have-to situation," Virgil said. "We do what we have to."

Virgil cocked the Henry.

Jimmy John put one end of the bow to the side of the sole of his boot. He put a strain on the other end of the bow, contracting the hardwood, and strung it tight with its string. He lifted his sombrero, slid the quiver over his head, and positioned it on his back. He replaced his hat, pulled an arrow from the quiver, and nocked it ready to fly.

We moved back up the wash to the ridge and started walking east toward the direction where Jimmy John heard the horse. We stayed just below the crown of the ridge as we moved through the post oaks and pine. The fog made it hard for us to see.

Whoever we were expecting to encounter would most assuredly not see us any better than we could see them.

We moved slowly, quietly, with our weaponry at ready. We walked for forty, fifty yards or so, moving silently between the trees, and we heard something. We stopped, waited, and listened. After a minute or two, we continued forward very slowly. I saw some movement in the fog ahead and stopped. Virgil saw it, too, as did Berkeley and Jimmy John. We crouched low behind two boulders that looked like tombstones and focused our attention into the fog ahead. There was motion again, faint as it was in the dense forest mist, but it was there, we saw something, a shadow moving in the mist. We heard a branch break on the forest floor, followed by another. Whoever it was, they were coming our direction.

Virgil touched Jimmy John's shoulder and pointed for him to get ready.

Jimmy John brought the bow up, pulled back the taut string to his cheek, and looked down the arrow, ready to let it fly.

I thought I could hear a horse breathing, and slowly, looming out of the fog, came a horse walking toward us.

94

The fog made it so we saw only the horse's legs at first. The big animal was taking one troubled step at a time coming our direction. It looked to be stepping awkwardly, as if it were crippled or something.

After a moment it became clear to us what we were seeing. The horse came into full view. There was no rider, just a saddled, riderless horse with troubled breathing and most certainly a crippled hind leg.

"No good son of a bitch," Berkeley whispered quietly. "That's that dun, Virgil, that belong to that big lumberjack in Standley Station."

Jimmy John released the tension he had on the bow.

No doubt this was Gobble Greene's dun, the second horse abused by Lassiter in less than twenty-four hours. We stayed put, squatted down, watching the dun as it slowly walked toward us. Nobody said a word. We just watched, and as he got closer we could tell the horse was done for. His back leg was broke and showing bone. Blood dripped from his nose, too, and his flanks were moving in and out rapidly. The dun stopped and just looked at us.

"Rode him out," Berkeley said. "Rode him until he couldn't go anymore."

"We know about this dun horse," Virgil said to Jimmy John.

"Fellow named Lassiter," I said. "One of the men we are after, rode another horse into the ground before he stole this horse."

"He damn sure did," Berkeley interrupted with a hiss. "My horse."

"Then he stole this horse from Standley Station," Virgil said.

Virgil stood up slowly. Berkeley, Jimmy John, and I stood up, too.

"He rode up the tracks, then cut off up to here, to this road from the pass switch," Berkeley said.

Jimmy John shook his head.

"Hard ride," Jimmy John said. "Rough ride. The back way I brought us up here to the west end of this line is longer but shorter in the long run. Riding up from the tracks to this road is tough going."

"He don't give a shit," Berkeley said. "He pushed this horse, broke it, just like he pushed mine, and now he's on foot. The son of a bitch. That what you think, Virgil?"

"I do," Virgil said. "Everett?"

"That sounds right," I said. "Unless he fell from the dun, was hurt, lamed himself or some such, but I doubt it. Figure he continued walking up the road to the camp."

"What now?" Berkeley said to Virgil.

"Now," Virgil said. "We get right with it."

"What about the dun?" Berkeley said.

We could not risk the sound of gunfire, but the dun had to be put down. A swift cut under the horse's jaw was necessary. Berkeley stepped up. He was not particularly eager to perform the task, but it had to be done. He figured since he was in some way connected to this animal's senseless demise, he would perform the unfortunate deed.

Afterward, nobody said a word as we walked through the thick fog back to our horses.

I thought about Gobble Greene and the muscular dun and how the two were a suited match. Gobble seemed like a loner. I'm sure Gobble's strong dun with the bull neck and Roman nose was a big part of his solitary world. No doubt Gobble would sorely miss his mistreated steed.

We mounted up and rode east on the ridge under the telegraph wire toward where the road dead-ended. Virgil was seemingly now more focused on our objective; at least his countenance and pace indicated more charge.

95

We moved over the crest of the ridge at a steady trot all the way to the last mining camp this side of the road. I was not certain if it was the dun having to be put down, or the passing of valuable time, or a combination of both that was causing Virgil's deliberateness, but whatever it was, he was in no mood for dally or delay. We dismounted, walked our horses for a ways through some tall brush and tied them behind a shed where the telegraph wire crossed over the road.

"What we know for sure is we're dealing with four of them," Virgil said.

Virgil pulled a second Colt from his saddlebag and secured it firmly under his belt.

"Wellington," Virgil said, "Lassiter, and two pickup riders."

"Could be more," I said.

"Could," Virgil said.

Virgil pointed with the Henry rifle in the direction we were getting ready to walk.

"Know soon enough," Virgil said.

"Figure the pickup hands will likely be on watch," I said. "Don't think they'll be expecting anyone, but they'll most likely be on the lookout."

Virgil nodded.

"That's most likely right."

"And we got a muleteer or some such to contend with, but late as it is now, he more than likely would be nearing the pass with the mule, don't you think?"

"That'd be my surmise," Virgil said.

"So you're thinking more than likely there is more than four we are dealing with?" Berkeley said.

"You just figure more," Virgil said, "always figure more."

Virgil nodded to Berkeley and Jimmy John, making sure they understood. They nodded back.

"Also, to reckon with in the unfolding," Virgil said. "We have the women hostages to deal with."

"Providing they are alive," Berkeley said.

"We go at this, every step of the way," Virgil said, "with the contention they most assuredly are alive."

"And Ernest, the telegraph operator, too,"

I said. "We got to take him into account as well."

"Ernest is no him," Jimmy John said.

I looked at Virgil and back to Jimmy John.

"Like a lot of the operators, Ernest C. is woman, about the same age as Jenny — pretty, too, like Jenny."

I had thought when Jimmy John previously asked which operator had pounded the note and I told him Ernest C. he found the news disparaging. I suspected there was a connection between Jimmy John and Ernest C., but I did not inquire and Jimmy John did not elaborate.

"Berkeley? Jimmy John?" Virgil said. "Either one of you need to forgo killing, now's the time to say so. I do not want to get into the fray and have one or both of you get weak-kneed on me."

"Unthinkable to abuse a horse, Virgil, but it's unconscionable to hold someone against their will," Berkeley said. "I'm all for a person being able to do what they want, free to choose, whoring or preaching. Don't want to make choices for nobody, and nobody should make choices for me or anybody else. The way I look at this is, those girls are being held against their will and that is just not right. Hell of a lot harder to lay down that dun horse than it will be to sort out these kidnappers."

"Choices and sorting out is one thing, killing is altogether another," Virgil said.

"You'll get no hiccup from me, Virgil," Berkeley said.

"Jimmy John?" Virgil said.

Jimmy John shook his head firmly.

Virgil looked back and forth between the two, waiting to see if there was a need to reconsider, but the two men both registered firm constitution.

"Jimmy John, that stick 'n string could come in real handy, but I need to know for sure you won't get fearful."

"If you walked away," Jimmy John said, "I would go at this alone."

"Why?" Virgil said.

"Because," Jimmy John said, "just because."

96

Virgil set the plan. We walked through the backside of the last mining camp where we'd tied the horses and made it to the dead-end part of the road.

Virgil pointed down the road to the west with the Henry rifle as he spoke to Jimmy John.

"So, there are two camps ahead of us here, that correct?" Virgil asked. "Before we get to the camp with the hot telegraph?"

"That's right," Jimmy John said. "The connected camp is the third camp?"

"We'll make our way there," Virgil said. "Foggy as it is, there is no need to walk the woods. We'll move on up the road, not in the middle but on the edge of the road, staying tight to the trees. When we get to the first camp we need to take it easy, make sure we don't see nothing, no people, no horses, nothing out of the ordinary, before we move through to the next camp."

"How are we going to address them?" Berkeley said. "Once we get there. We're not going to just walk up and knock on the door, are we?"

"Before we get to the third camp, we'll split up," Virgil said.

"Two of us come in from the west side," I said, "and two of us come in from this side?"

"That's right," Virgil said.

"Two of us go uphill, through the trees, cross over, then drop back to the road," I said.

"Yes, good," Berkeley said. "So there is no situation for them to escape."

"We'll have them covered that way," I said. "Catch them coming and going?"

Virgil nodded. "Two on this side will wait. We plan it so there is plenty of time for the other two to get set on the other side."

"Jimmy John and I are the most fleet," I said. "Figure we should do the cross over and come in from the west, don't you imagine?"

"I do," Virgil said. "Berkeley, you and me will come to the office from this side."

Berkeley nodded slowly.

"We'll move on this way on the road here. Berkeley, you and me will walk up the right side. Everett, you and Jimmy John walk up the left. Go through the other two camps, be on the lookout. Make sure there is nothing that needs our attention. Long as everything is clear, we continue on. When we get close to the third camp, we'll separate."

"Giving Everett and Jimmy John time to get to the other side?" Berkeley said.

"Yep," Virgil said.

"But how will we time this out?" Berkeley said. "We don't want to show up at the office at different times, do we?"

Virgil pulled his pocket watch and tapped it. "Off a get-go time we'll come at them from both sides," he said. "Let's set us a solid minute mark and check 'em after we get on a ways."

Berkeley and I pulled our watches. Jimmy John did not.

Virgil looked to Jimmy John.

Jimmy John shook his head slightly.

"On Indian time, boss," Jimmy John said.

Virgil nodded.

"Just make sure you and Everett stay together," Virgil said.

Jimmy John nodded. Virgil popped open his watch cover.

Berkeley, Virgil, and I set our watches to the minute.

"So once we are set," Berkeley said, "on each side of the office, what will we do on the minute, move in fast, move slow, what?"

"What we don't want to do is cause a ruckus outside, so we don't rush," Virgil said. "What we want to do is straighten their ass out without commotion, a second at a time."

"Fog can work for us," I said.

"Can," Virgil said, nodding.

"See them first," I said. "We will be looking."

"That's right," Virgil said, "and they won't."

Virgil showed the knife on his belt and pointed to the knife on Berkeley's belt and Jimmy John's.

"Under most circumstances, give a man the benefit of defense, an option," Virgil said, "but these disregards called it. That is the temper of this situation, that simple. We move in on them. Hopefully come from behind if we can, get 'em like a coyote, before they know something life-ending has happened. Without negotiation, offer, or noise, that is what we will do."

"What if we can't?" Berkeley said. "What if the situation is they spot us?"

"We shoot 'em, move fast inside the office," Virgil said. "Shoot whoever we have to inside, save the women, that sort of thing."

97

The two camps we walked through were vacant. We did not see anyone, or any sign of horses, no horse droppings, nothing, the camps were empty. Seeing the two camps gave us an idea of what we would be dealing with when we got to the third camp. They were laid out pretty much the same. The bunk quarters and mess quarters and privies, or what remained of them, were on our left, the south side of the road. They were like Jimmy John had said, wood-sided and canvas-roofed, but the roofs were gone and the wooden sides were dilapidated. On our right, across the road from the bunk and mess quarters sat the mining headquarters. The headquarters in both camps we passed through were constructed the same: complete wood construction and no canvas. The buildings were long narrow structures that paralleled the road with doors on both ends. We walked through them both. They were built just the same; half of the structure was a tool shed with a bunk and the other half had an abandoned desk, some chairs, and tables. We left the second camp and continued walking west. Berkeley and Virgil moved up the right side of the road and Jimmy John and I moved up the left, staying close to the trees. We walked for a ways and before we got anywhere close to the third camp we were closing in on, Virgil spoke up, very quietly.

"Far enough," he whispered.

Jimmy John and I stopped. Virgil and Berkeley crossed the road to where Jimmy John and I had stopped.

Virgil pulled his watch. "Let's see what we got."

I opened my watch and so did Berkeley, and we held them next to Virgil's watch. We all leaned in looking at them, comparing the time, and sure enough, they were all still showing the exact same minute after the hour.

"On the money," Berkeley said.

"Good," Virgil said. "We move in at exactly half past the hour. Everett, that gives you and Jimmy John a full forty minutes to go up and around to the other side and get back to the road."

I looked at Jimmy John, and he nodded.

"You ready to get this going, Everett?" Virgil said.

"I was going before I was gone," I said.

Virgil nodded. "Let's get on, then," he said. "Be seeing you boys subsequently."

Jimmy John and I split with Virgil and Berkeley. We left them on the road and made our way up into the woods. We walked uphill for about one hundred yards or so and started working our way back to the west. We navigated through the foggy forest until we got to the overhead telegraph drop that we knew went to the third camp. We continued west a ways and started making our way back downhill. We stopped before we got to the road and waited for a moment. After we made sure there was no one near, we edged out of the trees and onto the road. I looked at my watch. We had exactly sixteen minutes before we were to close in on the mining office but we needed to get ourselves closer, within immediate striking distance. We started moving back east toward the office. We stayed to the trees and moved very slowly, very quietly, taking one careful step at a time. It took us a while and before we had the structure in sight, we heard voices.

We kept inching slowly and within a moment we saw the building and someone sitting outside of it on a bench that faced the road. I pulled my watch from my pocket, opened the face, and looked at the time. I held up five fingers to Jimmy John, and he nodded. We could not see the man on the bench too clearly until he moved some, adjusting his body, and we could see him very well. It was one of the hands, no doubt. It was clear he wore Mexican spurs with oversized rowels. He was talking to someone as he cleaned mud off his boot with a stick, but we could not see whom he was talking with or hear clearly what was being said. The hand laughed, said something, making whoever he was talking with also laugh. The hand stood up and started walking across the road toward the bunk quarters. His spurs were noisy as he moved off at a leisurely pace. We lost sight of him in the trees and after a moment we heard a door shut.

"He's in the shitter," I said quietly as I pulled out my watch again and opened it.

"Almost time?" Jimmy John asked in a whisper.

I nodded and held up two fingers. "Two minutes," I said.

Jimmy John nodded.

"I'll go this way to the office and deal with whoever we can't see and you deal with the

401

hand in the shitter."

Jimmy John nodded.

I pulled my knife from its sheath.

"Think you can deal with the hand on the pot?"

Jimmy John pulled his knife.

"Yes," Jimmy John said.

"Okay then," I said.

I held the pocket watch up for both of us to see clearly. We watched the minute hand as it moved around the face of my timepiece. When it hit the get-go time, Jimmy John and I looked at each other and moved off swiftly, silently into the fog.

98

I thought about Emma and Abigail and what they had been through as I moved slowly toward the building. It seemed like a very long time since I had last laid eyes on them. I thought about Emma looking into my eyes, and me looking into her eyes. I thought about holding her hand and her holding mine. My heart pumped harder as I got closer to the building, wondering if she had been hurt, or raped, or if she was even alive. Sure, like Virgil said, we go at this every step of the way with the contention they most assuredly are alive. But what if they were not, what then? When I saw her on the train I felt like I had known her from before. Even though I never met her or seen her previous, I felt as though we had a history together, maybe from another life. Or maybe in this life, the mysterious powers of the universe had us a predestined union designed beyond our imagination or understanding.

Jimmy John slipped off into the trees toward the privy on my right, and I continued on, moving slowly up to the building.

As far as I could tell, I made it to the structure without being seen. I placed my back to the west-end wall next to the door and crouched down low. I edged my eye around the corner, and just as I did, I saw blood. Berkeley was right, he had no problem killing. Just like he slit the throat of the big dun horse, he just slit the throat of one of the getaway riders. Berkeley had his huge hand around the man's mouth, and his knife had opened a straight line across the man's throat, and his blood was gushing. I stepped around the corner and saw Virgil. He was just behind Berkeley. He pointed me to the door on my end of the building and pointed to himself and Berkeley and to the other door. Virgil held up his hand and showed five fingers, twice. A ten-second count.

I nodded and started counting. I sheathed my knife, pulled my Colt, and moved back around next to the west-end door.

One thousand one . . . one thousand two . . . one thousand three — I pulled my second Colt — one thousand four . . . one thousand five — I stepped back to kick the door — one thousand six, one thousand seven, one thousand eight, one thousand nine.

This was it. This was the moment.

I kicked the door hard just as two shots rang out from inside. The door busted from its hinges, crashing flat into the room and landing at the feet of a tall man.

"Don't shoot!" he cried out, and instantly raised his arms above his head.

With his one good arm, and his wood arm high above his head, I knew right away this fellow was the masquerading conductor, John Bishop Wellington, and the man who had escaped from prison with Bloody Bob. Wellington was healed with a backward side rig. The butt of a Smith & Wesson was sticking out facing me, but his arms were up and I had both my Colts pointing at him.

"Don't shoot!" Wellington pleaded again as he backed away from me. "Please!"

Behind him, the door separating the office from the bunkroom was open. I saw Virgil with his Colt standing in the smokefilled office. To my left there was a low bunk, but no women.

"Take that S 'n W out, slow," I said, "and pitch it over to the bunk."

Wellington did what I told him and kept both arms up.

"Don't see the women," I called out. "You?"

"No!" Virgil replied. "Two dead hands. No Lassiter. No women."

"Where are they?" I said to Wellington.

"Please, don't hurt me."

I raised one Colt with an eye-level bead between Wellington's eyes. "Where are they?"

Before Wellington could open his mouth I heard two distinct clicks behind me, and metal pressing into my back.

99

Distinct clicks I'd heard before. Many times before. And a voice: "Release the hammers on those pistols and drop them to the floor, Deputy," the voice said. "You too, Marshal," the voice called out louder, "or one shot of this eight-gauge blows a hole through your deputy's back and the other will be for you. Your call."

I recognized the voice, but I could not place it until he spoke again.

"Like I told you before, I have killed before, and I'm not afraid to do it again. I will give you three seconds!"

It was Captain Lowell Cavanaugh, the dandy from the first coach. The son of a bitch had my eight-gauge. The dandy was in on it.

"No need, Mr. Cavanaugh," I said.

I was looking directly at Virgil standing in the office.

"Now!" Cavanaugh shouted.

"Okay," I said. "Okay."

I released the hammers and dropped my Colts.

"Just take it easy."

"I will tell you how to take it, Deputy," Cavanaugh said. "From here on, I do all the telling!"

I was watching Virgil closely, wondering what he could do.

Virgil did not have a shot. Cavanaugh was small and standing directly behind me.

"There are three of us," Virgil said. "You only got two shots."

"Shut up!" Cavanaugh shouted as he jabbed the barrels of the eight-gauge hard into my back. "You don't have the upper hand here, Marshal!" Cavanaugh continued with a seething snarl. His jabbing got harder, punctuating each of his words as he talked. "If you value this man's life, you will do exactly as I say!"

"So, you're the one behind this?" I said, trying to keep him talking, thinking. "This was all your doing?"

"Shoot him!" Wellington said to Cavanaugh. "Goddamn it, just shoot him!"

"Don't move an inch, Mr. Wellington, not an inch," Cavanaugh said. "This is a perfect symmetry, you see. With the deputy demilitarized, his marshal has no recourse but . . ."

Cavanaugh stopped talking.

"But?" Wellington said. "Goddamn it, but what?"

I felt the barrels of the eight-gauge slip from my back and heard them hit the floor with a thud. Wellington looked down, saw the eight-gauge was no longer on my back, and he went for his pistol on the bunk, but he was too slow and too late. I snatched the back of Wellington's neck and jerked him away from the bunk. Virgil and Berkeley came in quick. Berkeley grabbed Wellington and slammed him into a loop of barbed wire hanging from the south wall and put a forearm stiff to his throat. Lowell Cavanaugh was still standing in the doorway. Both of his arms were at his side. The eight-gauge was in his right hand, but the barrels were planted firmly on the floor. He was staring straight ahead with a blank look on his face, and I saw why. Sticking through the left breast pocket of his dandy suit coat was a razor-sharp arrowhead.

100

Cavanaugh was dead on his feet with the eight-gauge propping him up but his hand released, the gun dropped, and he fell forward flat on his face with the arrow sticking out of his back. Berkeley had Wellington tight against the wall.

"Where are they?" I said.

Berkeley let up on Wellington, but Wellington gasped, trying to get some breath, so Berkeley — in his own way — helped him. Berkeley slapped him hard.

"You heard him!" Berkeley said.

Wellington just sucked air.

Berkeley slapped him again, harder.

"Berkeley," I said.

Berkeley let up on Wellington, but all Wellington could do was bend over coughing, trying to get his breath.

Berkeley lifted him up to face us.

"Where!" Berkeley said. "Where are they, goddamn it!"

Wellington's coughing got worse and his face got redder than it already was as he continued gasping for air.

Jimmy John came hurrying up to the door.

"Got one running," Jimmy John said pointing to the north. "That way!"

"Get on him!" Virgil said.

Virgil moved quick out the door, following Jimmy John on the run.

"Go," Berkeley said to me. "If there is anything to get out of this son of a bitch, I'll get it. Go!"

I picked up my eight-gauge and moved out the door, following after Virgil and Jimmy John.

They were running next to a coal track that traveled from the road toward the mines. Virgil and Jimmy John were ahead of me by about twenty-five yards. As I was on the run, I heard a horse to my left, and I saw movement in the trees. I heard galloping. I stopped next to a small watershed. Riding out of the trees, running directly toward me, came a rider. He was looking back over his shoulder toward Virgil and Jimmy John — they had run past him — and the rider had no idea he was riding directly at me. When he turned in the saddle to look forward, he saw me. It was Lassiter. He was too late to rein the mount away from me as I swung my eight-gauge and hit him square in the face with the heavy barrels. Lassiter flipped backward out of the saddle and hit the ground like a shot buffalo.

"Got him here, Virgil!" I called out, "I got him back here! It's Lassiter!"

Berkeley came running up.

"The mine shaft!" Berkeley shouted out as he came running, pointing. "He said they were stowed in the mine shaft!"

"They alive?" I asked.

"Don't know," Berkeley said, out of breath. "He went limp. I wrapped him in barbed wire." Berkeley looked at Lassiter on his back, spitting up blood and teeth. "Keep going! I got this bastard, and the other! Go!" Berkeley grabbed Lassiter and started dragging him back toward the office like a rag doll.

I moved off as Virgil and Jimmy John came up. "Mine shaft!" I said.

Virgil, Jimmy John, and I ran down the coal rail into the fog. My mind was racing again, thinking about Emma, and I was feeling scared. Hell, all the gun hands we'd faced through the years, I was never scared. Not of anything, ever, but I was now. Guess I didn't care about myself, or anyone else, enough to ever be scared. It never mattered really if I lived or if I died, but for some reason I felt different. I had a sick feeling in my stomach. We followed the rail as it curved around a tall outcropping and turned between low-growing evergreens before we saw the mine. Even though the shaft was within sight, it seemed like it was a mile away. A cluster of crows picked up out of dry hackberry trees surrounding the entrance to the mine as we got close. There were thick oak doors covering the entrance that were chained and locked.

Virgil stepped off to the side, put his Colt close to the lock, and pulled the trigger. The lock jumped but did not open. He shot it a second time, and the lock opened.

I unwrapped the chain looped between the two big doors' iron handles, and we pulled the heavy doors open. The first thing I saw made my heart drop.

101

Emma was looking up at me, shielding her eyes. She was cowering some, covering her sister's eyes from the light coming through the open doors. Though the late afternoon was covered with a hazy wet fog and the light was dim, the daylight was still a harsh contrast to the previous darkness of the mineshaft. When Emma's eyes focused, seeing it was me who was standing in front of her, she started shaking and burst into tears. I moved to her. She rose up and lunged for me, putting her arms around me. I felt her lips on the side of my face, close to my ear. One of her hands was at the back of my belt, pulling my waist to her, and the other held the back of my head. She was not clutching me tight. She was holding me gently. She was trembling, and I could feel her warm breath in my ear.

"It's you. . ." she said. "You are here, you came for us. You came for me. . ."

She stopped talking and kissed my face softly. She kissed me again, and again, and again.

Abigail was still shielding her eyes from the light. Next to her was Ernest C., a pretty woman with wispy, wheat-colored hair. Ernest C. saw Jimmy John behind me, and she looked at him as if she was looking at a ghost.

"Jimmy John?"

"It's me."

Ernest C. charged Jimmy John and was off the ground into his arms in an instant. Jimmy John held her tight. She wrapped her arms and legs around him and buried her face into his neck, sobbing, "Oh! Oh my God! Oh my God! Jimmy! Oh my God! Thank God!"

"It's okay," Jimmy John said. "I'm here. It's okay."

The women were dirty and scratched up. Their dresses were soiled and ripped up. Their hands and faces were smudged with black coal, but they were alive.

Virgil kneeled down, looking at Abigail. He held out his arms toward her as if he were encouraging a baby to take her first step, but she recoiled, moving back a little, shaking her head slowly.

"You're safe now, Abigail."

Abigail looked unsure of Virgil. It was clear she was in shock. She just gazed at Virgil with her big eyes and continued to shake her head slowly back and forth.

"It's all over," Virgil said.

Emma looked to her sister. "Abby, honey, it's Marshal Cole and Deputy Marshal Hitch."

Abigail frowned at Emma as if she did not understand.

"They are here to help us."

Abigail turned her attention back to Virgil.

Virgil nodded. "That's right," he said. "What your sister is saying is right."

Abigail looked at Virgil and nodded very slowly.

"You're gonna be okay now."

She lifted up some, looking at Virgil with a hopeful expression on her face.

"That's good," Virgil said.

She started rising, reaching out toward him. Virgil moved closer and just as she got fully to her feet, her body went limp and she fainted, falling into Virgil's arms.

Virgil gathered her up, holding her. He situated her head resting on his left shoulder and her legs draping over his right arm.

"Let's go," Virgil said.

102

The trip back down to Half Moon Junction was without incident. After loading the horses and tying Lassiter and Wellington inside the stock car, we bid Jimmy John and Ernest C. farewell, climbed aboard the Ironhorse and left Crystal Creek. The farewell was just a tip of the sombrero from Jimmy John. No real good-bye was exchanged as he rode off to Tall Water Falls with Ernest C. sharing the saddle with him. Jimmy John left us sort of like when he arrived, simply and quietly.

Jimmy John wanted none of the outlaw horses we had gathered after the ruckus, so we traveled them down the rail and left them with Gobble Greene. Gobble was sad to hear about his dun horse but was more than grateful for the gift of the other animals. Berkeley's black horse was still completely unstable. The horse had improved a little but remained in bad shape, so Berkeley told Gobble he should keep the black horse, too. If he recovers, Berkeley told Gobble, do with him as you see fit.

The time of travel was considerably less on the return to Half Moon Junction than our trip going up. Because the journey was downhill, Uncle Ted was able to maintain a much swifter speed on the Ironhorse and, when we arrived back to Half Moon Junction it was just getting light.

We got Abigail and Emma to Hotel Ark as the sun came up. Berkeley arranged for Rose to help them out with bathing and clothes. We did not see the reunion between the governor, his wife, and his daughters, but Rose relayed to us that the governor cried. They all cried, Rose said. Rose also shared with us some very fortunate news, that the outlaws had not raped the women.

When we left them earlier at the hotel, I told Emma it'd be a real pleasure to sit with her some before she and her family left for Texas. That notion seemed to make her sad, but she agreed.

After we got the women cared for, we secured the Texas money in the heavy vault at the Half Moon Junction Bank for temporary safekeeping. Following that, we got Lassiter and Wellington out of the stock car and locked them in the jailhouse with Vince and the other outlaw. Hobbs wired for the Texas Rangers to collect the four outlaws and according to the wire back, the Rangers were on their way.

Virgil and I spent the day getting ourselves situated. We got our horses shod, ate some brisket and beans, got a shave and a hot bath, and rested up some while the Chinese cleaned our clothes. Berkeley offered us a room at Hotel Ark, but Virgil preferred the open-air bunks behind the bathhouse that looked out to a hillside meadow.

103

It was late in the afternoon when I woke up. I found my clothes folded at the foot of the bunk I was sleeping on, and Virgil was gone. I looked out to the meadow behind the bathhouse, and trees surrounding it were swaying with the breeze and the air was much cooler now than when I fell asleep. I took my time getting dressed. I cleaned my teeth real good, drank three full ladles of water, then walked down the side hall leading out to the front porch of the bathhouse. When I stepped out the door I found the street was a bustle of activity. Up the street to the west, past the corner, I could see Berkeley talking with his deputy on the porch of the sheriff's office. I crossed the street and started walking toward the office.

"Everett."

I turned. Virgil was coming up the boardwalk from the east.

"Get yourself some good sleep?" Virgil said.

"Did," I said. "Needed it."

Virgil caught up to me, and we continued walking.

"You?"

"For a bit," Virgil said. "Then I went over to the depot and had Jenny send a wire to Appaloosa."

"Allie?"

Virgil nodded.

"Allie."

"What'd ya wire?"

"Let her know we were on our way back," Virgil said, "to be expecting us."

I thought about that for a moment. That was Virgil's way of telling her to keep her breeches on, but the fact of the matter was, her breeches had already been off. According to the telegram Virgil received when we were in Nuevo Laredo, her breeches had been off quite a bit.

"That's a good idea," I said.

Virgil nodded.

"I thought so, too," he said.

"A warning shot."

"Yep," Virgil said.

"Don't want to waltz in there and brush the dirt away from the lock-and-load."

"No," Virgil said. "Don't."

"But that don't change the fact when we get back to Appaloosa you got some house-cleaning to take care of."

"Don't have a house," Virgil said. "Allie burnt that down."

"That ain't the housecleaning I'm talking about."

We stopped at the corner and waited for a buckboard to pass. I looked to the north. Clouds were rolling in and it looked like more rain was headed our way.

"Chauncey Teagarden and me will have our go of it outside."

104

A dark wall of clouds covered the northern sky, and for the moment the town was shrouded in a dusky golden glow as the evening sun dropped below the horizon. Virgil, Berkeley, and I sat on the porch of the jailhouse, drinking whiskey out of tin coffee cups and watching the storm come in. Up high and heading our way was a crooked line of Canada geese moving ahead of the storm. They were working their way south.

"They got a jump on that Northern," Berkeley said.

"Did," Virgil said.

We watched for a while as the geese got closer. Nobody said anything else as we watched. After a bit we could hear their honking getting louder as they neared. The flock was large and they were not traveling very high. We watched a little longer and the honking got noisy as they got closer. After a few moments the formation passed over our head and was gone from our sight.

We sat silently, drinking our whiskey. Then Berkeley spoke up.

"Hell of a deal," he said.

Virgil nodded.

"Was," Virgil said. "Good of you to throw in like you did."

Berkeley nodded some and took a drink.

"So you boys will be heading out in the morning?"

"Will," Virgil said, "after the Southbound Express shuffles off the governor and his family, we will."

Across the street Doc Meyer walked up the boardwalk. He was wearing his shabby dentist coat and his hair was sticking out in every direction. He turned the corner and just before he entered an establishment called Sleepwalkin' Cindy's, he looked up and saw us sitting on the porch. He stepped into the street and was almost run over by a team passing by. The teamster and Doc Meyer exchanged a few harsh words with each other before Doc made his way over to us. He started talking before he was close.

"You have the best pussy in town, I'll give you that! But I've never really valued you for your skills as a constable, Mr. Berkeley, and of course when you are needed, you are not to be found. I was looking for you! You leave this godforsaken hellhole without so much an ounce of authority left to deal with the misbegotten disregards!"

By the time Doc Meyer was close to us he was out of breath and his face was as red as an apple.

"What is it, Doc?" Berkeley said.

Doc Meyer held up a single finger, providing him with some space, before saying his next words, and us listening to his next words. He put a hand on the porch post, took a few good pulls of air, and said, "I was looking for you, and you, too, Mr. Cole, I was looking for you, too!"

"When?" Virgil said.

"Yesterday!"

"I was not here yesterday," Virgil said.

"That I goddamn know!"

"Why were you looking for me?" Virgil said.

Doc Meyer was still laboring to collect air as he talked.

"You got company, Mr. Cole."

"Company?"

"Bad company."

"Who?" Virgil said.

"I don't know."

"What are you getting at," I said.

"I was lucky I was not murdered!"

"Murdered?" Berkeley said.

425

"Goddamn right," Doc Meyer said. "By the animal that came to see me."

"What animal?" Berkeley said. "Who?"

"Goddamn it, I don't know his name!"

"What he come to see you about?" Virgil said.

"Wanted medical supplies."

I looked at Virgil. "What kind of medical supplies?" I asked.

"He'd been shot, twice," Doc Meyer said.

"Where is he?" Virgil said.

"Now? I do not know, I have no idea," Doc Meyer said. "Before, he was in my goddamn office."

"When was this?" Virgil said.

"Yesterday, an hour past dark," Doc Meyer said. "I was about to leave my office and there he was, standing in the door. Scared the hell out of me. An unpleasant reptile of a man. He took the bullets out of himself, he said. With a knife. His wounds were infected, and he wanted me to clean and dress them. Goddamn disgusting."

"He told you he was looking for me?"

"He did. I was just trying to keep the reprobate distracted, keep his heinous thoughts from drifting into the territory of having the passing notion to gut me or what have you. So I filled the unpleasant passage of time with vague niceties. I was rambling about the price of grain, or mung beans or some shit when he asked me if I knew where to find Virgil Cole."

"What did you say?" I said.

"I simply told him I had no earthly idea where you were but that if you were still in town you would not be too hard to find because you stuck out like a sore thumb," Doc Meyer said. "I ascertained he had some particular deep-seated disdain for you Mr. Cole, and that was my feeble attempt to create some kind of kinship with him — however awkward, mind you — some simpatico if you will."

"What did he say?" I asked.

"Nothing," Doc Meyer said. "He just growled."

The Northern was slowly closing in on Half Moon Junction, and darkness was most definitely looming.

105

Bloody Bob was alive and as far as we knew the mean, murderous son of a bitch was still in Half Moon Junction. Berkeley rounded up all of his hands. We left Deputy Larson and two other of Berkeley's men to keep watch on our prisoners and went in search for Bloody Bob. We first went to the Hotel Ark. We went through every room in the whole place including the kitchen, bathrooms, and broom closets before we got the place secure. The only rear door to the establishment was in the kitchen, and it was secured with a heavy oak beam. Berkeley positioned two of his hands, a couple of brothers, Gabriel and Jesse, to guard the hotel. The brothers were big, strapping fellows with surly dispositions.

Virgil told Hobbs to make sure the governor and his family did not step foot out of their rooms.

"Under no circumstances," Virgil said.

"Make sure they do not so much as pee."

It was raining hard by the time Berkeley, Virgil, and I were out looking for Bloody Bob. Virgil figured since we were dealing with a monster who has proved hard to put down, it'd be best for us to stay together as we searched for him.

The three of us wore our slickers as we worked our way slowly around town in the pouring rain, looking for any sign of Bloody Bob. Each bar and whore establishment we searched with a plan. Virgil gave one of us time to get positioned by the back door before two of us came through the front. We did this in all the bars and brothels and found nothing. We walked through the livery stables, looking thoroughly through each loft and stall. We rooted through every tent and shed. We checked the depot and every train car in the yard. High and low we scoured the whole of Half Moon Junction looking for Bloody Bob or anyone who might have seen him, and by ten o'clock we came up empty-handed. After we looked through the Chinese laundry we stopped by the whore church. Virgil pointed me around the back, and him and Berkeley positioned themselves in the front. When I got to the back of the church I found the door open. Inside was dark but there was a single lamp burning, and I could see Betty Jean lying bloody and naked on the floor. I pointed my eight-gauge into the darkness.

"Hold up, Virgil," I shouted. "Look alive!"

"What do you got?" Virgil called out from the front.

"Got one dead for sure," I said. "Take her easy."

"The big one or little one," Virgil said.

"The big one," I said.

"That'd be Betty Jean," Berkeley called out.

I heard Virgil ask Berkeley what was the name of the other whore. Berkeley answered him and Virgil called out.

"Laskowski," Virgil said. "You in there?"

We listened for a moment, but there was no answer.

"Bob?" Virgil said. "You in there?"

106

Virgil waited, but there was no response from the whore Laskowski or Bloody Bob Brandice.

"If you are in there Bob, now's the time see what you're really made of."

Virgil stopped and we listened, but there were no sounds.

"I know living and dying you don't think much about, Bob, both are pretty much the same to you, but on the living side of things I know you'd like to bring me down. Here is your chance. If you are in there, why don't you not act like the no-good coward you are and let me know."

After a moment we heard a woman's voice. "I don't see him," the voice said.

"Laskowski?" Virgil said.

"Yes," she said from somewhere in the dark.

"Where is he?" Virgil called out.

"I don't know," she said. "I think he left."

"Single," Virgil shouted.

"What?" Laskowski asked.

Single was our word for a five-count. I started counting, and I entered the back door on five. The church was small, a one-room situation with a partition creating two sections where the whores took care of business. I moved to see both sides, and there was no Bob. I saw Virgil and Berkeley but no sign of Bloody Bob or Laskowski.

"No Bob," I said.

"Laskowski!" Virgil called out.

"Yes," she said.

We all looked up and saw her. She was naked, straddling a rafter about twelve feet off the floor.

"You okay?" Virgil said.

"No. I'm scared and I ain't no damn monkey," Laskowski said. "Somebody help me, catch me."

She threw one of her legs back over the beam, slipped down, and hung from the beam.

"I got you," I said.

I stood under her. Laskowski dropped, and I caught her in a sitting position like it was a practiced circus act.

"You hurt?" Virgil said.

"He didn't touch me," she said. "But he tried."

"When did this happen?" Virgil asked.

Laskowski grabbed a blanket to put over Betty Jean. She turned back to us with no thought of covering herself.

" 'Bout thirty minutes ago," Laskowski said. "I just finished a customer, and when he left I heard some slappin', things sounded kind of tough. I called out to Betty Jean, then I peeked around the separation here, and the mean bastard reached for me. He had me cornered. I couldn't make it to neither of the doors so I crawdadded my ass away from him and climbed this wall like a blistered barn cat. All the time, he was just a-reachin' an' grabbin' for me. He caught my foot a bit, but I kicked the hell outta him and he let go."

"And then he left?"

"He cut Betty Jean and then he left. It was like he just forgot about me. He cut her, then he walked out the door. I thought maybe he was just actin' like he was gone, so I just stayed up there."

We got Laskowski settled in with the working gals at Sleepwalkin' Cindy's place, rustled up the city undertaker to take care of Betty Jean, and started looking for Bloody Bob again. We looked everywhere. For hours we looked. We checked all the places we previously looked and we found some more places to look, but we found nothing.

107

Lightning flashed as we entered Hotel Ark, and for a brief moment the animals on the walls looked eerily alive.

Berkeley's two hands, Gabriel and Jesse, were leaning on the counter, playing blackjack with the front desk clerk, Burns, when we entered.

"No commotion?" Berkeley said to his men.

"Nothing," Burns said.

Gabriel and Jesse shook their heads.

Berkeley nodded, turned to Virgil, and unbuttoned his slicker.

"Maybe the son of a bitch moved on," Berkeley said.

Berkeley removed his hat and slicker and hung them on an antler coat rack next to the doors.

"Might be," Virgil said.

"Murder and move," I said. "Not unlike him."

"Is," Virgil said. "Gives him a sense of purpose."

"Nobody has reported they've had a horse stolen," Berkeley said.

I leaned my eight-gauge next to the door and took off my slicker.

"He might have had a horse already," I said.

I shook rain from my slicker and hung it up on the antler rack next to Berkeley's.

"Bloody Bob don't really need a horse, though," I said.

"Don't," Virgil said.

"Be more inclined to kill a horse before stealing one," I said.

Virgil nodded. "Kill anything, anybody," he said, kind of sad-like as he took off his slicker.

Virgil shook his head and hung his slicker on the rack. His hand remained on the slicker for a bit of time as he looked at the floor.

"Whiskey?" Berkeley said.

Virgil nodded slowly and looked to Berkeley.

"That sounds right," Virgil said.

"Does," Berkeley said.

I could tell Virgil was downhearted about the death of Betty Jean. What Bob really wanted was to kill Virgil. Killing Betty Jean was just Bob's way of satisfying his blood-thirsty nature. If he couldn't kill Virgil, he'd kill someone else, and Virgil was feeling the unpleasantness of that notion.

Berkeley opened up his bar. It was musky and stuffy when we walked in. Berkeley lit up a lamp and opened a set of Frenchstyle doors that looked onto the street, letting in some fresh air. The rain was coming down steady and a solid waterfall fell from the hotel eaves.

"We've been through this town pretty thorough," Berkeley said.

"Have," I said.

Berkeley went behind the bar. He got some glasses and a bottle of whiskey and set them on the bar in front of Virgil and me and poured.

"I'm good to get back out," Berkeley said, "keep looking; just say the word, Virgil."

Virgil did not say anything. He just looked at the glass of whiskey in front of him and threw it back. Berkeley poured another.

"He could have made it out to one of the mining camps," Berkeley said.

"Hard to say where the son of a bitch is," Virgil said.

Virgil sipped on his second shot. Berkeley poured me a second, and then he poured one for himself.

"You want to go back out?" Berkeley said. "Keep looking?"

"Not at the moment I don't," Virgil said. "Right now I'm gonna drink a bit of whiskey and smoke one of them Romeo and Julieta cigars."

Virgil pointed to a box of cigars behind Berkeley.

"That is," Virgil said, "if you don't mind."

"By all means," Berkeley said.

108

Berkeley rapped his knuckles on the bar like an amenable barkeep and got a cigar from the box and clipped the tip. He handed the cigar to Virgil, dragged a match under the bar, and cupped the flame. When Virgil got the cigar flaming, Berkeley waved away the match fire. Virgil worked on the cigar, securing its ride, before he spoke.

"I've shot Bob four times."

Virgil took a pull of the cigar and blew out a roll of smoke.

"Not all at once," Virgil said. "Four times altogether."

"Tough bastard," Berkeley said.

"Is," I said.

"All high body shots," Virgil said. "Including the one in the neck."

Virgil pulled on the cigar again.

"Would have killed most men," I said.

Virgil nodded and blew a stream of smoke that drifted across the bar and swirled around in the glow of the lamp.

"Next shot will be to the head," Virgil said.

Virgil put his middle finger to his forehead just above his eyebrow.

"One-way ticket," Virgil said.

Virgil picked up his whiskey and moved to the door, looking out at the pouring rain. He leaned against the jamb and smoked.

"We gave this place a good go-through," Berkeley said.

Berkeley stepped out from behind the bar and moved to the door by Virgil.

"Hard to look in every commode and confessional," Berkeley said. "We've burrowed 'n rooted best we could in the dark. We can start looking when it's light. Maybe this rain will lift and we'll find him in the light of day. We can look outside of the town proper, too. There are abandoned dwellings and homesteads, farms, and of course the mining camps. Hell, this is not New York or Frisco or Chicago, or even godforsaken Dallas, he can't be that hard to find."

"That little fellow there," Virgil said. "He ain't hard to find."

Berkeley followed Virgil's point.

"No he's not," Berkeley said. "That's Miner. He just mines his way from kitchen to kitchen."

I looked out, they were talking about that

mangy cur Virgil and I had seen coming and going all over Half Moon Junction. He was walking slowly down the middle of the street in the pouring rain. He stopped and looked over at us. He walked toward us, just shy of the boardwalk and looked up at us as if we might have something to eat.

"I don't have anything to eat, Miner," Berkeley said. "Not at the moment I don't."

Miner stayed looking up at us but soon got bored and pawed casually at what looked to be a cluster of flowers on the ground. He put his nose to the ground, sniffed the cluster a little, and walked off on down the street.

"He doesn't go hungry," Berkeley said, "I'll guarantee you that."

"What's that he was pawing at?" Virgil said. "Those flowers?"

I got the lantern off the bar and stepped out and got a look.

"Is flowers," I said. "Petunias."

"Ah, hell, same flower in our window boxes," Berkeley said. "Planter must have filled up with water and broke off."

Virgil looked at me, I followed him, and we stepped out off the boardwalk, past the eaves, turned and looked back up at the second story of the hotel.

"Good goddamn," Virgil said as he pulled his Colt.

109

Berkeley and I followed Virgil moving quickly out of the bar and into the main room of the hotel.

Virgil spoke quiet to Berkeley's men, Gabriel and Jesse, who were still playing cards with Burns. "You two! Get around the back of this building. Keep your eyes open, you see the buckskin fellow we described to you, kill him, don't let him get close to you and don't you shoot nobody else."

Gabriel and Jesse looked at Berkeley.

"You heard him," Berkeley said quiet-like, "go . . ."

Gabriel and Jesse hurried out the front.

"That window with the broken planter," Virgil said. "Who's in that room?"

"I don't know," Berkeley said, looking at the desk clerk, Burns. "Don't think anybody. Room eight?"

Burns shook his head. "There's nobody in room eight."

"Which door would that be in the hall up there?" Virgil asked Berkeley.

"Turn right at the top of the stairs," Berkeley said. "Eight is the second-to-the-last room on the right."

"What about the girls," Virgil said. "What room are they in?"

Berkeley looked to Burns.

"They are in the same room with their mother and father. Stateroom on the third floor," Burns said. "They did not want to be separated."

"Where are the stairs up to that room?"

"When you get to the second floor, you go all the way past room eight; the stairs to the third floor are there, at the end of the hall on the left."

"Hobbs," Virgil said. "He in the same room he was?"

"No," Burns said. "We haven't got the doors fixed yet after you and your deputy knocked 'em in. He's in the room right across from where he was. Room two."

"Don't think we'll need him," Virgil said, "but get the keys."

Burns turned and got the master ring from a drawer and set them on the counter in front of Virgil. Virgil handed them to me and pulled his second Colt.

"I know I don't need to tell you boys,"

Virgil said looking at Berkeley and me, "but watch yourself."

With that, Virgil cocked the second Colt and we started up the stairs. We moved slowly and quietly. Virgil led the way with his dual Colts, followed by me with the eight-gauge and Berkeley with his .38 Smith & Wesson Lemon Squeezer. We moved one step at a time.

The sconces were burning, but the light was very dim on the stairs and on the second-floor hall. Virgil stopped shy of the hall and lay down on the steps. He removed his hat and peeked out into the hall, looking first to his left, then to his right. He moved back, looked at us, and shook his head. He put on his hat, stood up, and stepped out into the hall. He held his hand up with his palm pointing toward us, for us to hold up and not move. He pointed to his eyes, to himself, and moved slowly down the hall to the right. I moved up to the top step. I could see the hall in the opposite direction Virgil had started walking. The direction I was looking was the short side, with only two rooms across from each other. The room I could see was the room with the broken door where I barged in on Hobbs. I inched out and looked in the other direction, watching Virgil as he walked the long hall.

He was moving slowly with a Colt in each hand. He stopped when he got to room eight. He looked down to the floor and continued walking until he got to the stairs leading to the third-floor room at the end of the hall. Virgil looked up the stairs. He looked back toward me and motioned for us to come. I stepped into the hall and walked slowly, quietly toward Virgil, and Berkeley followed. When we got to room eight, Virgil was by the door and pointing at the floor. There was a path of blood at the bottom of the door that led down the hall and up the stairs. Virgil stepped to one side of the door, motioned for us to get to the other side of the door, and pointed to the door handle with his Colt.

I nodded and turned the handle gently. The handle moved. The door was not locked. I looked at Virgil. He nodded. I turned the handle fully, and the door swung open freely.

110

We did not move. We stayed to each side of the door out of sight of the room and just listened. All I could hear was the sound of the rain outside of the open window in the room. We stood there for a long moment, waiting, but there was nothing. Not yet.

I kept my eye on Virgil, and when he moved, I moved, and in a second we were in the room.

We saw no one in the room.

I looked quick under the bed and there was nothing. The curtains were blowing and outside the rain was pouring, but the room was empty. There was broken glass, dirt, and pansies on the floor from where the window had been broken open and the flower box's soil had been dragged into the room. And there was blood, blood across the window seal, the floor, and on the inside doorknob.

I whispered, "Looks like he got cut by the

window glass."

Berkeley nodded.

Virgil pointed at the blood on the floor leading out the door and into the hall. He pointed up.

"Rattlesnake got to the nest," Virgil said, quietly shaking his head.

I moved first out the door. Berkeley and Virgil followed. When I got to the steps leading to the third floor, we heard laughter coming from behind us. We stopped.

We turned, looking down the long hall. It was empty, but we heard the laughter again.

No doubt it was Bloody Bob's raspy laughter, but it was hard to tell exactly where he was, where his voice was coming from. Then, we saw him. He stepped out of Hobbs' old room with the busted door at the far end of the hall. He was holding Abigail in front of him. He had his big knife to her throat. Abigail was wearing a white nightgown, and we could see it was bloody. I could not tell whether the blood was Abigail's or Bob's, but there was blood. Bob held Abigail off the floor, and her face was directly in front of his. Virgil stood square in the hall facing Bob, Berkeley was behind Virgil, and I stood behind Berkeley. Bob was at least sixty feet away.

"Been looking for you, Virgil," Bob said.

"So I heard," Virgil said.

Lightning flashed, and the window behind Bob let in a purplish-blue color.

"Ya'll were quiet as this twat's tears sneaking up here, I'll give ya that," Bob said. "Didn't hear ya, but I smelt ya."

"Let her go, Bob," Virgil said. "Let her go so you and me can have our jig."

Bob shook his head.

"Nope," Bob said. "I got some bloodlettin' to do first . . ."

"You do," Virgil said.

There was a loud boom, and a plume of smoke kicked away in front of Virgil's Colt. Abigail dropped to the floor.

I'd been in enough gunfights to know where the flight of a bullet ends up, and that shot from Virgil's Colt hit a small piece of Bob's head that was leaning out, looking past Abigail. There was another boom, and more smoke kicked out in front of Virgil's Colt. Bob stumbled back, and Virgil shot him again. Bob crashed through the window behind him, and in a second was gone from our sight. Abigail did not look back. She got up and ran toward Virgil. Virgil laid down his Colts, and in an instant, Abigail was in his arms.

Virgil looked back to me and said, "The others!"

Berkeley followed me, running quickly upstairs to the governor's stateroom. The door was locked. I pounded on it.

"It's Everett Hitch!"

I didn't hear anything.

"Deputy Marshal Hitch!" I said, beating on the door.

I thumbed through keys. Quickly losing patience, I stepped back a ways, and just before I kicked the door, it opened.

It was the governor, and huddled in a corner behind him were his wife and Emma.

111

The Texas rangers arrived in Half Moon Junction to collect the prisoners and to escort the governor and his family back to Texas. There was a bunch of them. They stepped off the Northbound Express and walked in a pack up Half Moon Street, heading for Hotel Ark. Little Charlie — acting as their pathfinder — led the way. Virgil and I were sitting on the corner of Half and Full Moon Street, eating breakfast at KK & Sandra's Café when they turned the corner and walked past us. There were ten of them, and they were all dressed the same.

"A sight," I said.

"Is," Virgil said.

"There's a bunch of 'em."

"Ten big men, wearing ten-gallon hats."

"Following a ten-year-old boy."

"Looks like they are outta the same litter," Virgil said.

"Does."

We watched them walk a ways, and Virgil went back to work on his breakfast of posole and cornbread.

I pulled out my watch and had a look at the time.

"The Southbound Express back to Texas will be coming through here in about an hour and a half."

"You gonna talk to that woman?" Virgil said.

Virgil was focused on his breakfast. He scooped up a big spoonful of posole.

" 'Bout what?"

" 'Bout what she wants to talk about," Virgil said.

He scooped in another spoonful.

"What do you think she wants to talk about?"

"You."

"Me?"

Virgil nodded.

"What do you think she wants to talk about me?"

"Most likely 'bout your problems."

" 'Bout my problems?"

Virgil nodded as he chewed his food.

"That's what they like to talk about," Virgil said.

"They?" I said.

"Women," Virgil said. "That's what they

want to talk about, mostly."

"Mostly?"

"That's what Allie talks about, mostly," Virgil said. "My problems."

Virgil cleaned his plate with a piece of cornbread.

"Way women are," Virgil said.

Virgil ate some more.

"Keeps them from having to talk about their own problems," Virgil said, "and if you ask me, talking about your problems is a hell of a lot easier than talking about their problems, so you just make peace with it. Just listen real good. Let her go on. Don't say nothing."

"You finished?"

"I am," Virgil said.

112

We paid up at KK & Sandra's and walked down to the livery stable to get our horses. When we got them saddled up, we walked them over to the general store. At the store we got ourselves out-fitted for our journey back to Appaloosa. We bought ourselves enough supplies for a week. We got coffee, beans, bacon packed in bran, pemmican, Chollet & Co. desiccated vegetables, jerky, boiled butter, dried fruit, sunflower seeds, and some whiskey.

After we got ourselves rigged out good, we walked our animals over to Hotel Ark, where some of the Rangers were sitting out front on the steps, smoking cigars.

We tied up our animals and started up the steps. A young Ranger held out his hand for us to stop.

"Hotel is off-limits for the moment," the Ranger said.

Hobbs spoke up as he was coming out the

door of the hotel with Berkeley.

"Don't even think about halting those men!" Hobbs said.

"Sorry, Mr. Hobbs," the Ranger said, "governor's orders."

"Goddamn it, son!" Hobbs said. "The governor, his family, and me included would not even be alive if it weren't for these men!"

The Ranger looked back and forth between Virgil and me. His eyes rested on Virgil.

"You Virgil Cole?" the Ranger said.

"I am," Virgil said.

The Ranger just looked at Virgil for an extended moment, kind of an odd moment. He took off his hat and held it in front of him over his belly.

"You are the reason I became a lawman," the Ranger said. "That so."

The young Ranger nodded slowly, kind of nervous-like. He was having a hard time saying what he wanted to say but did manage to get his words out.

"My . . . my father was the foreman on the Sweetwater Ranch in the panhandle who was killed by Bob Brandice, along with my mother. That was eleven years ago. I was twelve years old at the time. You hunted Bob down, near killed him, put him behind bars, and now you done away with him for good."

Off in the distance I heard the whistle of the Southbound Express approaching Half Moon Junction: two long, a short, and a long blast, and I saw her walk out the door followed by her mother, father, and sister. She was wearing a pale yellow dress, obviously a dress she got from Rose, and even though the dress might not have been her taste and style, she looked beautiful. I could no longer hear the conversation between Virgil and the young Ranger as she looked past Virgil, past everyone, and rested her eyes on me. I could not hear anything other than the beat of my heart as she moved down the steps toward me. When she was close she reached out her arm and grabbed my hand. She turned to the Ranger talking with Virgil.

"Darling," Emma said to the young Ranger as she hooked her arm in his, "these are the lawmen I was telling you about. Everett, this is my . . ."

Emma continued to talk, but her words faded away, and now all I could hear was the sound of the locomotive as it got closer to town. I kept looking at her as she was talking, but I wasn't really listening. I guess I didn't want to hear what Emma was saying. I could feel Virgil looking at me as

Emma kept on talking, but I did not meet
his eye.

113

The Southbound Express pulled out of Half
Moon Junction with the outlaws in shackles,
the ten Texas Rangers, Hobbs, the governor,
his wife, the money, Abigail, and Emma just
past noon on Friday.

It was a bright, warm afternoon, and there
was not a cloud in the sky as Virgil, Berkeley,
and I walked back from the depot to Hotel
Ark, where our horses were hitched in front
of the French doors that led to the hotel
bar.

"You boys sure you don't want to stick
around a few days?" Berkeley said. "You
deserve a respite. Why don't you for a while?
You can stay right here, ease up some, least
give yourself a daybreak start."

"Appreciate it," Virgil said, "but we need
to get on back, tend to the garden."

"Something makes me think you're not
much of a gardener, Virgil," Berkeley said.

"Whatever gave you that notion?" Virgil said.

Virgil threw the stirrup over the saddle of Cortez and tightened the cinch.

"I'm a hell of a gardener," Virgil said.

Berkeley smiled.

"Plant something, watch it grow," Virgil said.

With that, Virgil climbed into the saddle.

I moved my roan around in a small circle. Made him back up a bit. I swung up in the saddle and nudged him up next to Virgil.

"Well, goes without saying," Berkeley said, looking at both Virgil and me. "But I'll say it anyway. You're welcome around this camp anytime. So if you find yourself in these whereabouts, don't hesitate to get your asses over here and drink some whiskey with me."

"Will do," Virgil said.

I nodded.

"Of course, I came to this part of the country," Berkeley said, "to get away from the so-called civilized ways spreading west of the Mississippi, but they're closing in now. There is a whole spindrift of bullshit sprawling east to west that'll be cutting me out, so there is no telling how long I'll be here."

Virgil had both of his hands draping over the horn of his saddle, looking at Berkeley, who was now looking off down the street.

"Oh," Berkeley said. "Hold on a minute."

Berkeley went into the hotel bar and after a second came out with the box of Romeo and Julieta cigars. He opened the box and held it up for Virgil.

"By God," Virgil said. "Don't mind if I do."

Virgil took out a cigar, and Berkeley handed him a match. Virgil moved Cortez up by the porch post. He dragged the match on the post and cupped it around the tip of the Romeo and Julieta cigar. Once he got it going good, he flicked the match in the street and circled Cortez about. He looked at me, ready to go.

Berkeley walked out to Virgil and held up the box of cigars. He opened Virgil's saddlebag and placed them inside.

"For the road," Berkeley said.

Berkeley refastened the straps on the bag.

Virgil nodded and backed up Cortez a bit.

"Much obliged, Constable," Virgil said. "Much obliged."

Berkeley nodded and took a step back.

I turned my roan around facing the same direction as Virgil.

Virgil took off. I tipped my hat to Berkeley. Berkeley nodded, offered a smile, and I took off following Virgil.

We rode out of Half Moon Junction, making our way up the long sloping grade north out of town, and when we got to the top of the rise Virgil stopped. He turned Cortez so as to have a look back at Half Moon Junction. When I caught up to Virgil I circled my horse around behind Cortez and stopped alongside Virgil and looked down on to the town. From where we were, the town was almost out of sight. We sat there for a moment as Virgil puffed on his Romeo and Julieta cigar.

"Look at it this way," Virgil said.

"Look at what this way?"

"Least you don't have to talk about it."

"Talk about what?"

"Your problems," Virgil said.

"Problems?" I said. "What problems?"

Virgil just looked at me. I looked at him back. He nodded at me a bit, turned Cortez, and rode on. I looked back to Half Moon Junction and the iron road tapering off in the distance. Then I turned the lazy roan and followed Virgil.

Virgil was ahead a ways, working Cortez through patches of flowering brush when a covey of quail kicked up around him. I watched the birds rise up into the northern breeze. They turned back, catching the current, and glided off south behind me, fan-

461

ning out, and slowly, one by one, they rested
gently back to the earth.

ACKNOWLEDGMENTS

Much obliged to G. P. Putnam's Sons' president, Ivan Held, for getting this night train out of the depot, and to all my rough and ready compadres for stepping aboard in the storm: Reeder Railroad's head honcho, Richard Grigsby (without him we'd surely have run out of steam); telegraph operator Roger Reinke; tracker Jamie "Whatnot" Whitcomb; gunsmith Keith Walters; wrangler Rex Peterson; the Oklahoma Historical Society's Larry O'Dell and Jeff Moore; my ex-oil field pard', Lowell Reed; mountain guide Rob Wood of Rancho Roberto; mechanical chieftain Jim Timplin; and Ed Harris, the extraordinary man who so expertly brought Robert B. Parker's Virgil Cole to life on the silver screen: "Feelings get you killed."

My deepest sympathy to all the beguiled and besieged who stoked this engine as it struggled upgrade into the mountains: Alison Binder, Josh Kesselman, Jayne Amelia Larson, Kathy Toppino, Alice DiGregorio, Chet Burns, Carol Beggy, Ginger Sledge, Lt. Col. Charles Austin, Minda Gowen, Lisa Todd, Mike Watson, my sisters — the Clogging Castanets — Sandra Hakman and Karen Austin, Grant Hubley, Rex Linn, Kevin Meyer, Corby Griesenbeck, them damned kids Gabriel and Vanessa, Julie Rose (the brightest light on the track), and to Michael Marantz, who is up there somewhere chewing the fat with a rustler's moon.

Muchas gracias to Michael Brandman and Ace Atkins, for jumping off the trestle and into swift Parker waters before me, and to Helen Brann, for shoving me off to follow and shouting, "Cannonball!" After I touched mud and came to the surface, a gasping holler went out to my editor extraordinaire, Chris Pepe, and her faithful fireman, Meaghan Wagner, for keeping me from drowning with my boots on.

And a GRAND BLAST OF THE WHISTLE to the notorious Parker clan, Joan, David and Daniel, for issuing a warrant for me to saddle up and ride where no other hombre has ever rode . . . and last, to Robert B. Parker, for allowing all of us, with the tap of a spinning spur, the opportunity to continue our gallop over the rails and across the open plains.

ABOUT THE AUTHORS

Robert B. Parker was the author of seventy books, including the legendary Spenser detective series, the novels featuring Police Chief Jesse Stone, and the acclaimed Virgil Cole–Everett Hitch westerns, as well as the Sunny Randall novels. Winner of the Mystery Writers of America Grand Master Award and long considered the undisputed dean of American crime fiction, he died in January 2010.

Robert Knott is an actor, writer, and producer. His extensive list of stage, television, and film credits includes the feature film *Appaloosa,* based on the Robert B. Parker novel, which he adapted and produced with actor and producer Ed Harris. This is his first novel.

The employees of Thorndike Press hope you have enjoyed this Large Print book. All our Thorndike, Wheeler, and Kennebec Large Print titles are designed for easy reading, and all our books are made to last. Other Thorndike Press Large Print books are available at your library, through selected bookstores, or directly from us.

For information about titles, please call:
  (800) 223-1244

or visit our Web site at:
  http://gale.cengage.com/thorndike

To share your comments, please write:
  Publisher
  Thorndike Press
  10 Water St., Suite 310
  Waterville, ME 04901